Rescuing Emily

Rescuing Emily

Delta Force Heroes

Book 2

By Susan Stoker

Cover Design by Chris Mackey, AURA Design Group
Cover Photographer: Darren Birks
Cover Model: Chris Connolly
Edited by Kelli Collins & Missy Borucki

Manufactured in the United States

Table of Contents

Dedication

To the *real* Mrs. Ogliaruso, you were the best second grade teacher Gilbert Linkous Elementary School in Blacksburg, VA, ever had. You had a huge impact on my life, and I will always be thankful for that.

For Shannel. The best day in Oliver's life was when you signed up to be his foster mom. From foster to adoption, you're my hero.

Danee, thank you for telling me the story about your bedtime ritual of reading. It was perfect for this story!

Prologue

SLAMMING HIS APARTMENT door behind him and shaking the entire wall while swearing loud and long, he threw his hat across the room, not satisfied at all when it fluttered to the ground a few feet away. He paced, knowing he'd never forget the humiliation he'd felt while standing in front of the colonel, seeing the disgust in the officer's eyes.

His squad had been so excited to be picked to go through the special training, sure they'd be able to get through the makeshift city undetected. They were infantry soldiers; they'd trained for hours—no, years—in order to be stealthy in urban situations. The thirty days they'd spent at the National Training Center out at Fort Irwin in California had taught them everything they needed to know.

But somehow their entire plan had fallen apart within five minutes of the whistle being blown. Instead of being able to sneak through the city and get to the rendezvous point unscathed, every single one of his squad had been "killed," hit with lasers from specially designed nonlethal weapons, before they'd made it even halfway through the training scenario.

Remembering how nonchalant the other unit had been after "killing" them all had felt like salt poured into an open wound. They'd acted as if they hadn't just ruined his career, his reputation. Sure, the colonel had said it was *just* an exercise. Had said that his squad had done well. But he'd been *lying*.

They hadn't done well.

And it sure as hell wasn't just an exercise.

He'd seen the colonel laughing with another officer about how fast they'd been killed. And the team that had beat them acted as if what had happened wasn't a big deal. They'd patted each other on the back and given each other high-fives. To add insult to injury, their team didn't even have one casualty. *Not one!* They'd taken out his entire squad as if it was child's play.

He went into the small bathroom in his apartment and stared at himself in the mirror for a long moment.

His entire life, he hadn't been good enough.

Because you're pathetic.

He shook his head at the voice in his head. He wasn't. It was them. *They* were pathetic. And it was up to him to show the colonel that he was just as good as the other team.

Nodding as if he'd made a momentous decision, he

started planning in his head. He and his friends had a lot of work to do, but by the time they were done, the other unit would regret their casual dismissal of his squad on the simulated battlefield, and he'd redeem himself with the general in charge of the post.

Knowing your enemy was the first rule in battle, and he vowed to himself then and there that he'd find a weakness in the other group of soldiers and exploit it to his advantage.

The asshole soldiers wouldn't know what hit them. By the time he was done with them, they'd regret their cocky attitude and their brush-off of his squad. He might have been beaten today, but the battle wasn't over.

He *would* take them down. No matter who he had to use to do it.

Chapter One

CORMAC "FLETCH" FLETCHER looked at the monitor sitting on the kitchen counter at the woman standing at his front door. His security cameras caught every inch of his property, starting from just outside the garage to around the back of the yard. He could tell who was driving up his driveway and who was at his door without leaving his house. Hell, he could even log into the app and check the tapes when he was thousands of miles away on a mission. All he needed was a Wi-Fi connection.

The woman at his door was probably five-nine, taller than the women he was typically attracted to. It was hard to guess her age because she looked tired. He figured probably late twenties or early thirties. Her brown hair was pulled back into a ponytail. Fletch couldn't tell what color her eyes were as she kept them downcast, never looking up at the door to be captured by the camera hidden in the ornate door knocker.

He'd received several messages about the rental apartment over his garage, and Fletch had a few interviews lined up with people who had inquired. The apartment really wasn't anything special. It had a single bathroom with a shower/bath combo, one bedroom, and a small kitchen. There were a couple pieces of furniture: a double bed, a refrigerator, and an old couch and coffee table. It wasn't fancy by any stretch of the imagination, but it was clean, and safer than anyone probably knew, considering who he was and what he did for a living.

He didn't have a lot of enemies, but there were always people who were jealous of him being in Delta Force. It wasn't widely known, in fact, not many people knew at all, but there was some suspicion that he and his team were more than simple soldiers. They were damn good at what they did and didn't seem to have any trouble attracting the ladies. The combination had spelled trouble for some of the other Deltas in the past, even without anyone knowing about their Special Forces background. Renting the apartment would mean there'd be someone on his property to keep an eye on it when he was away on a mission.

Fletch wiped his hands dry after rinsing the last dish in his sink, and turned off the security monitor. Not advertising the fact that he had such intensive security was key in catching anyone dumb enough to try to rob or vandalize his property. He walked to the door and opened it wide. The woman standing there looked up with a gasp and took a step backwards after seeing him.

Fletch knew he could be scary. He was six feet two inches tall, and muscular. He'd spent much of his life making sure he was in shape and that no one would mistake him for anything other than what he was…dangerous.

He had tattoos on his forearms and biceps. They were bright and somewhat gaudy. He looked like a stereotypical sailor. Some of the tattoos he'd gotten when he was young and dumb. He probably wouldn't choose them if he had to make the decision again, but what was done was done. Fletch knew when people who didn't know him caught a glimpse of him, they were weary. He was big and knew how to use that to his advantage to intimidate people. But the woman on his doorstep wasn't someone he wanted to scare away. He pasted a smile on his face as he greeted her.

"Hi, you're Emily Grant? Here about renting the apartment?" Fletch asked, trying to put the woman at ease.

Emily looked up at the man standing in the doorway. If she hadn't been so desperate, she probably would've turned around and gotten right back into her 1998 Honda Civic and driven away. She wasn't sure what she'd expected out of the man who'd invited her to come check out the apartment, but it wasn't someone who, while only a few inches taller, could easily bench press her.

His tattoos were also a surprise. She'd seen lots of tattoos on the soldiers on the base, but they were usually more subdued. Black tribal designs or something similar. Instead, the very masculine man had what looked like cartoon characters on his forearms. He was wearing a plaid shirt, open at the throat—enough for her to realize he didn't have a carpet of fur on his chest—and with the sleeves rolled back to his elbows. She didn't get an in-depth look at the tattoos, knowing it would be rude to stare, but they still surprised her. Somehow, though, they worked for him.

Putting aside thoughts of his tattoos—and whether he had any others hidden—Emily brought her gaze up to the man's. She needed this apartment. It was one of the only places she could find that was close enough to work and school, and was within her small budget.

She took a deep breath. "Yeah, I'm Emily. I appreciate you meeting with me today." She bravely held out her hand in greeting.

Fletch smiled at the woman. He could see right through her bravado and knew she was scared to death of him. But he gave her points for not backing farther away and for reaching out to shake his hand.

He took her hand in his, careful not to squeeze it too hard. "Nice to meet you. Come on in, we can talk about the particulars, then I'll show you the apartment."

Emily nodded and gripped her purse hanging off her shoulder tightly as she followed him into his house. Fletch saw her looking around as if trying to figure out more about him. He knew what image the house projected: not one of a bachelor. It was neat as a pin, with not one item out of place...exactly how he liked it.

They walked into a small dining room off of a kitchen that could've been featured in any cooking magazine. Fletch pulled a chair out from the dark mahogany table and helped her scoot in once she'd sat.

"Would you like something to drink? Water? Iced tea?"

"No, thank you," Emily told him, knowing she'd be stupid to take something to drink from a man she didn't know. It would be easy to drug a glass of tea or water. Especially when she was inside his house. He could render her unconscious before she realized what was happening. She normally wasn't a paranoid person, but lately, when she couldn't sleep, she'd been watching too many forensics and crime shows.

Fletch could practically see the woman's brain churning. She sat uncomfortably in the chair at his table. Her purse was in her lap and she was holding it as if she thought he'd reach over and snatch it from her. He wasn't offended, far from it, he was impressed she was being as cautious as she was. He made sure to sit across from her, keeping the table between them to give her space.

"Do I know you?" Fletch thought the woman looked familiar, but he couldn't quite place her.

She shrugged. "I work at the PX. You might have seen me there."

Fletch nodded. Now that she mentioned it, he thought he did remember seeing her there a time or two. "That must be it. My name is Cormac Fletcher, but everyone calls me Fletch. I own the house and live here by myself. I work on base and am called away on trips somewhat frequently. I'm discreet, and won't get in your business, and I expect anyone who rents from me to do the same. I'm past the point in my life where I need or want late-night parties. I like to live quietly and I'd like for anyone who resides on my property to be similar." He paused, gauging her reaction to his words. Emily sat still, giving him her complete attention.

When she didn't immediately protest or even show any emotion other than curiosity, he continued, relieved. "The apartment isn't fancy, I've had two people look at it recently and wrinkle their noses and decide it wasn't for them. Rent includes all utilities. It's too much of a pain in the ass for me to separate out how much electricity you use versus what I use. All I ask is that you don't get a wild hair to grow marijuana or something that would make the bills spike every month."

"No marijuana, check," Emily mumbled under her

breath as she nodded.

Fletch wanted to smile, but he controlled it and went on with his well-rehearsed speech. "You can use one side of the garage for your car, but any boxes of other stuff you want to store will have to be either in the apartment or you'll have to rent a storage unit. There's simply no room in there for more. I usually park at the side of my house, so don't worry about taking the empty spot inside the garage for your own vehicle.

"When I'm gone, I'd appreciate it if you could get my mail and look after the place, but if that's outside anything you want to do, it's not a deal breaker for renting. Rent's due the first week of the month, whichever day works best for you. Any questions?"

Emily tried not to fidget under Fletch's direct gaze. His eyes were ice blue, and had her pinned in place. His hair was longer than she thought anyone in the Army was allowed to have, and it looked like he hadn't shaved in a couple of days. He was good looking, but even though she was attracted to him, Emily wasn't looking for any kind of relationship at the moment. She had enough on her plate.

Knowing there was one thing he had to understand before she could accept the apartment with any good conscience, she cleared her throat.

"You should know, I have a kid. Her dad's not in the picture. She's six and in the first grade. I didn't know if that would be a deal breaker for you or not. I didn't see anything in the ad that said whether or not kids were allowed."

"Does she scream all day?"

"Uh…no."

"Steal? Draw all over the walls? Destroy property?"

"No!" Emily sat up straighter, getting irritated. "She's *six*. She's not a thug. She doesn't hang out on the street corner with her homies every night. She plays with her toys, reads books, and watches cartoons."

"Then I don't think we'll have a problem," Fletch said with a smile, amused at how easy it was to rile the woman sitting in front of him.

Emily chewed on her lip, as if contemplating her next words. Fletch saw the moment she worked up the nerve to tell him what was bothering her.

"She *can* be very inquisitive though. She asks questions…*lots* of questions. Some people have gotten annoyed with her in the past."

"Annoyed?" Fletch asked, raising an eyebrow.

"Yeah, annoyed. The thing is, Annie's smart. Really smart. I try to keep her busy and find things to help stimulate her, but she has an unrelenting need to learn. Some of my neighbors in the past have gotten irritated with her asking them questions all the time. But she doesn't do it to be annoying, she just likes to figure stuff out."

"Of course she does. She's a kid. I have no problem with questions, Emily."

"Okay, but—"

"Is she gonna break into my house and come up to my room in the middle of the night and interrogate me about how the garage door opener works?"

Emily giggled. "Maybe not in the middle of the night, but I'd say there's a pretty good chance that sooner or later she's gonna want to know. And, as far as I'm aware, no one has taught her how to pick a lock...yet."

"Good to know," Fletch said with a grin.

"I just...some people don't like kids and I don't want to live anywhere again where she's made to feel like a freak."

"Again?" Fletch asked in a low voice. "You lived somewhere where someone made her feel like a freak? A six-year-old *kid*?"

"She was four, and yes." Emily's answer was succinct and she didn't offer any other details.

"I haven't been around kids all that much, but anyone who sees the thirst for knowledge as anything but a good thing, is an asshole, and you're better off not being around them or having your daughter around them."

"Yeah. Thanks," Emily said softly.

Fletch tried to relax his shoulders. It pissed him off that someone would be cruel to a kid. Growing up, he'd also been smarter than his classmates, and he'd experienced some of what Emily was describing himself. Probably not to the extent of her daughter though, if Emily's protectiveness was anything to go by. "Want to see the apartment?"

"Yeah, but…uh…can I ask how much the security deposit will be? There's no use in me seeing it if I can't afford it."

Fletch tilted his head as he looked at Emily. Really examined her. He hadn't taken the time before because he wasn't sure if he'd be renting to her or not. But he liked what he'd heard so far.

She was wearing a T-shirt and jeans. She had an old pair of sneakers on her feet. She looked casual, but Fletch could see something he hadn't seen in any of the other people he'd interviewed so far—desperation. He saw it all the time at work at the missions they went on. People frequently put on a front, but he could see that this woman *needed* this apartment. He didn't know her story, but recognized that for whatever reason, renting the little space above his garage was vitally important to her.

Fletch was also impressed with her candidness about her daughter. He'd interviewed someone just that morning who he knew had been hiding something from him. Given time, he would've figured out exactly what, but he didn't feel like going through the hassle. He

13

SUSAN STOKER

didn't get good vibes from the man, and it wasn't worth the effort to find out something that would make him want to kick the man out later when his intuition was telling him to turn him down from the get-go.

But Emily laid it out there, making sure he knew not only that she had a young child, but that she was gifted, and that others had found her annoying in the past.

He made a quick decision and cut a couple hundred dollars off of what he'd planned to rent the apartment for; he didn't need the money anyway. He'd prefer to have someone reliable and responsible living on his property to keep an eye on it when he wasn't around.

"I haven't had good luck in renting it so far," Fletch told her in a nonchalant tone, "so if you're willing to help out with the house when I'm away, I'll rent it to you for five hundred a month with half that for the security deposit."

Emily gaped at the man. Five hundred dollars? And only two-fifty for a deposit? Was he kidding? "Is that a joke?" She couldn't stop her incredulous question.

Fletch smiled at the disbelief on Emily's face. He didn't blame her; he knew he could probably get double that if he pushed. But it was obvious she needed a break. "No joke. You interested in seeing it? Don't agree until you check it out. It's only got one bedroom, so you'd have to share with your daughter. It's nothing special,

14

you might hate it."

"I won't hate it," Emily said, still in shock at her luck. She'd taken the day off work, knowing that even though the missed hours would hurt her budget, she *needed* to find a better place to live for her and Annie. The landlord at the seedy apartment complex they were currently staying at had gotten more aggressive in his pursuit of her, and Emily knew it wasn't because he was actually interested in *her*—but because of Annie.

Her daughter was beautiful. Yes, she was only six, but she was tall for her age and slender. She had long, beautiful blonde hair that she'd inherited from her father. She had blue eyes and never met a stranger. Annie was friendly and bubbly and Emily knew the landlord, damn him, had a sick interest in her daughter.

Money was always an issue. Ever since Annie's father had left while Emily had still been pregnant, she'd fought to provide Annie with a safe and happy life. She worked at Fort Hood in the PX, the Post Exchange. It was the general store on base. She wasn't able to work full time, because she didn't have the money to pay for childcare for Annie. She'd relied on neighbors to look after her daughter before she'd started kindergarten full time, but now that Annie was in the first grade, and in class all day, Emily could work a full six hours every day. She dropped Annie off at the elementary school at seven-thirty, and was able to get to work by eight. She worked until two, without a lunch break, then picked Annie up around two-thirty.

Emily had no health insurance and no retirement plan, but Annie was loved and happy. It was worth it. But to be offered a reliable, secure, and quiet place to live for only five hundred dollars a month? It was as if Emily had hit the lottery.

Even before seeing the ad in the paper for this apartment, she'd planned on leaving the scummy place she lived in before the month was up, even if she had to live in her car. She'd done that when she'd been pregnant, and had sworn to herself that Annie would never know that kind of life. But Emily had been losing hope of finding anything appropriate.

The cheapest apartment she'd been able to find had been eight hundred a month, and it looked scarier than where she was now. Since the building was close to the Army base, Emily had thought she'd feel safe living with other soldiers, as the landlord had told her most of the other occupants were single men and women who worked at Fort Hood, but unfortunately, that hadn't been the case.

Annie's father had taught her in more ways than one that just because someone was a soldier, it didn't mean they were a good person. While *she'd* thought they were starting their lives together, *he'd* apparently just been in it to get laid. Somehow he'd arranged to get transferred to another base not too long after she'd happily told him she was pregnant with his baby, and informed her that he didn't want her following him.

Emily knew she could probably go to the Army and do a paternity test and force him to pay child support, but she didn't want that for Annie, or herself. Years of relying on someone else to send her money made her stomach churn.

She and Annie had been okay so far, and Emily knew she'd continue to do whatever it took to keep her daughter safe and happy...without help.

Nodding at Emily, Fletch stood up. "All right, let's go and check it out, then if you like it, we can come back here and do the paperwork, okay?"

"Okay."

Ten short minutes later they were back at the dining room table in Fletch's house. Emily had immediately said the small space was perfect, even though Fletch told her there were all sorts of things he should probably do to upgrade it.

"I'll need to make a copy of your ID," Fletch told Emily, being as nonchalant as he could. He didn't really need it for her to sign the lease, but there was no way he'd let anyone live on his property, no matter how fragile and lovely she seemed, without doing a background check. It wasn't completely legal, but his friend, Tex, was discrete and could have it done within an hour.

Tex was a medically retired SEAL living out in Pennsylvania. He used to live in Virginia, but had moved his entire operation after meeting a beautiful woman named Melody on the Internet. Tex was the eyes and ears behind the scenes for their Delta Force team, and several other Special Forces groups. The man was pure genius with a computer and could find information that someone would swear was locked up tighter than the money at Fort Knox. No one ever questioned how he was able to pull off some of the things he did, they were just grateful he was on their side.

Fletch watched as Emily bent her head and pulled her wallet out of her purse. She handed her license over to him, saying, "If you laugh at my first name, I'll have to hurt you."

Emily watched as Fletch looked down at the small plastic card she'd handed him and he tried to hold back his smile. His lips twitched, but he looked up and said with a mostly straight face, "Miracle?"

Emily sighed, obviously used to telling the story about her given name. "Yeah. My parents were older. They'd always wanted kids and when I was born, they called me their little miracle."

"But you go by Emily?"

She nodded. "Yeah. Definitely."

"Miracle is a pretty name."

Emily made a face. "Maybe, but memories of being made fun of throughout my elementary and middle school years made it not so pretty after a while."

"Kids are cruel."

"Yup."

"Your parents still around?"

Emily didn't really want to get into this with Fletch. He was still a stranger after all—but she didn't want to be rude either. "Unfortunately, no. They died when I was in college."

"Tough."

That was the understatement of the year, but she merely said, "Yeah."

Fletch carried Emily's driver's license to the small printer he had off to the side of the living room and made a copy.

"So, you're not married?" Emily asked, deciding if he could be nosy, so could she.

"Nope."

Emily waited and when he didn't elaborate, she pushed. "This place looks like you're married."

Fletch barked out a laugh. "It does, doesn't it? I actually hired someone to decorate it. I didn't give her much assistance, and this is what I got when she was done."

"She did a good job," Emily observed, looking around.

"Yeah. Apparently it's fun to spend someone else's money."

Emily didn't smile, but continued to run her eyes over every inch of the room she could see. "I bet it is."

Fletch leaned against the wall next to the printer and watched Emily check out his house. He wondered what she saw. He looked around to try to see it from her eyes. He had two leather couches that looked stiff and formal, but when you sat in them, you melted into the cushions. He had a large flat-screen television on the wall and a coffee table that looked perfectly normal, but had a secret compartment under it that currently held a Sig Sauer 40 caliber handgun. He was always prepared for the unknown. But thinking about the various weapons lying around the house made him realize that he needed to make certain they were all secure. If there was going to be a child in his house he wanted to be sure to protect her.

Not that her daughter would be hanging out with him, but if she came over with her mom to bring in the mail, the last thing he wanted was for her to find one of his weapons and accidentally set it off. He shuddered at the thought, and vowed to move them all way above kid level as soon as Emily left.

There was a pair of boots lying on the floor next to one of the couches; he'd left them there the day before when he'd gotten back from the base. Other than that, everything else was in its place and there were no stray papers or magazines or any kind of "stuff" that could be seen.

"I'm a bit of a neat freak," Fletch told Emily unnecessarily as he came back to the table to sit next to her.

"Yeah, I can see that," she laughed, turning her eyes back to him. "But it's nice. She did a good job. It's formal without being fancy. Comfortable without being stuffy. I hope you don't expect mine to look like this," she teased. "Annie and I are *not* neat freaks."

Fletch laughed and handed her license back to her. "No, I don't give a shit what your place looks like, as long as there aren't mice and cockroaches."

Emily shuddered. "Oh no. We might not be neat, but we're clean."

"Then we're good."

They smiled at each other. Fletch pushed the lease papers over to her. "Take these home. Read them over, get them looked at by a lawyer if you want, but I want to make sure you completely understand everything and agree before you sign."

Emily looked at him in confusion. "Did you hide anything weird in here?"

"Weird?"

"Yeah, weird."

"Weird how?" Fletch asked.

"I don't know. Like my car only gets four-point-two

feet of space in the garage and if I violate it, I'm out. Or weird like if you see Annie after four in the afternoon, I owe more on the rent, or weird like if I'm late one day on giving you the rent money, I'm gone."

Fletch started out smiling at her, but was frowning by the end of her comments. "Fuck no. Look, Emily, I'm a lot of things, but I'm not an asshole. If you're having issues paying the rent, just talk to me and we'll figure something out. I already told you that I don't care if your daughter is around. I might get upset if she plays with something inappropriate in the garage, but only because it could hurt her, not because I care about anything out there. It's all just stuff. Stuff that can be replaced. The lease is a simple one, I printed it off the Internet. There's nothing weird in there."

"Okay. Thank you." Emily's voice was low, but she didn't break eye contact. "I just wanted to be sure."

"Good. Look it over, make sure it's amenable to you. Bring it back and you can move in whenever you're ready. Today's the twentieth, if you want to move in before the first, feel free. I won't charge you for this month, consider it a gift." Fletch narrowed his eyes. "If someone is giving Annie a hard time for asking questions, I'm okay with you getting out of there and moving in here now. No kid should have to feel bad for being herself."

"Again, thank you." Emily had no idea how she'd

gotten so lucky, but she'd never been so glad in all her life that she'd seen the ad in the paper about the apartment. She'd been actively looking, and had found the Sunday paper in the recycle bin behind her current apartment. She usually looked over the paper when she was at the PX, but since she wasn't working that Sunday, she'd grabbed it from the recycleables.

"Can I drop this by after work tomorrow?" Emily wanted to have her boss look it over. She couldn't afford to take it to a lawyer, but Jimmy liked her and he'd be able to tell her if she'd missed anything.

"Of course. I'll leave a key under the mat by the stairs that go up to the apartment."

"Uh, you know that's the first place burglars would look for a spare key, don't you?"

Fletch barked out a laugh. If someone *did* manage to somehow get on to his property undetected, his face would be recorded from so many different angles, he'd be caught before he could get too far away. "I think it'll be okay for a day or so, Em."

Emily smiled shyly at Fletch, teasing him. "Okay, but if I come back and someone has stolen the couch up there, I'll expect you to replace it."

"Deal." Fletch smiled back. Maybe having another renter wouldn't be so bad after all. After the last one he'd thought long and hard about trying again. Fletch would make sure Tex got the background check done on one Miracle Emily Grant before she returned the signed lease the next day. It'd be child's play for the man.

Fletch would sign it after making sure she was everything she seemed to be. He didn't think he had anything to worry about. The woman seemed open and honest, and relieved to have a place for her and her daughter to live, even if it was a small, barely furnished hole in the wall.

Being safe trumped material things, and he understood that in a way not a lot of other men would. He'd seen too much in his ten years in the Army, and five years in Delta Force. People would lie, cheat, steal, and kill to feel safe. He'd seen it over and over. Mothers who did whatever the local terrorists and bullies ordered them to, simply to protect their children. Kids who joined gangs, just to feed their families. The horrors of the world went on and on.

But Fletch could tell that the woman sitting in front of him now was a completely different person than the one he'd invited into his home thirty minutes ago. She was more relaxed and at ease, whereas before she was tense, cautious, and suspicious. Simply because she'd been offered a safe place to live for her and her daughter.

Fletch liked that he could give that to her. It felt good. He'd helped too many people to count in his lifetime, but he could feel the relief emanating from the woman all the way to his gut. "Go tell Annie she has a new home and I'll see you when I see you. Yeah?"

Emily nodded. "Yeah."

They stood up and Fletch walked her to his door. He stood in the entryway with one arm braced on the doorjamb and watched as Emily walked toward her car. She stopped when she was halfway there and turned to him. "Thank you, Fletch. I know you're totally giving me a break on the security deposit and rent, and I appreciate it. I'll do what I can to help around here, you just need to let me know what you want me to do. I can rake, mow, sweep and—not that it looks like you need any help—I can even clean your house if you wanted me to."

"You're welcome, Emily. But I didn't hire you to be my maid or groundskeeper. I'm actually getting as much out of this arrangement as you are. I have a responsible tenant living on my property who isn't interested in robbing me blind or throwing crazy parties. It's a win-win situation. I'll see you later."

Fletch mentally rolled his eyes at her offer. It was sweet, but there was no way he'd ask her to do manual labor. She could look after his house when he was on a mission, but other than that, there wasn't much needing to be done that he couldn't do himself.

"Okay. See you later."

Fletch closed his front door and heard her car start

up, complete with the muffler backfiring. After turning on the security monitor, he watched as her car backed out of his driveway and disappeared onto the road next to his house. He picked up the piece of paper with Emily's information on it and called Tex. He was ninety-nine-point-nine percent sure Emily was just who she said she was, and what she looked like—a woman who was down on her luck and wanted a quiet place for her and her daughter to live.

Suddenly, he was looking forward to meeting her daughter. From the little bit Emily had said, she sounded precocious and fun. Fletch hadn't ever really thought about having children, or even been around many, but it occurred to him that it might be fun to teach a child things like how a garage door opener worked.

As far as he was concerned, the sooner Emily and Annie moved in, the better he'd feel. They'd be safe in the small apartment above his garage. He'd make sure of it.

Chapter Two

"**W**HATCHA DOIN'?"

The question came from behind Fletch, and wasn't all that surprising. He'd been working on the vintage 1968 Dodge Charger all that week, and he'd seen the little girl peeking in on him every afternoon. But it wasn't until today that she'd gathered up the courage to talk to him.

The signed lease agreement had been stuck inside the storm door of his house the day after he'd met with Emily. He'd left a key under the mat, as he told her he would, and given her his extra garage door opener as well. She'd moved in one day while he'd been on the base. Fletch had planned to help her, but she either didn't have that much stuff, or she'd gotten assistance from someone else, because when he'd knocked on her door to make sure she'd gotten moved in all right, she'd opened it a crack, leaving the chain on the door, and told him everything was perfect.

Fletch had let her be. He'd gotten the locks updated on the small apartment, wanting to make sure Emily and her daughter felt secure. He'd added a new deadbolt as well as two chains on the door. One was around Emily's eye level, and the other was three feet from the floor. Fletch wasn't sure why he'd thought about putting in the second lock so low, but he supposed it was the thought of the single mother being alone in the little apartment, and wanting her daughter to be able to lock the door as well.

Without looking up, Fletch continued to work on the engine. He was leaning over the car, changing the spark plug wires. "I'm trying to fix this old car."

"Why?"

"Because I want it to work again."

"Why?"

"Why not?"

"Because it's old. You can go buy a new one."

"Why would I want to buy a new one when I have a perfectly good car right here?"

"I don't think this one is perfectly good."

Fletch couldn't really argue with the little girl. He had a lot of work to do on the Charger before it'd be street-ready again. He looked over at her. "Annie, right?"

"Uh-huh."

"Sometimes old isn't a bad thing." Fletch could see Annie digesting his words.

"Someday I'm gonna own stuff that isn't old."

Fletch felt his gut clench, but Annie continued before he could examine her words or his feelings.

"Can I help?"

"You want to help with my car?"

"Uh-huh. Mommy says I'm a good helper."

Fletch stood up from under the hood of the car and looked at Annie carefully. She was wearing a pair of jeans that were just a tad bit too short for her. He could see white socks and a well-worn pair of sneakers on her feet. She was wearing a black T-shirt that hung a bit loose on her slim frame. Her blonde hair was pulled back by two barrettes on either side of her head, but wisps had come loose and were hanging freely around her face. She had a smear of dirt on one cheek and her hands were filthy. Not only that, but on a second glance, he realized the girl was covered in dust and dirt.

"What have you been up to, sprite?" Fletch asked, wiping his own dirty hands on a cloth nearby.

"Playing."

"Playing where?"

Annie pointed behind her and Fletch took a step toward the garage door to see what she'd been pointing at. Around the corner, he saw a pile of plastic and metal cars strewn around a patch of ground that had always been resistant to growing grass. It was in the shade of the garage and it looked like the little girl had made a race track of sorts in the dirt. Some was piled up here and there, and Fletch could see marks in the dirt where she'd kneeled to play with the toys.

"You like cars?"

Annie shrugged. "They're okay."

Fletch tried not to smile. It was more than obvious the little girl liked cars. "What about dolls? You like playing with dolls?"

Her face scrunched up in disgust. "No. Dolls are stupid."

"Stupid, huh?"

"Uh-huh. I like boy toys. Mommy doesn't like when I call them boy toys, but it's what everyone else calls them."

"What kinds of boy toys?" Fletch asked, leaning against the Charger and smiling down at the earnest little girl.

"Anything. Trucks, monsters, cars, *Star Wars*. And I really like military stuff."

Fletch was surprised. With her blonde hair, blue eyes and angelic appearance, she looked delicate and girly; it was amusing to see she had another side to her. "Not stuffed animals, dress-up clothes, or dolls?"

"No."

"Your mom said you like to read."

Annie looked up at him and asked somewhat belligerently, "Are you gonna make fun of me if I do?"

Fletch frowned and kneeled down so he was at eye

level with the little girl. "No, Annie. I'm not going to make fun of you. I was just interested in *what* you like to read."

She studied him with a look in her eyes that was much wiser than her six years. "Adventure stories."

"Adventure stories." Fletch felt a little foolish repeating her answers, but she continued to surprise him.

"Uh-huh. And mysteries. Mommy read me *The Lion, the Witch and the Wardrobe* and now we're on *The Boxcar Children.* Then we're going to start on the Hardy Boys and Nancy Drew books."

"You are, huh?"

"Uh-huh. And I can read them too, but I'm too slow. Mommy's working on it with me, but I like when she reads to me 'cause we get through the stories more faster."

Fletch was amazed. He hadn't spent a lot of time with kids, but Emily hadn't been lying. It was obvious Annie was way ahead of other kids her age. "Those are cool stories."

"You've read them?" Annie's voice was awestruck. "Really?"

"Yup. They're great."

"Cool!" the little girl breathed.

"Annie!" Emily's voice rang out from the door at the top of the stairs around the corner. "Where are you?"

"Here, Mommy!" Annie said, stepping around the

corner so her mom could see her.

"You're supposed to stay where I can see you."

"I know, I'm sorry, Mommy. I was talking to…" Her voice trailed off and she looked up at Fletch. "What's your name?"

"Fletch."

Annie's brow scrunched up and she frowned. "Fletch? Is that your first name?"

Fletch smothered a laugh. Annie was adorable. "It's a nickname. My first name is Cormac and my last name is Fletcher. My friends call me Fletch."

Annie nodded. "Yeah, that's much better. I'll call you Fletch too."

Fletch snorted in laughter. Leave it to a kid to totally insult him but make him laugh at the same time.

"I'm with Fletch!" Annie yelled up at her mom.

"I'm right here, Annie, you don't have to yell," Emily told her daughter, putting her hand on top of her head. She'd come down the stairs as Annie was talking to Fletch. "What have I told you about leaving Mr. Fletcher alone when he's working?"

"I know, but Mommy, he was banging around in here and saying some of those words you told me I wasn't allowed to say. I came in to see if he needed help and we started talking."

Fletch hadn't smiled as much as he had today in a long time. "It's fine, Emily. We were just getting to know each other."

"I hope she wasn't a bother."

"Never."

Emily smiled at Fletch shyly, the disparaging remarks of others who were annoyed at her child obviously fresh in her mind. "Okay. Come on, Annie, show me what you've made today. I can see you worked very hard to make the perfect race course."

"Oh yeah, Mommy, it's awesome! Come see! The mean ol' blue car didn't get to win today, his car broke down, like ours did that one time, and the red *and* green car zoomed past him in the last second."

Fletch watched as mother and daughter went around the side of the house to where Annie had made her race track in the dirt. He bent over the engine of the Charger again, all the while listening to Annie chatter away to her mom about her cars. The kid had an amazing imagination and Fletch looked forward to getting to know her better.

It wasn't only the little girl he wanted to know better, either. Emily was fascinating to him. He'd caught her checking him out, but despite Fletch being friendly and open toward her, she didn't go out of her way to speak to him or otherwise interact other than polite hellos and goodbyes. She was attentive and loving to her daughter, but it was more than that. He'd been fighting a surprising attraction to her since she'd knocked on his door a couple weeks ago. Surprising because he was usually attracted to women who were more...polished, for lack of a better word. Those who styled their hair, had perfect makeup, and showed off their bodies with provocative clothes.

Most of the times he'd seen Emily, she'd looked very natural. Usually in jeans and T-shirts with her hair pulled back. She rarely wore makeup, but she didn't need it, and it all made her seem...approachable. Down-to-earth.

And her slightly mussed look made him think about what she might look like after making love, or first thing in the morning when she woke up in bed.

Fletch shifted and groaned. The last thing he needed was a woody. He grinned, but the visual of what he would look like to her if she walked back into the garage was enough to will his erection to go down.

Fletch made the decision right then and there to get to know Emily better. It probably wasn't smart to get involved with a tenant, but the hell with it. Something inside was pushing him to see where a relationship with Emily could go. He relied on his instincts a lot. They'd saved his life more than once. And right now his instincts were telling him that Emily was just the type of woman who would understand who he was and what he did.

Satisfied with his decision, Fletch went back to work

on the car, whistling, happier than he'd been in a long time, turning over through his mind how he'd approach Emily. The anticipation of a courtship coursing through his veins.

EMILY KISSED ANNIE'S forehead and closed the latest episode of *The Boxcar Children* she'd been reading to her. She made sure to stop at the public library every week, loading up on enough books to keep her daughter entertained until she could go back to get more.

"Mommy, why is it okay for Fletch to draw all over his arms, but I can't draw on mine?"

Emily held back a smile and tried to look stern. "They're called tattoos, honey, and they're permanent. They aren't drawings."

"He has a lot. How did he make them pernanent?"

"Permanent. It means they won't ever go away. They're put there with a needle." Emily tried to make the process sound as unappealing as possible, knowing if there was one thing in the world her daughter disliked, it was needles. "Ink is put into the needle and it's pushed into his skin over and over until the drawing is under his skin and it won't come out."

"Needles?" Annie asked in horror.

Emily nodded solemnly.

"Yuck. Why?"

"Some people use them as decoration, others use them as a way to express themselves."

Annie scrunched her face up. "His are pretty, but I don't understand."

Emily had to agree with her daughter on the first part, Fletch's tattoos *were* pretty, not that she'd ever admit it. She changed the subject. "Do you remember what we talked about tonight?"

"Uh-huh."

"What?"

"That I'm never ever allowed to let anyone into our apartment. That it's *our* house and our safe place."

"That's right, baby. And what about the door locks?"

"That I should always lock the door behind me when I come in. Including my own special chain lock."

"Good. And why should you do that?"

"Because this is our house and no one is allowed in unless we invite them in."

Emily nodded. "Yes. I don't want you to be scared of people, honey, but there are some bad men and women in this world that want to take what doesn't belong to them."

"Like robbers?"

Emily nodded, knowing her daughter didn't really understand. "Exactly, like robbers. When we're here in our apartment, we're safe from robbers. It's our home."

"And like the scary men where we used to live…right, Mommy?"

Tears welled up in Emily's eyes. She kissed the top of her daughter's head to try to hide her emotions from her too-observant eyes. "Yes, Annie, like the scary men at the other place. But they aren't here. It's just a good habit to get into, locking the door behind you. Right?"

"Right, Mommy. But Fletch isn't scary."

"No, he's not. But, Annie, you should really leave him alone when he's working. He might not like you interrupting him."

"He said his friends call him Fletch. I'm his friend. He doesn't mind when I interrmupt him."

Emily leaned down and kissed her daughter again. "I love you, Annie."

"And I love you, Mommy."

"Sleep well."

"Okay, you too."

Emily pulled the covers up on her daughter's side of the double bed they sometimes shared. Annie liked to feel snug when she slept, so Emily would tuck the covers in as tightly as she could, then throw a blanket over herself when she went to bed. Most of the time, however, Emily found it easier to sleep on the couch so she wouldn't disturb Annie when she went to sleep after her bedtime. She turned on the small table lamp she'd found at a yard sale for a dollar and left the room, closing the door behind her.

She puttered around the small living area, wiping down the kitchen counter and washing the few dishes that were in the sink. She put some crackers into a small baggie, packed an apple and made a sandwich for Annie's lunch the next day. She eyed the last two apples sitting on the counter and shook her head. She needed to save those for Annie's lunches. Emily knew she'd get paid again at the end of the week, so she'd be able to splurge and get them both a treat.

Stomach growling—it seemed like she was always hungry, but there was no way she would ever take food away from her child—Emily went to the small hall closet and pulled out a blanket. She walked to the couch and lay down, covering herself with the fluffy blanket she'd found last year at the church rummage sale. She clicked on the small television Fletch had put in the apartment sometime between when she'd toured the place and when she'd moved in.

He'd left a note that said simply:

Had an extra TV. It's hooked up to my satellite dish. No extra charge. Enjoy. -F

Her thoughts turned to Fletch. He'd surprised her. She'd become too jaded since Annie's father had left, painting all soldiers with the same tainted brush she'd learned to use after giving birth alone and broke. But her new landlord was different. In the few weeks they'd lived there, he always went out of his way to talk to Annie, not just listen to her absently, but to engage.

It wasn't only that he was nice to her daughter. It was the attention he gave to *her* as well. He looked at her like he enjoyed what he saw...which hadn't happened in a long time. Emily felt feminine for the first time in ages. And it felt real. She wasn't parading around in low-cut shirts and shorts that barely covered her ass cheeks. She might be reading the signals coming from Fletch wrong, though. It'd been a good while since she'd even thought about trying to flirt or gain a man's interest. She'd gotten used to getting through her life one day at a time, and ignoring everything and everyone around her except for Annie.

But Fletch made her want to try. Made her want to be pretty for him. She smiled into the empty room. Fletch was hot. He was buff and built, and the longish hair curling against his neck made her want to tangle her fingers in it and tug as he devoured her mouth.

Lord, it'd been so long since she'd had any kinds of sexual feelings, it was almost surprising, but it felt good. It probably wasn't a smart idea to get involved in any way with someone who controlled her rent and could kick her out at a moment's notice, but she couldn't help thinking about it. If he crooked his finger at her, she'd probably obey his every command.

Thinking about Fletch made her squirm on the couch. She hadn't been with a man in quite a while, but that didn't mean she didn't have a healthy sex drive. Emily's hand drifted down her stomach and pushed under the elastic waistband of her sweats. Closing her eyes, she imagined one of her favorite scenes from a romance novel she'd read once, superimposing Fletch's eyes, hands, and body into the dream.

She was lying on a huge bed, naked, while Fletch was standing next to the bed, also nude. In the book, the man crawled over the heroine and ate her to an orgasm, then took her from behind, but in her mind, Fletch took hold of his impressive cock and stroked himself, encouraging her to do the same.

Emily's fingers swiped through her soaked folds as she imagined Fletch telling her how beautiful he thought she was, and how he couldn't wait to get inside her. She flicked her fingers faster over her clit, moaning, as dream Fletch's blue eyes stayed glued to what she was doing.

It didn't take long, Emily was primed and ready. The orgasm peaked quickly and she moaned quietly as she climaxed, so as not to wake Annie. As her hips jerked and she lightly stroked herself, prolonging the delicious feelings, Emily imagined Fletch's own orgasm, his hand tightening around himself as he groaned, the sight of her going over the edge pushing him over as well.

Sighing and pulling her hand away from between her legs, Emily stretched, sated. She might not have a boyfriend, but she knew how to take care of herself. She'd been doing it for a long time, and it had always felt great. But tonight was different. Probably because instead of a nameless, faceless hero in her mind, it'd been Fletch. But there was no way a guy like him was single. And if he was, something had to be wrong with him.

Emily tried to put her sexy landlord out of her mind. It was no use wishing for something that wasn't smart, and probably wouldn't happen anyway. She might be able to daydream about him, but that was all it would ever be.

Emily fell asleep on the sofa, dreaming about being flung down on a bed and being made love to by a man with bulging muscles and a sexy smile…and feeling safe for the first time in a long time.

Chapter Three

"WHO IS IT?" Emily called through her closed door.

"Fletch."

Feeling her heart rate increase just at hearing his voice, she tried to get herself under control so she wouldn't jump him the second she opened the door. Emily unlatched both chains and unbolted the lock before opening the door. "Hey, Fletch." She tried to sound calm and composed, when inside she felt like a giddy teenager, happy to see her crush.

"Hi."

"What's up?"

"Two things." Fletch didn't beat around the bush. "I brought something for Annie."

Emily looked down at Fletch's hands and saw he was holding a bag.

"I've enjoyed spending time with her over the last couple of weeks and saw this and thought of her."

"Oh...um..." Emily wasn't all that thrilled that a man she really didn't know all that well was giving her little girl presents.

When she didn't reach for the bag, Fletch put it on the ground near the door. "The other thing is that I came over to tell you I'll be out of town for a while."

"Oh, okay."

"I brought the keys to the house, and I hoped you might still be willing to look in on it and make sure everything is okay, as well as bring the mail in?" He pulled a keyring out of his pocket with a single key dangling from it.

"Of course. I'm happy to help," Emily told him.

"Mommy!" they heard from inside the apartment. "Hurry up! I can't read as fast as you and I wanna know what's gonna happen!"

The adults smiled at the impatience in Annie's voice. Emily turned her head to yell back at her daughter, not even thinking about how it probably wasn't the most ladylike thing to do in front of Fletch. "Keep your pants on! I'll be right there!"

Fletch smiled wider. Emily and her daughter were adorable.

Emily stepped out and closed the door behind her then held out her hand for the keyring. "Any special instructions?"

"Yeah, I have an alarm. When you enter the house, you'll need to enter the code or you'll have the cops descending on this place within minutes."

43

Emily laughed nervously. "Oh, okay. Although you should know, I suck at alarms. They make me uneasy and inevitably I panic and put in the wrong code, or don't put it in on time or whatever. I'm not allowed to open or close the PX anymore because I set it off too many times and my boss finally realized that I was hopeless."

Fletch grinned at the fidgety woman. She was wearing a pair of black yoga pants and a purple tank top. She wasn't flirting with him or trying to catch his notice in any way, and maybe that's why he *did* notice. She was slender, but had curves in all the right places. He could almost picture his hand smoothing up her stomach to her tits and—

He shook his head. Not the time or the place. He had a mission to prepare for and didn't have the headspace at the moment. Fletch cleared his throat and tried to reassure her.

"It's easy. You want to come over and see how it works? Or I can write down the code and you can figure it out later."

"I'd better come now. With my luck, I'd lose the paper or not be able to find the keypad when I got in." She turned the knob and eased the door back open before yelling inside, again not caring that Fletch was standing there. "Annie! I have to go next door for a moment. Come lock the door behind me!" Emily knew it was probably overkill, since she was just going to Fletch's house for a few minutes, but she'd gotten used to locking the door every time she left when she lived in the other apartment complexes; it was hard to break the habit.

They waited and heard little feet running to the door before Annie's voice whined, "I wanna go too!"

"I'll just be a second, baby, you can stay here…"

"I wanna goooooooo!"

"Ann Elizabeth Grant," Emily warned her daughter in a stern voice.

Annie stuck her head out the door and looked up at Fletch. "I wanna come, Fletch. Please?"

Fletch looked at Emily. He would never go against anything she said in front of her daughter, but he gave her a look that he hoped said he didn't mind if the little girl tagged along.

Emily laughed and shook her head. "Lord, what a hangdog look. Fine, Annie, you can come, but don't touch anything in Mr. Fletcher's house."

"Yay!!"

"Go put on your sneakers. Don't bother changing out of your pajamas, we won't be gone that long."

"Okay! Be right back. Don't leave without me!"

Emily smiled as her daughter ran back into the apartment to find her shoes. She turned and looked up at Fletch. "Thanks for letting her come too. We won't stay long. Just show me the code and what to do and we'll get out of your way. I'm sure you have a lot of stuff to do before you leave tomorrow."

Fletch found himself lying. "Nah, I don't have too much I need to get done. It's fine." Actually he had orders he needed to review, maps that needed to be examined, and it was his responsibility, as it was all the guys on the Delta Force team, to come up with a plan of action. They'd all explain their plans the next morning, and they'd figure out the best way to go forward. But he couldn't resist spending a few minutes with Emily and Annie. They always made him smile.

Annie came rushing back at them and almost tripped over the bag sitting on the floor in the doorway. "What's that?" she asked with childlike curiosity.

"It's for you," Fletch told her, picking it up and holding it out.

Annie didn't even reach for it, instead she looked up at her mom as she'd been taught. Emily nodded, letting her daughter know it was okay, and only then did the little girl reach for the bag Fletch was holding out to her.

She looked in and Fletch swore her eyes grew three sizes in her face. She looked up at him. "For me? *Really?* It's not even my birt-day."

"Yes, squirt. For you. I don't know when your birthday is, but I saw them and thought you might like them. It's a special thing, though. Don't expect a present every day. Call it a 'welcome to your new apartment' gift."

Annie kneeled down on the landing and reached into the bag and pulled out two packages. They were GI Joe dolls. Fletch had seen them in a store that morning and thought of Annie. They seemed like the kind of thing she'd like. They were dolls, yes, but Fletch figured the military thing would cancel out the fact that they were the very kind of toy she previously said she didn't like to play with.

Annie reverently put them on the wooden boards of the landing and gazed down at them. She ran her little fingertip over the plastic on one of the boxes and looked up at her mom. "Mommy, they're *new*."

"I see that, sweetie."

"*Brand new*," Annie breathed again, leaning over and putting her face right next to the package, as if talking to the plastic soldier inside. "Hello, soldier man. I'm Annie."

Fletch watched the little girl in confusion. He'd never seen anyone accept a present as Annie had. It was touching, cute…and sad all at the same time. Most children would gleefully rip open the packaging to get to the toys, but Annie didn't look like she was in any hurry to actually get her hands on them. She was gazing down at one of the dolls through the packaging as if it was precious and fragile.

"Annie, do you still want to come with us? Or do you want to stay here with your new toys?" Emily asked in a gentle voice.

The little girl looked up and answered immediately. "With you and Fletch. Will you wait while I put these inside where it's safe and they won't get dirty?"

"Of course, baby. Go on, we'll wait. Take your time."

Fletch watched as Annie carefully picked up one of the packages and placed it back inside the bag. Then she did the same with the other one. She stood up and eased inside the door, disappearing into the apartment again.

"How'd you know she liked military figures?" Emily questioned.

Fletch shrugged and put his hands in his pockets. "She told me the other week."

Emily opened her mouth to say something else, to explain why her daughter was so enamored with the fact that the toys were new, but Annie returned before she could think of how to explain.

The little girl went straight to Fletch and grabbed him around his thighs. She held on tight and squeezed hard. "Thank you, Fletch. Thankyouthankyou-thankyou."

Fletch ran his hand over Annie's head. "You're welcome, sprite."

He stood there awkwardly for a moment, feeling his

heart expand at the sweet affection Annie showed him until Emily urged her daughter, "Come on, let's get going, it's your bedtime, Annie."

The little girl looked up at Fletch, and nodded absently. "It's the bestest thing I've ever gotten. Thank you."

Fletch nodded, thinking that if the ten-dollar GI Joe figurines were the best things Annie had ever received, it was kind of sad, and he'd have to see what he could do to spoil her further...without hurting Emily's feelings, of course. If she couldn't afford to get her daughter new toys, he didn't want to upset her in any way. He cared about both of them...especially Emily. There was just something about her that made him want to wrap her in his arms and hold on tight.

The trio walked across the yard toward the house and Annie held both her mom's hand and Fletch's. She babbled on as they went, apparently back to her old self. They entered the house and Fletch showed Emily where the keypad was for the alarm. He didn't let her know that not only was the alarm system hooked up to the local police department, it was also wired to alert a few other special people Fletch knew and trusted, including Tex back in Pennsylvania.

"The code is two-six-four-three-seven. When you come in, hit those numbers, then the green button. That will disarm the alarm. When you leave, hit the same numbers, two-six-four-three-seven, then the red button. You have one minute to get out of the house when you leave and to punch in the numbers when you enter. If you'll be in here for any length of time—feel free to watch a movie or whatever—hit the same numbers, two-six-four-three-seven, and the yellow button. That will arm the house, but the motion sensors inside won't be activated so you can walk around freely without worrying about setting it off. Got it? Want to practice?"

"Uh…yeah, although I still don't think this is a great idea. I didn't know you had motion sensors."

Fletch watched as Emily nervously keyed in the numbers and set the alarm. Then she punched in the same buttons and hit the green button to turn it off.

"You got it. Easy. I told you."

"That's if I remember the numbers," Emily joked.

"It's easy, Mommy," Annie told her. "It's my name."

"What?"

"My name. Well, it's spelled sorta wrong, but it could still be my name."

Fletch crouched down so he could look Annie in the eye. "How's it spelled, sprite?" Fletch thought to humor the little girl.

"A-N-I-E-S. Like it's mine, but with only one N instead of two."

"What are you talking about, Annie?" Emily asked in confusion.

Annie looked at Fletch and whispered, "It's like the Indian code talkers…it's code. We learnded about them in school."

"The Navajo code talkers?" Fletch asked.

"Uh-huh."

"You wanna let me in on the secret code?"

Annie nodded solemnly. "It's the phone code."

Fletch looked into Annie's blue eyes. She'd leaned into him so trustingly. It was then that he realized *exactly* how smart Emily's little girl was. "The phone code. Yeah, you're right. It is."

"Do one of you want to enlighten me?" Emily asked, crossing her arms over her chest. Watching the handsome man who she thought about way too often kneeling on the ground, talking with her daughter as if she wasn't abnormally smart, was making her heart pound and making her wish for things that were probably only dreams.

"Should we let her in on the secret code?" Fletch asked Annie playfully and winked at her.

She giggled. "Yeah, she's mommy, I think she should know."

Fletch nodded in agreement. "Yeah, keeping secrets from Mommy isn't a good thing." He looked up at Emily. "The phone code. Each number on a phone has certain letters assigned to it. For example, the number two has A, B and C. The number three has D, E and F, and so on."

Annie picked up where Fletch left off. "Yeah, and four is G, H, and I. So the number to his code two-six-four-three-seven can spell lots of things, but one thing it spells is Anie's...with one N instead of two."

Emily looked down at her daughter, dumbfounded. Jesus, she had to look into getting her into a gifted school.

Fletch ruffled Annie's hair as he stood up. "You're one smart cookie."

"I know," Annie told him, smiling.

"Seriously, I said it before," Fletch told Emily, "but please don't hesitate to come over if you want to watch a movie or something. You can put my mail on the counter in the kitchen. I don't think you'll forget the code *now*, will you?"

"No, I don't think I will," Emily agreed, still a little shell-shocked after hearing proof of how smart her daughter really was.

"Good. I'll let you keep that key for whenever you might need it. Come on, I'll walk you back to your place."

"We'll be fine, it's just across the yard."

"I'll walk you back."

Annie took Fletch's hand and pulled him toward the

door. "Hurry up, Mommy, I wanna get back and look at my toys!"

They walked back across the yard and up the stairs to the small apartment over the garage. Emily unlocked the door and Annie tore inside, not bothering to say goodbye to Fletch, too excited to get back to her new toys.

It didn't escape Fletch's notice that Annie said she wanted to get back to her room to *look* at her toys, not play with them. He didn't think it was a mix-up in words. He'd learned over the last few weeks that Annie said what she meant most of the time.

"Thanks for the gift again, she loves them," Emily told Fletch.

"You're welcome."

"How long are you going to be gone? Soldiers get deployed for months at a time, don't they?" she asked.

"Yeah, but I'm in a special group, not with a platoon or unit. I can't really talk much about it, sorry. I'm not sure how long we'll be gone this time. Our missions sometimes last one day, or they can be long-term, up to a year, but I'm pretty sure this one will be short, hopefully around a week."

Emily gaped at him. "A year? Really?"

"Yup, although they've never been that long in the past."

"Oh. Okay."

"You'll be okay here?"

"Yeah, we're great. The apartment is perfect for us. I love it."

"Good. I appreciate you keeping your eye on things while I'm gone."

"Who's looked after it in the past?"

"I've had some friends from work stop in every now and then," Fletch told her.

"Ah. Okay, well, I'm happy to get your mail and make sure all is good for you."

"Thanks. I guess I'll see you when I get back."

"Yeah, sounds good."

"Take care of yourself and Annie while I'm gone."

The words were surprising, but they made her feel good. "I will. Don't worry about us, we'll be fine. *You* be safe. Okay?"

"I will, thanks. See you soon."

"See ya." Emily closed the door behind Fletch and leaned against it. How the hell she'd be able to keep her hands off of him in the future was beyond her. He was beautiful. But as much as she'd hoped he might make a move, he was apparently immune to her. She was way out of practice in flirting. She loved Annie with all her heart, but the little girl wasn't a very good wingman.

Oh well. Maybe when Fletch got back from his mission, she'd see if she could turn on the charm. It probably wasn't very smart and she might make a fool out of herself, but Fletch was so damn sexy and it had been way too long since she'd even been attracted to a man. In the meantime, she'd continue to dream about him.

FLETCH LOCKED THE door behind him and set the alarm. He checked the monitors and watched as the lights went off in the apartment across the yard. He sighed. He was having a hard time keeping away from Emily. She seemed to be everything he liked in a woman. Hardworking, compassionate, easy on the eyes...and she was a great mother. That much was obvious. He'd found himself daydreaming more and more about stripping off her clothes, how she might look up at him with passion in her eyes as he caressed her body.

He'd had a doozy of a dream the other night where he'd stood over her and watched as she masturbated for him. It was hot as hell, and not something he thought he'd get off on. But he'd woken up with a hard-on so intense, he actually turned his head to see if somehow it wasn't a dream. Unfortunately for him, he was alone in his bed, but Fletch immediately shut his eyes, bringing back the image his unconscious mind had dreamed up, and within minutes he'd brought himself to orgasm.

Thoughts of Emily were actually turning into sort of an obsession, one that Fletch knew he needed to do something about. He'd never been the kind of man to sit around and wish for something. He went after what he wanted—and he wanted Emily.

And then there was Annie. Fletch had never thought of himself as the fatherly type, but remembering the look of awe in the little girl's eyes as she saw the military figures he'd brought her, he knew he wanted to see it again and again. He felt protective of her, and wanted to do everything in his power to make her happy.

But he wasn't a good bet when it came to a relationship. Not only was his job extremely dangerous, he'd never felt the need to claim a woman for himself for all time. He never wanted to be so consumed by someone that it affected his work...but he was afraid it might be too late. His new tenant had gotten under his skin.

He wanted Emily *and* her daughter for himself, but he had to be smart, go slow. When Fletch got back from the upcoming mission, he'd make a move and see if Emily had thought about him at all. Even with all the pitfalls in his way, he wanted to make it work...somehow. He hadn't wanted anything in a long time like he wanted Emily.

Chapter Four

THE MAN WAITED at the end of the driveway impatiently, hidden. He knew the asshole soldier and his friends were currently on some mission and it was time to put part two of his plan into action.

He smirked, pulling the black baseball cap down farther on his head as he waited for the woman to get home. It had been so easy to put part one of his plan together. One of the soldiers who he drank and gambled with was a clerk in the same building where the team often had meetings. In return for some debt being overlooked, the clerk had been eavesdropping on their casual conversations for several weeks.

The group was amazingly boring and never openly discussed anything related to missions, but they talked *all* about their personal lives. The clerk had passed along all sorts of random information about the group, including who had profiles on which dating sites and their favorite bar to drink at.

But most useful—that Fletch's new tenant was poor as hell and only paying five hundred bucks a month in rent. Apparently Fletch was an easy mark who felt sorry for the stupid woman and her kid.

The clerk had said the men laughed all the time about the things the woman's daughter said and did. She was some sort of freak brainiac.

The man took off his cap and wiped the sweat from his brow with the bottom of his tank top, then replaced the hat on his head.

The woman's a slut.

The man nodded in agreement with the voice in his head. She was. All women were. Even his ex-girlfriend had only pretended to like him in order to use him.

She'll get hers though.

He smirked. Yeah. She'd get hers. He was smart enough to always find something to hold over people's heads. He never knew when it'd be useful. And now he had all the information he needed to start on the second part of his plan.

The asshole soldier and his entire team would rue the day they embarrassed him and his squad on the battlefield. No one fucked him over and got away with it. *No one.*

When a car pulled into the long driveway toward the garage, the man silently and carefully made his way down the pavement, keeping to the trees as he went.

EMILY PULLED INTO the garage and sighed wearily. It'd been a long day, longer than most for some reason. Maybe it was the gigantic sale they were having at the PX, and the craziness that ensued whenever that happened. Maybe it was because she was actually missing Fletch. It wasn't that she'd spent a lot of time with him, and it had only been three days since he'd left, but it was comforting to come back to the apartment and know he was right across the yard.

Or maybe it was the fact that Annie was being extra talkative today. Emily told herself a long time ago she'd never tell her daughter she was talking too much. She was just expressing herself, it was what kids did. But, not for the first time, she would kill for some silence right about now.

"And then John told the teacher she was stupid!" Annie exclaimed, obviously shocked someone would talk back to an adult, and her teacher at that.

"He did? What happened then?"

"Well, Mrs. O told him to prove it."

Emily smiled. Mrs. O's name was actually Ogliaruso, but that was quite a mouthful for six-year-olds, so she'd happily told her students to call her Mrs. O instead. Emily reached in the backseat for the two plastic bags of groceries she'd picked up at work. The granola bars and the loaf of bread had been marked down since their expiration dates had passed, and the six cans of soup were discounted because they were dented. "And could he prove she was wrong?" she asked, waiting for Annie to step outside the garage so she could push the button to close the door and run out herself.

"No. He tried though, and when he couldn't, he pouted and threw his pencil across the room."

"Oh, that sounds dangerous."

Annie nodded and hitched her GI Joe backpack higher up on her back. "It was. And that's why he got sent to the principal's office. Mrs. O told us that he was in trouble, not for telling her she was wrong, but for throwing things. She says that it's okay to question...atority, but not to remort to violence."

"*Authority*, and *resort* to violence," Emily corrected automatically.

"Yeah, that's what I said," Annie grouched at her mother.

"Hello."

The voice surprised both Emily and Annie and they twirled around as the garage door closed behind them. A man was standing way too close to Annie for Emily's peace of mind, and she reached out with her free hand and pushed her daughter behind her.

Emily had never seen the man before. He held himself with the same sort of...conceit that she'd seen in Fletch, but it seemed different with this man. Fletch was confident, but in a protective way. He knew that he was stronger and more dangerous than most others around him. But not once had Emily felt as though he was dangerous to her or Annie.

But this man was egotistical in the way bullies were. His lips were quirked upward in a smirk, as if he knew she was scared of him. His black tank top clung to the muscles on his chest, and Emily could see a black skull tattoo on his forearm. He wore camouflage pants, like she saw every day at work, and had a ballcap pulled low over his forehead, making it hard to see his eyes. It was obvious he was a military man. Emily concluded he must be there to see Fletch.

"Fletch isn't here."

"I know." His answer was immediate and cocky. "I'm here to see you, Emily."

"Annie, go upstairs." Emily used her "mom" voice, the one Annie had learned never to disobey. Call it a mother's instinct, but everything about the stranger made the hair on the back of her neck stand up straight. Emily had no idea how he knew her name, but her protective side took over and she wanted her daughter as far away from this man as she could get her.

Annie took the keys her mom held out to her with a shrug, turned around and went up the stairs on the side of the building without a word.

"She's pretty."

"What do you want?" Emily asked, trying to get his

attention off of her daughter.

"Interesting question. Here's the thing...Emily...your landlord owes me money."

"Why don't you wait until he's back and you can ask *him* for it," Emily answered with a hint of snark. She didn't like that this man knew her name. She didn't like that he'd been able to surprise her. She *especially* didn't like the way he'd watched Annie.

"Because. I talked to him before he left, and he told me *you* would have the money for me."

"*What?*"

"Yeah. He said that he rented this place to you for a steal, and that you would pay me monthly to make up what he owed."

Emily wrinkled her brow in confusion. It didn't sound like something Fletch would do at all, but she hadn't known the man for that long, and they'd really only talked in passing.

"Come sit with me," the soldier demanded, reaching for her groceries and setting them on the ground gently. "Don't make a fuss about it and do everything I tell you, and no one will get hurt. Understand?" He took her hand in his as a lover might, but instead of holding it tenderly, he grasped it tightly, hurting her as her fingers were squeezed together.

Not knowing what the man wanted—and more importantly, what he might to do her or Annie if she

RESCUING EMILY

"made a fuss"—she followed along behind him without a struggle. "What's your name?" she asked, as she was towed over to a large rock alongside the driveway.

The man pushed her down, giving her no choice but to sit. He turned her slightly, putting her back to the main house, and took her other hand in his as well. He held them tightly as he kneeled down in front of her.

"My name doesn't matter. What matters is that Fletch owes me a truckload of money."

"I don't—"

"You're going to pay me two hundred a week."

Emily recoiled in shock. Two hundred...a *week*? There was no way she could pay that on top of her rent, food, and gas. Again, she didn't think Fletch would put his debts on her, no matter how desperate he was. "I don't believe you. Fletch wouldn't make me pay his debts."

"No? He thought you might say that. He knows you've been eyeballin' him, but he's so far out of your league, he thinks it's hilarious you thought he might be interested in you that way. The other day, when we talked about your situation here, he told me how he was only charging you five Benjamins a month. You told him with the money you were saving on rent, you were working on building up your savings account. How much you got saved already? A thousand bucks? Two? He owes me twenty times that.

"Your landlord has a gambling problem, Emily. He owes me a shit-ton of money, and if you want to continue to live here with your too-smart daughter, safe from those predators who are all over the city, you'll pay me."

Emily paled, but the man continued on, seeming to enjoy her distress.

"And if you don't? If you decide I'm bluffing and go to your landlord to try to straighten this all out? Get him to pay his own debts? Child Protective Services will receive a call about an abusive situation. They'll hear all about how a little girl is living on a property with a single man who has parties with his male friends all the time. How she's left alone for long stretches of time while her mom works."

"They wouldn't believe you," Emily said in a tone that wasn't as strong as she wanted it to be.

"Maybe. Maybe not. But they'd have to investigate. And when CPS looks into allegations of abuse, the child is taken out of the home and placed in foster care. You want to see your daughter in foster care, Emily?"

"No!" Emily exclaimed, horrified. The mere thought of being separated from Annie, of not knowing if she had proper meals, if she was being allowed to read what she wanted, ripped her heart out. "Of course not. But, I don't have anything to do with him, I barely know him. I—"

Emily now recognized the look in the man's eyes as evil as he brought one hand up to her face and caressed it, brushing a stray lock of brown hair behind her ear. She flinched at the tender gesture, knowing it was anything but.

"I don't care. And I know you're lying. You know him. He's told us how you've undressed him with your eyes every time he sees you. He'd have no problem fucking you, if that's what it takes; he'd never turn down a chance to get some. But Emily, know this—I'll do everything I can to get your precious Annie taken away from you if you don't pay me every week."

He must've seen the rebellion in her eyes, because he leaned in close and snarled, spittle hitting her in the face. "I'm a sniper, Emily Grant. You think I can't take your daughter away from you? I can put a bullet between her eyes and no one will ever know I was there. Maybe you don't give a shit about Fletch for more than a way to get off. But what about Annie? She likes to play outside, doesn't she? You can't keep her inside all the time. You can't protect her while she's at school during recess, can you?" He paused, then crowed, "I always get my way, babe. Don't fucking doubt it."

Emily was trembling by this point, but she could see the man was one hundred percent serious. She jerked her head up and down once, letting him know she understood his threat perfectly.

The scary man stood, keeping his head tilted down, and held out his hand to her as if he were a gentleman at a ball asking her to dance. "Good, I'm glad we had this talk."

She ignored his hand. "How will I get you the money?"

"When Fletch isn't home, I'll come here. When he is, I'll come to the PX."

"Not my job!" Emily protested, not wanting him anywhere near her coworkers. He could cause her a lot of trouble and she needed her job, especially if she was going to have to come up with an extra thousand dollars or so a month to pay him what Fletch owed and to protect her daughter.

A little voice in the back of her head was screaming that something wasn't right...that she only needed to talk to Fletch and he'd take care of this for her. But then she remembered what the man had said. The threat that if she went to Fletch he'd call CPS. And that he and Fletch had laughed at her obvious attraction to him. She hadn't thought she'd been that transparent. There was also the man's threats against Annie. How could she— or how would Fletch, for that matter—fight against a bullet? She was so confused and didn't know what to do.

The soldier leaned down, grabbed her hand and pulled her upright, putting both hands on her shoulders and leaning in, having the nerve to rest his forehead against hers in a pseudo-intimate way. He ground out in a low, menacing voice, "Yes, your job. Don't fuck with me, Emily, and I won't fuck with you. Two hundred a week. No more. No less. I'll see you next week for our first installment. Say hello to pretty Annie for me."

He kissed her forehead, and all Emily wanted to do was scrub her arm across it to remove the slimy feel of his lips on her skin. He pretended to tip his hat to her after stepping away then headed up the driveway toward the road. She had no idea if he had a car parked somewhere nearby or not.

She moved toward the garage, not turning her back to him for a moment. She picked up the groceries the man had placed on the ground and when she reached the bottom of the stairs, hurried up them. She pounded on the door when she reached it.

"Annie, it's me. Open the door!"

Her daughter must've been waiting for her, because Emily immediately heard the lower chain being removed and the door opened within moments.

"Mommy!"

Emily burst into the room and slammed the door behind her, locking the chains and making sure the bolt was fastened. She knew she was breathing too hard and likely scaring the shit out of Annie, but she couldn't control it.

"Mommy?" This time the word was a question.

Emily looked down and saw her daughter wringing her hands, eyes full of tears and her eyebrows drawn down in worry. "Who was that man?"

She squatted on the ground and gathered Annie in her arms. Emily held her, caressing the back of her head, giving as well as taking comfort from the embrace. "Nobody to worry about, baby."

"I didn't like him."

Out of the mouths of babes, was Emily's first thought. She didn't like him either. But she didn't want to worry Annie. She was sensitive enough already. Emily needed to make sure Annie was cautious, but not scared out of her skull. She pulled back and put her hands on Annie's small shoulders. Emily tried to find the right words to explain what the hell had just happened.

"He wanted to talk about adult stuff with me, baby. I was proud of you for instantly obeying me when I told you to come up to our house. Thank you."

Annie bit her lip, and still looked worried. Emily spoke quickly. "You remember our old landlord, right?" When Annie nodded and got a disgusted look on her face, Emily explained, "I want you to do what you did when you saw *him*, if you ever see the man who was here today again."

"Run away and hide?"

"Exactly."

"Is he bad?"

Emily shook her head, not wanting Annie to share that with anyone. She loved her daughter, but she was notoriously bad at keeping secrets. The last thing she wanted was for her to tell Fletch about the "bad man" who was hanging around. He'd want to know more, and anything she told him would probably get back to the man who'd threatened Annie.

Emily didn't like her blackmailer, but she knew how it felt to be stuck between a rock and a hard place. Fletch had done her a favor by letting her live here for such a low rent. She felt positive he hadn't done it with the intent of having her pay the money to someone else. Sometimes shit just happened and you had to deal with it. She wasn't happy with the way Fletch had decided to deal with *his* problem, but she'd help him, and in return, would make sure Annie was kept safe. While she paid some of his debt—and looked for another place to live—maybe she'd suggest he find some help for his addiction.

Resigned to doing what she had to do for the moment, Emily resolved to talk to Fletch and get him to own up to his problem, and hopefully deal with his friend *without* involving her and Annie. If she could convince him to take over his debt sooner rather than later, she'd be off the hook and they could each move on with their lives.

"He's not bad," Emily told her daughter, "he's just *my* friend, and you shouldn't be around him. Okay? So if you see him, you get up here to our place. And if for some reason you can't get up here, go to Fletch's."

"And get the key hidden in the fake piece of grass hidden under the bush next to the door and then put in the code. Right, Mommy?"

"Right. You remember the code?"

"A-N-I-E-S."

"Yes, two-six-four-three-seven."

"I'm allowed to go into Fletch's house when he's not here?"

"If you see that man, and I'm not around, then yes. Otherwise no. Only with me. Okay, baby?"

"Okay, Mommy. I'm hungry."

Emily hugged her daughter to her once again, holding on tight and vowing to herself that no one would ever hurt Annie as long as she was around.

Finally, when Annie wriggled in her grasp, she pulled back. "Why don't you check out the soup I bought today and pick out which one you'd like tonight," Emily told her.

"Yay! I love soup!"

Emily smiled and stood up. Annie did love soup. They didn't have it a lot, and it looked like once the six cans she'd bought today ran out, it would be a while before she had it again. It was expensive compared to other things she could buy.

Hearing her own stomach growl, Emily put a hand on her belly and took a deep breath. She had a feeling that the man knew she didn't have an extra two hundred dollars a week to give him, but didn't give a damn.

She'd been through tough times before. She could do this. She made just enough money each week to pay the man and cover their few monthly expenses. She'd be okay for a little while, because she *did* have some money saved up, he was right about that. But before too long, she would reach the end of her savings and it'd be a whole different ballgame. But she'd cut off her own arm before Annie went hungry.

Emily looked around the apartment with new eyes, mentally calculating what she could and couldn't do without. She had some things she could sell, nothing of Fletch's, but the small microwave she'd bought, the little end tables and the frames she'd gotten from Goodwill and spruced up with some doodads from the craft store. She could sell them.

They'd be all right. They had to be.

Chapter Five

FLETCH SCOWLED DOWN at his phone as he watched the tapes from his security system. The cameras were set to record when they detected movement. Their mission had only taken a week, as he'd told Emily, and he was sitting on the plane at Robert Gray Army Airfield at Fort Hood waiting for them to be cleared so they could go inside, debrief, shower, and head home.

"What are you frowning about so fiercely?" Keane "Ghost" Bryson, his friend and teammate, asked.

"My security tapes," Fletch told him shortly.

"You have a break-in?"

"No." Fletch had watched the first couple of days, where Emily and Annie had pulled out of the garage in the morning and arrived back each day around the same time. He'd smiled in amusement because he could see Annie's mouth moving nonstop as she chattered to her mom. He could only guess what she was telling Emily.

The duo had gathered his mail and brought it up to the apartment. Fletch figured Emily had probably collected it and would bring it over when he returned, or maybe drop it off in chunks rather than entering his house each day. She really *did* have an aversion to alarms.

But the third day he was gone was different. She'd pulled into the garage as usual—and then suddenly there was a man with her.

The cameras hadn't recorded any other vehicles entering the property, so he'd obviously walked up to the garage, and managed to avoid being recorded while doing so. He didn't like the fact that someone could get onto his property and avoid the cameras, and Fletch made a mental note to adjust them so they'd record every angle of his driveway.

As soon as she saw the man, Emily had sent Annie up to their apartment while she'd stayed and talked with him. He'd held her hands, kneeled down while they'd spoken, and had even put his forehead against hers before he'd said goodbye.

She hadn't seemed overjoyed to see him, but she hadn't seemed too alarmed, either. They'd held hands while they talked and while he couldn't see either of their faces, she hadn't pulled away or run from him, making him assume she knew the man.

The kiss the man had bestowed on Emily's forehead had made Fletch's stomach lurch, and he swallowed hard just thinking about it. He'd had no idea Emily had a boyfriend. She hadn't mentioned him before. Not once.

"It's nothing," Fletch said, waving his hand in dismissal.

"Sure looked like something to me," Ghost insisted.

"It's not. I just realized while watching the tapes that there was something I should've done before I left, but it's too late now." Fletch wasn't trying to be coy, but he hadn't talked about his attraction to his sexy renter with any of the guys on the team, or anyone else. He'd talked about how he had a new renter, and even about little Annie, but not how much he admired and liked her and how he wanted to get to know her better. He'd been respecting her privacy, but also enjoying what he'd thought had been flirtatious looks she'd been sending his way. Obviously he'd been way off with that one.

Ghost frowned, suspecting something was up with his friend, but not wanting to push. He shrugged, dismissing the topic since Fletch had inferred it wasn't a big deal. "We've got the next two days off, then we're slated to play the bad-guys-in-the-desert scenario."

"Again?" Coach griped from next to them, obviously listening to the conversation.

"Yup," Ghost affirmed.

"Damn. I hate always being the bad guys," Beatle commented, saying what all of them were thinking.

The Army had decided that every base around the country would go through training exercises, much like the National Training Center in Fort Irwin, California, offered. The Army spent a lot of money building "cities" on bases, and platoons would rotate through training exercises, learning the best ways to navigate and fight. Since Fort Hood was a base that had deployments to the Middle East frequently, training situations were held regularly.

The Delta Force teams had some of the best firsthand knowledge about enemy tactics, so they were often tasked to play the bad guys. The fact they were Delta was a highly kept secret, and not many on the base were privy to that information, but those who did know liked to use them in training, since they were the best of the best. If the regular troops could hold their own against the Deltas, they would be in good shape to be deployed overseas.

While it was good training, for both sides, it *did* get old for the team to always play the role of the enemy.

"The last time we did this, that infantry squad got really pissed. It was as if they didn't realize it was just an exercise," Truck commented unnecessarily.

They all knew the other soldiers were upset that they'd been taken out within minutes of entering the "city" because, that night, after the Deltas had gone out for a beer to celebrate, ten of the infantrymen had ambushed them in the parking lot. The soldiers had lost as badly in the dim light of the bar parking lot as they had in the exercise—and hadn't taken it any better. No matter how many times Ghost had told the men, "It was only a training drill, chill out," they hadn't listened.

The incident hadn't been reported by either side, but Ghost's team hoped the feelings of animosity had lessened since they'd been gone. While it had been just another day on the job for the Deltas, the other soldiers obviously didn't feel the same way. They'd taken it personally, instead of treating it as a learning experience.

"We don't have a choice," Ghost said, obviously frustrated. "I told the colonel that it wasn't a good idea to always use us, that they needed to rotate the troops in and out of the scenarios, on both sides, but so far he hasn't been able to convince his superiors."

"Shit. Well, keep your heads up. The last thing we need is to be fucking shot by one of our own because of this shit," Blade groused.

"I'm gonna be pissed if someone shoots me on US soil," Beatle agreed. "It'd be a bitch to survive the shit we go through only to be killed by a namby-pamby infantryman."

Fletch nodded in agreement as his teammates griped about the upcoming training scenarios. They were a good diversion from their everyday jobs and from planning real life-or-death missions, and the laser weapons were fun to use, but with the increasing tensions between the regular troops and the "bad guys," it wasn't worth it. It was well past time for the Army to use the regular platoons and squads as the bad guys. They could learn just as much, if not more, from the exercise.

Outwardly, Fletch looked as if he was paying close attention to his friends, but in reality he was bemoaning the fact that Emily appeared to have a boyfriend. He'd waited too long to make his move. He hated the fact that she and the mystery man appeared so close on his tapes, how the other man had held her hands, and how he'd felt comfortable enough with her to not only rest his forehead on hers, but to kiss her as well.

It had to be a fairly new relationship, though, because if Emily was his woman, he wouldn't be content with a chaste kiss on her forehead. He closed his eyes and pressed his lips together. Damn. He'd dreamed about her lips on his, and even though he'd thought she was clearly indicating interest, he'd obviously misread her signals.

Fletch couldn't see the man clearly in the tapes because of the hat he'd worn pulled low over his face, so he had just his general build and height, but he and Emily looked close. Closer than *he'd* ever been to her, that was for sure.

His finger hovered over the delete button of the video on the app on his phone. There was no reason to keep the recording…but something stopped him.

Maybe it was how the man had just appeared without having triggered any of the cameras on the property. Maybe it was something about the way Annie tore up the stairs. Maybe he was just a glutton for punishment.

If nothing else, Fletch would keep the recording so he could remind himself Emily was taken when he had a moment of weakness around her. He closed the app and, hearing they were finally cleared to deplane, reached for his bag.

Well shit. You snooze, you lose. He should've remembered that statement earlier. He hadn't thought Emily was dating anyone, especially with her schedule being exactly the same, day in and day out. But she was pretty, and worked on base. She had to come in contact with hundreds of other soldiers. It was no wonder one had finally caught her eye.

Her boyfriend was tall, in shape, and although Fletch couldn't see him all that clearly, he supposed he could see the appeal. He just hated it.

He mentally shrugged. There wasn't anything he could do about it now. He'd just have to wait things out and see if they lasted. Maybe they wouldn't be compatible and he'd have his chance later.

"MOMMEEEEEEEEEEE! FLETCH IS back!" Annie

screeched as she heard the garage door going up below them.

"I hear, baby. Can you please try to use your indoor voice?" Emily was nervous to see Fletch. She'd stressed all week about the mysterious man and what he'd said about Fletch. She knew she needed to clear the air and talk to him about what was going on. But it was easier said than done. Not only did she have to worry about the man going through with his threats to call CPS if she brought it up with Fletch, she hated conflict and didn't want to embarrass the man. But surely he didn't want her to have to pay his debts? He just didn't seem the type of man to rely on a woman for any kind of monetary support, whether that was paying for a dinner when they went on a date or paying his gambling debts. He was just too…manly.

"Can we go down and see him? Please, please, please?" Annie was in full whine mode and Emily knew nothing would shake it out of her except allowing her to get her way.

"Okay, but be careful on the steps," Emily told her daughter as she raced to the door and got to work on the security chains, straining on her tiptoes to reach the upper one.

Annie tore down the stairs, not even waiting for her mom to turn on the light so she wouldn't trip on her way down. "Fletch! Fletch! You're back! I missed you!"

Her daughter disappeared around the corner of the garage and by the time Emily got to the bottom of the stairs, Annie was engulfed in Fletch's embrace.

"Hey, sprite. Look at you. I think you grew an inch while I was gone!"

"You're silly," Annie told him seriously. "Humans don't grow that fast!"

"You got me there. Were you a good girl this past week?"

"Yes."

Fletch leaned over and put the child on the ground and smiled down at her.

"Did you get me a present?"

"Ann Elizabeth," Emily scolded. "You know that's not how you behave."

Annie scuffed her shoe in the dirt on the ground. "Sorry, Fletch. Love is the best present I could ever get. I'm glad you're home safe and sound." She was obviously repeating what her mom had told her often.

Fletch got down on one knee and looked into Annie's eyes. "I was traveling for work, not for pleasure, sprite. There wasn't any good place to shop where I was."

She nodded at him solemnly. "It's okay. I have my Army men you gave me. You want to come up and look at them with me? They're still safe inside their boxes."

Emily felt a lump in her throat. She'd never been

able to give her daughter new toys. Birthday and Christmas presents all came from the thrift store or yard sales. She cleaned them up so that they looked as new as possible, but they both knew they weren't. Every night, Annie talked to her Army men, safe inside their plastic packaging. She refused to take them out, wanting them to stay in perfect condition. Having a new toy was an anomaly, one that Emily knew she'd forever be some-what jealous of Fletch for giving to Annie.

"I can't, sorry. Another time, yeah?"

"Okay." Annie was rarely disappointed. If Fletch said he'd come up another time, she'd hold him to it.

"Welcome home, Fletch. Bye!"

Emily and Fletch watched as Annie raced back up the stairs. She almost never walked, always in a hurry to go somewhere.

"Did you have a good trip?"

Fletch nodded, but didn't say anything.

"I brought your mail." Emily held out the bundle she'd grabbed before heading down the stairs. "If you weren't back in a day or so, I would've brought it over and made sure all was well in your house, but I didn't think I needed to yet since it's only been six days."

"Thanks." Fletch reached out and took the stack of mail from her. "Everything go okay here?"

Emily nodded, sensing something was different with Fletch, but not able to put her finger on it. Maybe he was worried about his gambling debts—or maybe he felt guilty about her paying them. She opened her mouth to bring it up, but he beat her to it.

"I saw you had a visitor this week," Fletch said in a monotone voice.

"What?"

"A visitor. I told you this place is wired; I have cameras set up."

"Oh," Emily breathed out in relief. Fletch had seen the man come by. He'd bring up the money and make it right. Annie would be safe.

"I might not have made it clear before, but of course you're welcome to have guests. The apartment is your home; I don't want you to feel bad about having people over."

Emily looked at Fletch in confusion. "What?"

"Emily, this is your home now. I wouldn't appreciate any wild parties, but you can certainly invite your friends, or boyfriends, up to your apartment."

Still confused, she opened her mouth to ask Fletch to please talk to his friend, to take care of his own gambling debts—and to make sure he knew about how the man had threatened to have Annie taken away from her—when he continued.

"There are things about me, about my life, that I can't share with you. But you being here makes my life easier, and I appreciate it. It's nice that you can help me out."

Emily bit her lip and stared up at Fletch in disbelief. Not only did it sound like he knew about the man and his demands, but that he *expected* her to pay the other soldier.

"I want my friends to be *your* friends too. They're important to me, and they know everything about me. Eventually you'll meet them all. But I don't want you to feel uncomfortable about bringing your own friends around either. All right?"

Emily could only nod. She was in shock. She'd been sure he'd tell her not to worry about the payments his friend was demanding. But he wasn't saying *anything* about it—and it sounded as if the payments were a part of her agreement to stay on his property.

"I'm beat. I'm going to head inside. I'll talk to you later, yeah?" She needed to get away from Fletch. She'd trusted him, enough to rent the apartment over his garage. It wasn't as though Fletch lived in the center of town, his place was somewhat isolated. But she'd felt safe with him nearby.

She wanted to confront him. Wanted to yell at him for sucking her into his problems, but now she was scared of him. Scared that the man she'd thought she was coming to know had only been an illusion. She was frightened and discouraged. She needed to take a bit of time and go over what she wanted to say to him. If it had been just her, she would've had it out right then and there. But she had to think about Annie. Her daughter was her life, and if she was somehow taken away from her, Emily didn't know what she'd do.

"Okay." Fletch nodded and turned his back to her and headed for his front door.

Emily swallowed hard and dropped her gaze to the ground in despair. She slowly turned to her stairs and climbed them, mind whirling with what had just happened.

Fletch was a gambler, he owed his friend money, and he expected her to pay his debt.

She swallowed the sobs that threatened. She had no idea how she was going to get out of the mess Fletch had put her in, but she'd do it. She was a fighter, this wasn't going to bring her down, and it would *not* touch her daughter. No way in hell.

PUTTING DOWN HIS monocular, the man hiding in the bushes smiled. He scooted backward very carefully, not rustling the leaves and branches as he moved. He backed up until he was well away from the house—and the cameras that the soldier thought he'd so cleverly hidden.

It looked like Emily and the sergeant suddenly weren't so buddy-buddy anymore. Perfect. So far, everything was working out as he'd planned. Soon, he'd be able to start putting the next part into motion. The sergeant and his team would regret dismissing him so easily. They'd see who the better soldiers were. Feeling in control over another human's life was icing on the cake.

She deserves to be miserable.

He agreed. She *did* deserve it. Since the father wasn't around she had to have denied the man access to his child. And that was wrong. His *own* mother shouldn't have divorced his dad the way she did.

He smiled and nodded as the voice continued to praise and reinforce his plan as he walked to his car, which he'd stashed half a mile down the road from the soldier's place. As he drove back to his apartment, going through different scenarios in his mind on how the final battle would take place, he grinned. It was perfect. He and his squad would prevail. He couldn't wait.

Chapter Six

"HOW'S THAT PRETTY neighbor of yours?" Ghost asked Fletch a couple of weeks later during a break in their PT.

"Good, I guess."

"You guess?"

Fletch shrugged. "Haven't seen much of her since we got back from that op."

"Really? I thought you guys were getting to know each other?"

Fletch had thought so too. But ever since he'd gotten back from that mission, she'd been detached. He still saw Annie every once in a while, but Emily was keeping her distance from him. He figured it was probably because of her boyfriend, so he hadn't pushed. "Yeah, well, she has a boyfriend, so I'm guessing she doesn't want to give me any ideas."

"Did you have ideas before the boyfriend was in the picture?" Ghost asked perceptively.

Fletch rolled his neck, trying to get the stiffness out of it. "Doesn't matter if I did or didn't. She's taken."

"You met the boyfriend?"

"Nope. She's not bringing him around...at least not while I'm there."

"Really? Does that seem odd to you?"

"Not really. I saw he came by earlier this week. I'd already left for PT and Emily was leaving for work and to take Annie to school. The cameras don't have the range I might like, but he was waiting for her at the end of the driveway. He met her at her car, she got out, they spoke for a minute or so, she gave him a letter or something, they hugged, and he followed her down the road."

"For someone who says it doesn't matter if she has a boyfriend or not, you watched that tape pretty carefully," Ghost noted dryly.

Fletch ran his hand through his hair and shrugged. "I don't poach, Ghost. I'll never be the reason a woman cheated on her boyfriend or husband."

"I know. I'm just making an observation."

"Anyway, she's only been renting the apartment for a couple months. It's not my business."

"It might make you feel better if you didn't check your cameras compulsively like you've been doing."

"Yeah."

The two men were silent for a beat before Ghost asked, "Any more trouble with the infantry guys?"

Fletch shook his head. At least the colonel finally got

someone to listen, and all the troops would now be taking their turns rotating through the city scenario. "No, they've been quiet."

"Quiet makes me nervous," Ghost spat, uncharacteristically harsh. At Fletch's surprised look, he continued, "I know, I know, but something Hollywood said the other day had me thinking."

"What'd he say?"

"Blade brought up the fact that most of the time, soldiers are hotheads, we bluster and bitch about shit, but then let it go. It's women who let stuff sit inside and don't talk about it. They plot and plan in their heads and come to conclusions based on information they *think* they know."

"Yeah, and…?"

"And these guys aren't acting like men…or soldiers. That time they ambushed us in the parking lot should've clued us in. They aren't going to just sit back and let go of what they think is a diss to their manhood and skills as soldiers."

"So they're plotting instead of coming to us like men to work it out," Fletch concluded.

"Exactly."

"So we need to be on our toes against retaliation," Fletch commented unnecessarily.

"Yup. You should talk to Emily and her daughter as well."

Fletch looked sharply at Ghost. "They're just my tenants."

"Right, but they're also women, and living on your property. What if those assclowns decide it'd be fun to burn down your garage and that sweet Charger you've got in there? Cameras aren't going to keep them safe if someone wants to cause problems."

Fletch's face paled. Jesus, he hadn't thought of that. He was an idiot. "I gotta go."

"Yeah, figured you might. I'll see you later."

Fletch absently waved as he headed to his car, looking at his watch. Emily would be at work by now, he'd swing by the PX and talk to her really quickly, make sure she knew to be aware of strangers on his property, and to let him know if she saw anything unusual. He might not be dating her, but she and Annie meant a lot to him. He'd never forgive himself if something happened to them and he hadn't warned her ahead of time.

EMILY TRIED TO concentrate on the shelf she was stocking, but it was no use. Having Fletch's friend show up at the end of the driveway—when Annie was in the car with her—had freaked her out. He knew exactly when she'd be there, and when Fletch would be gone.

He'd blocked her car so she had to stop and walked

up to her window as calmly as he pleased. Emily, not wanting Annie to overhear him, grabbed the envelope she'd been carrying around in preparation, and got out to meet him.

"Hey, babe. Got something for me?"

Emily had held out the envelope without a word.

He took it without looking inside. "Thanks. I'll make sure Fletch knows you've been making regular payments for him, and that you're doing what he expects." He leaned close, putting an arm around her waist and pulling her into him. He brushed his lips across her cheek and then put his mouth next to her ear.

"Don't fuck with me, babe. I can see you're pissed by those pretty eyes of yours. Don't even think about doing something stupid. Annie's looking real cute in her jumper this morning. You wouldn't want anything to happen to her, would you? I bet there's a foster daddy who'd take a shine to her…if you know what I mean."

Emily had stood stock still in his embrace and shuddered. She might've tried to convince herself that maybe the man wasn't going to go through with his threats, but with those words, she knew she'd been wrong. She felt something shrivel up inside her, knowing Fletch and that monster were friends. That after the present he'd bought Annie, and how nice he'd been to her, and how outraged he'd been on her behalf after hearing how the little girl had been treated by others, Fletch would still knowingly put Annie's life in danger, and wouldn't care if she was taken away from her mother to live with strangers.

Emily sighed and sagged on the little stool she was sitting on as she stocked the shelf with bottles upon bottles of perfumed shower gel. She was heartsick. She'd misread a man...again. It had been bad enough with Annie's father, but with Fletch, it somehow hurt ten times more. He'd been so nice and open with her daughter. Even after their first meeting, she'd gotten good vibes from him, going so far as to think he might be interested in her, but obviously her "bad man" meter was broken.

"Hey, Em."

Emily was startled so badly she would've slipped off the stool if it wasn't for the hand on her arm, catching her. She looked up into the eyes of the man she'd been lambasting herself over for the last twenty minutes. Quickly standing up, Emily took a step back and away from Fletch.

"Hey. What're you doing here?" Her words came out harsher than she'd intended.

"I had a chat with one of my friends this morning and wanted to come and talk to you about something. You have a minute?"

Not able to help the hope that soared through her, Emily nodded quickly. Maybe he was coming to tell her that he'd talked to the asshole and he'd had second thoughts about her paying off his debt. "Yeah, you want to go out back?"

"That'd be great, thanks."

Emily led the way through the store and passed by Jimmy's office on the way out the back door, telling him she was taking a ten-minute break.

Fletch held the door for her as they headed outside. The day was already warm, not surprising for Texas. Emily waved at two of her co-workers taking a smoke break and led Fletch over to one of the picnic tables under some trees. Management had set them up so the employees had a comfortable place out of the sun to eat lunch or take breaks.

They sat on opposite sides of the table and Emily waited for Fletch to tell her why he was there.

"So, as I said, I was talking to my friend, and I wanted to let you know that you need to be careful."

Emily's brows came down in confusion. "What do you mean?"

"My job isn't the safest, and sometimes there are others that get...irritated with me. I'd hate for something to happen to you or Annie."

Emily could feel her heartbeat pick up and the adrenaline course through her system. Was he going to tell her that she didn't have to worry about the other man anymore? That he'd make sure no one took Annie from her? "Annie and I aren't safe?"

"Look…" Fletch ran his hand through his hair, clearly agitated. "I'm not saying this right, but the bottom line is that if my fuck-ups leak into my personal life, I don't want you and Annie to get stuck in the crosshairs of that."

"Maybe we should just go then," Emily said, wondering if she'd be able to get out of the bind she'd found herself in so easily.

"No. You aren't going anywhere, that's not what I meant. Stay. I like having you guys around."

"If you're having…problems…maybe you should talk to your friend? Maybe you guys can work it out between the two of you and I don't have to be involved," Emily tentatively suggested.

"But you *are* involved, you live on my property," Fletch said resolutely. "And I've talked to my friend. Believe me, we've spent a lot of time discussing the situation, and you and Annie. You're better off where you are, doing exactly what you're doing. Look, if someone comes around that you don't like the look of, just tell me. I'll take care of it for you."

"What if it's your friend?" Emily asked quietly.

"My friends won't hurt you or your daughter. They'd rather die first."

"Are you sure?"

"I'm sure. If they ask you to do something, do it.

They have your best interests at heart."

"Do they have yours?" Emily asked, thoroughly confused. How could Fletch sit there and say that his friend threatening to take away or shoot Annie was "in her best interests"?

"Of course. They'd do anything for me. Just as I would for them. No one fucks with what's ours."

Emily's heart dropped. There was her answer. His friendship with the asshole meant more to him than a struggling single mom. Money was obviously very important to him, to both men.

Emily wanted to cry. She felt so far out of her league it wasn't funny. Not only was she scared, but she was hungry, her savings was steadily being drained every week, and she was thoroughly disillusioned.

This was the last time she was getting involved with any military man, ever. They were all scum. No matter how they seemed on the outside, deep down, all they cared about was themselves.

"Okay."

"Okay?"

"Yeah, okay. I'll do what your friend wants. Do you think…after this is over…you'll consider getting some help?"

"Help? Help with what?"

"You know…your situation."

"Don't worry about that. My friends and I are dealing with it. I know what I'm doing."

"Hmmmm."

Fletch leaned over the table and picked up one of her hands. He brushed his thumb against the back of it. "I appreciate you being understanding about this. All I want is for you and Annie to be safe."

Emily almost choked on the bile that rose from her throat. Yeah right. Safe from who? "We will be. I'll never let anything happen to my daughter."

"I know."

"I know you do," she told him sadly, finally understanding that was why he'd rented the apartment to her in the first place. She was an easy mark. Lure in the single mother and get her grateful, then sic his friend on her. She was an idiot.

Fletch's head cocked as he examined her. "Are you sure you're okay with this?"

"Yeah, I'm sure. I don't really have a choice."

He squeezed her hand once more then stood up. "It's for your safety. Just remember that. I'll see you later, yeah?"

Emily nodded and sat stock still as Fletch leaned over and brushed his lips against her cheek in a chaste goodbye kiss. "Later."

"Bye."

Emily sat on the table in the hot Texas morning long after Fletch left. She thought through a million scenarios and couldn't figure any way out of what was happening to her. She had held out hope that Fletch had no idea what his friend was doing, but it was obvious after their "talk" that he was fully aware...and didn't give a shit.

Finally, she pulled herself up and went back inside the PX and to the shelves that needed stocking. She was no closer to figuring out a solution to the situation now than she'd been that morning, and she felt more alone than ever.

Chapter Seven

THE KNOCK ON Emily's door startled her out of a restless sleep. Since her discussion with Fletch a couple months ago, she wasn't sleeping more than four hours a night. She was stressed out, hungry, and had lost around fifteen pounds.

Breakfast and dinner were meals she usually skipped to make sure that Annie was getting enough to eat, but she was failing even with that. Too many times, Annie asked for more after she'd finished whatever it was Emily had made for her.

Occasionally one of her coworkers would take pity on Emily and get her something for lunch, but most of the time she raided the bargain bin in the PX and got whatever was cheapest. It wasn't good for her health, Emily knew that, but she didn't know how else to fix her situation.

Fletch's friend continued to show up weekly, like clockwork. He never said much, only more threats to either her or Annie, and he made a point of telling her how pleased Fletch was with her cooperation.

Emily had sold as much of their stuff as she could...at least what she could make a couple bucks on. Annie wasn't dumb, she knew something was up, but Emily refused to talk to her about it. She was the mother, she had to protect Annie as much as possible, just like she always had and always would.

That night, when Emily told her daughter that she just wasn't hungry and the ramen noodles were all hers, Annie had looked at her with eyes at least twenty years older than her six years. She'd scooted her chair out from the table and went to her room. She reappeared with her beloved Army men in her hands. They were still in their packages, pristine.

"Sell my Army men, Mommy. They're brand new, so you can get a *lot* of money for them."

Emily's heart officially broke. Annie loved those toys, and not just because they were new. Her idol, Fletch, had given them to her, and she loved the man as much as Emily loathed him for putting her in this position in the first place.

Putting her hand on the top of Annie's head, she desperately tried to hold back the tears and looked her daughter in the eyes. "I'm not selling your toys, baby. They're yours."

"But you aren't eating. I can feel your backbone when I hug you."

"I'm eating. Promise. I'm just not hungry. We're

fine. We have this wonderful apartment to live in where we're safe. You're the smartest girl in your class. We're *fine*, baby."

It was obvious Annie didn't believe her, but she was also relieved she didn't have to give up her precious toys. "Okay, but maybe Fletch has a sandwich you could eat?"

Lord. That was the last thing she needed. Emily had curbed the amount of time Annie spent with Fletch as much as possible, but it was obvious when he got home since they lived over the garage. Emily had watched him carefully, and he was always gentle with Annie. Not once had he said anything to her that was out of line or threatening. Annie didn't have a lot of friends, and Emily couldn't bear to take away the man who obviously meant a lot to the little girl.

"I'll talk to him. Okay?"

"Okay!" Annie declared happily, deciding the problem was fixed, and digging into her noodles as if they were the best thing she'd ever eaten, rather than the same thing she'd had for dinner every day that week.

Emily crawled off the couch where she'd been sleeping for the last month and staggered to the door. "Who is it?"

"Fletch."

The last person Emily wanted to see was her landlord, but she couldn't exactly not open the door to him either. She unlocked the locks and slipped out, making sure to close the door tightly behind her. "Hey."

"Hey, Em, I wanted to come over and let you know that I'll be out of town for a while."

"Yeah?"

"Um hum, we got called on a mission fifteen minutes ago. I have thirty minutes before I'm supposed to report to base."

Hating that she cared, but worried nonetheless, Emily asked, "Everything all right?"

Fletch shrugged. "Duty calls. Can you get my mail and watch the place for me again?"

"Yes."

His eyes narrowed at her terse response. "If it's too much to ask, you don't have to."

"It's fine. It was part of the deal."

"Fuck the deal. If you've got other things to do, I'll understand."

"I *said* it's fine," Emily snapped.

"No guests."

"What?"

"I don't want anyone over there but you and Annie. Don't bring your boyfriend into my house."

"My boyfriend?"

"Yeah. Think you can handle that?"

His voice had gotten hard, and Emily wasn't sure what he was talking about. She didn't have a boyfriend;

why would he think that?

"Of course. Fletch, I don't—"

"And I hope you're feeding your daughter more than yourself. Kids shouldn't be on a diet."

"I'm not—"

"I'll leave the key on the seat of your car in the garage. I don't know how long I'll be away, but I hope I can trust you to take care of things around here while I'm gone?"

Emily could only nod. Her coworkers had noticed her weight loss, but Fletch hadn't said anything about it until now.

"I'll see you when I see you then."

"Bye."

Fletch didn't say anything else, simply turned and headed down the stairs and into the darkness.

Emily looked at her watch: four-fifteen. Whatever he was getting called off to do, it must be serious if he had to leave at this time of the morning. She opened the door and headed back inside the small apartment, wondering if his friend would be going with him, or if he'd be around to pick up the payment for the week.

GHOST LAY ON the ground, keeping his binoculars trained on the building in front of them. They were in

Egypt, trying to figure out how many hostages were being held in the government building in Cairo, and where. The flight out had been busy, the Deltas and a team of SEALs had spent the hours coming up with best- and worst-case scenarios for getting the Americans and other hostages out alive.

Even though they didn't have a lot of time to chit-chat, Fletch wanted to talk to Ghost. He'd been acting weird for a few months, and it was obvious the man was head over heels for a woman. His own life might be screwed up, but he'd do anything for his team leader and friend.

"What's up with you, Ghost?"

Ghost sighed, but remained silent.

"Does it have anything to do with that new tattoo on your leg?" Fletch pushed.

"I told you before, I'm not talking about it," Ghost ground out between clenched teeth.

Fletch smiled sadly, reading between the lines to what his friend wasn't saying. He recalled the conversation they'd had about the one-night stand Ghost had many months ago. Typically, Ghost didn't have a problem sharing details about his love life, but for some reason, had been reluctant to talk much about this woman.

Fletch ignored his friend's snarled words and kept pushing, knowing he needed to talk about whatever it was that was bothering him. Especially if it involved a woman. He'd never seen Ghost be close-lipped about someone he'd slept with before. That alone told him Ghost had feelings for her.

"I might not be the smartest man on the block, but if I had a sweet, feisty woman who left me with the memories *you* obviously have until the next time I could get home, I'd do anything in my power to do something about it."

Ghost nodded, but didn't answer.

Before Fletch could delve any deeper into Ghost's non-relationship with his mystery girl, the shit hit the fan. A bomb detonated in the building they were watching and there was no more time for talk. They had a job to do.

HOURS LATER, WHEN they were all on their way home, and Ghost's mystery woman was miraculously lying injured, but alive, on a pallet at the back of the bird they were flying in, Fletch felt the need to reach out. He'd seen the love and care Ghost had for Rayne, the woman who'd surprisingly been in the middle of the Egyptian coup they'd just foiled. Fate seemed to have had a hand in bringing them together again.

They settled in and shot the shit about Rayne, how

she had a tattoo that looked remarkably similar to the one Ghost had inked on his leg a few months ago. Not liking to see his friend so uncertain, Fletch tried to bring things into perspective for him.

"I've met someone," he said quietly. "She's funny and amazing and is more stubborn than anyone I've ever met. She's got secrets, and won't let me in. But the worst thing is that she seems to already have a man."

They'd talked a bit about Emily and her boyfriend before, but in the quiet and dark of the plane, his words seemed more stark and sad.

Ghost looked up at him. Fletch was standing with one shoulder against the wall, seemingly relaxed, but every muscle in his body was tense.

"Every time I see them together I want to pound something. She's got an amazing little girl who's scared of this guy."

"Fletch—"

He didn't let Ghost continue. "I heard what that SEAL said when you went off about wanting to keep your distance from Rayne to keep her safe, and he's right. We aren't even dating, but the thought of someone doing anything to hurt Emily or her daughter makes me crazy. If Emily looked at me with a tenth of the love Rayne looks at you with, I'd move her and her daughter into my house so quickly their heads would spin. Don't give her up, Ghost."

Fletch wandered back to his seat, leaving his friend to think about his words and to be alone with the woman who'd turned his life around. Seeing how Ghost was with her was eye-opening for Fletch.

Something was up with Emily, and he didn't like not knowing what. She'd pulled back from him, and he hated it. He'd thought that after their conversation at the PX, she understood she could be in danger because of his job…and maybe she did. Maybe that's why they hadn't really talked since. Maybe she was nervous because of what he'd said.

She continued to see her mysterious boyfriend, but Fletch never saw the man go up to her apartment. So she was either seeing him at work, or somehow spending time with him without Fletch realizing it.

But it wasn't only Emily. Annie was being affected too. When they'd first met, the little girl was always happy and bubbly and would come clomping down the stairs every time she heard him come home. She didn't do it very often anymore. If he was paranoid—which he was, it came with the job—he'd think Emily was keeping Annie from seeing him. And that hurt.

Didn't she know that he'd protect them from any harm? That he'd never let anything happen to them?

Probably not. They were still essentially strangers.

Emily was a perfect tenant. She paid her rent on time every month; an envelope with a check for the five hundred dollars showed up in his mailbox on the first each month. She was quiet, didn't hold crazy parties, and didn't throw herself at him, which was a welcome break from the last tenant he'd had.

Except…a big part of him *wanted* her to throw herself at him.

Fletch knew he should be happy, but he wasn't. He wanted the old Emily back. The old Annie. The females who smiled at him, who seemed happy to see him.

Fletch sighed. He was as much of a mess as Ghost. He needed to talk to Emily again, but first he wanted to make sure Ghost was good. It looked like Rayne, the woman his friend had found after not thinking he'd ever see her again, was back. And he hoped like hell Ghost wouldn't be stupid enough to let her go a second time.

Once Ghost and Rayne were settled, he'd have that talk with Emily and find out what was going on once and for all.

Chapter Eight

"**W**OULD YOU GUYS like to come over for dinner?" Fletch's question was obviously off-the-cuff and not something he'd planned to ask, but they'd pulled into the garage at almost the same time. Emily could only stare at him.

The last two months had gone by quickly—too quickly for Emily. She wasn't sure if she'd be able to come up with the next payment for Fletch's friend, but had no hope he wouldn't be around to collect it in the next couple of days. The damn man was like clockwork...always on time. He hadn't missed collecting even one of the weekly payments.

Fletch had come and gone a couple of times since appearing at her apartment early in the morning weeks earlier. He'd politely asked her to look after his place and she'd agreed just as politely. They'd exchanged greetings every time they'd seen each other, and Annie had even begged to go over to his house one Saturday and watch cartoons after a casual invite by him. Her daughter had gazed up at her with such a pleading look,

Emily couldn't deny her.

But this was different, this wasn't Fletch asking to spend time with Annie, he was asking for her to come too. Emily stared at him for a moment, digesting his words.

Would she like to come over for dinner? Emily thought about what she currently had in her house. An apple, two pieces of wheat bread, one slice of processed cheese, one slice of bologna, the final batch of carrots, ketchup, mustard, a stick of butter, one hotdog, and a package of beef ramen noodles. The hotdog and noodles were going to be their dinner...for the fourth night in a row. If asked, she'd say she was sharing it with Annie, but they both knew that was a lie.

Annie wasn't stupid. She knew they didn't have a lot of money, but after that one time where she'd offered to allow Emily to sell her cherished Army men, she hadn't said another word about it. Annie was made fun of at school enough already—for being smart, for her clothes that didn't quite fit and were clearly secondhand—so she didn't dare tell another kid or a teacher about how little food they had at home.

Obviously Emily had taken too long to answer Fletch, because he began speaking again, thinking he needed to convince her. "I was going to put steaks on the grill. I've got corn on the cob and the makings for salad. I'll let you guys put together the salad if that would make you feel better."

Emily felt a tug on her pants and looked down. Annie was staring up at her with eyes as big as saucers. She knew better than to beg when Fletch was around, but it was obvious what her decision would be.

Just once Emily wished she could be the mom who could go to the store and put things in her cart without thinking about prices. It was her habit to go through the Dumpster behind the PX for the extra newspapers that were thrown out. She would collect the coupons that were always in the Sunday paper, cut them all out and plan their meals down to the penny.

She currently had twenty dollars and thirteen cents in her bank account. The thirteen cents was her "cushion" so she didn't go below the twenty dollar minimum and get the service charge added to her account. She would be paid soon, but the four hundred dollars would go quickly, especially when half of it went to Fletch's friend for his gambling debt.

She wanted to be able to buy a pack of cookies or a candy bar as a surprise for Annie. But there was never enough money. Annie's favorite cereal was Puffy-O's. The bag claimed they tasted exactly the same as the Cheerios that were sitting right next to them on the shelf, but which cost an extra dollar and a half. Emily couldn't remember if her daughter had ever even tasted real Cheerios. She'd always had the generic brand.

It was that thought, along with her daughter's pleading eyes, that made her decision for her.

"Yes, we'd love to come over for dinner." Emily knew she'd be an idiot to decline. She had no desire to spend time with Fletch, but for her daughter's health, she'd do it.

"Yay!" Annie exclaimed. "Can I bring my Army men?"

"Of course. Fletch, we'll just go up and change and then we'll be over. That okay?"

"Yup. Give me twenty minutes. I'll take a quick shower and turn on the grill."

"See you soon, Fletch!" Annie told him with a huge smile on her face.

"See you, sprite."

Emily started to go up the stairs after her daughter, but was stopped by Fletch's hand on her arm.

"Hang on a sec, Em."

She turned to face him and raised her eyebrows questioningly.

"Are you upset with me? Because the last couple of months I've definitely sensed some ice-queen vibes from you."

Emily couldn't believe Fletch was accusing her of being frosty to him—as if he didn't know why. She tried to work through what she wanted to say to him, but before she'd thought of a suitable comeback, he spoke again.

"Just because you have a boyfriend doesn't mean that we can't be friends. I've missed Annie. She's funny and sweet and I enjoy spending time with her. Maybe you've just been busy, or maybe you really are avoiding me, but I hope that you'll at least consider loosening up a bit around me. I haven't had my friends over for a barbeque in too long. Now that my best friend has hooked up with a woman, I'd like to invite them all over and introduce you properly."

Emily was horrified. He thought she was *dating* his friend? That they'd hooked up? He was delusional. "I don't think that'd be a good idea."

Instead of looking upset, Fletch looked determined. Lord, the last thing she needed was him deciding they should be friends and hang out together. She was afraid of the *one* friend of his she'd met, and hanging with more wasn't even something she wanted to think about.

"Why?"

"Fletch, look, I appreciate that you let me and Annie move in, but that's all we are. Your tenants. We'll come over tonight, because I already told Annie we would, but I'd appreciate it if, after dinner, you don't try to get us any more embroiled in your life than we already are."

She almost felt bad for the look of confusion and sorrow that flitted across his face before he locked it down. There was no reason Emily should feel sorry for

Fletch, not after everything that had happened over the last few months. No way in hell.

"All right. I didn't know you felt that way, but fine. I'll see you in a bit." Fletch spat the words out, spun around and stalked across the yard to his front door.

Emily swayed where she stood. She was so tired. Tired of being hungry, tired of being scared, tired of being worried, and tired of always watching to see if that man was lurking about. All she wanted was to keep Annie safe; she hadn't thought that was too much to ask, but apparently it was. She sighed and held a hand to her tummy, which was letting her know she'd skipped lunch…and breakfast.

She headed up the stairs to her apartment, wondering how she was going to get through dinner.

HOURS LATER, EMILY realized she shouldn't have been concerned. Fletch was super-attentive…to Annie. He'd given Emily a glass of wine, and then proceeded to give all of his attention to her daughter. They laughed as Annie tossed the salad, and spilled most of it on the counter in the process. He sliced the corn off the cob so she could eat it without burning her fingers. Fletch even cut her steak up into tiny bites so it was easier to eat.

At one point, he'd brought up the shooting that had

happened recently at her elementary school. A man had gone into the school Annie attended and had injured a few people and held an entire gym full of children hostage. Luckily, he hadn't actually known kids were hiding in the gym, but it had been horrific all the same. It turned out that one of Fletch's Army friends, a man named Jones, happened to be in the area for a hostage negotiation seminar, and had been able to help take down the bad guy.

Annie had chattered away with Fletch about the experience as if it was the coolest thing that had ever happened to her. She'd been in her own classroom, far away from the gym, and Mrs. O had quickly gotten all the kids out of the building through the window so they'd had no idea what was really going on.

Emily knew what Fletch was trying to do…make the entire experience not seem as horrifying as it was…and she appreciated it. But she couldn't think about that day and not remember how insanely scared she'd been. There were a couple of hours that had almost broken her, when she didn't know if Annie was one of the missing students. Thinking she might've lost the best thing that had ever happened to her was something she never wanted to go through again—and was what made her go along almost docilely with the whole blackmail scheme of Fletch's friend now. She couldn't lose her daughter.

Emily listened as Annie spent more time talking about how happy she was that one of the other first-grade teachers and her favorite gym teacher were apparently now dating after the experience. Fletch didn't interrupt her, and carefully steered away her questions about what had actually happened that day, which Emily appreciated. It was almost beyond her comprehension how Fletch could be so great with Annie, but be a total dick and insensitive as to what his friend was making her do.

Emily let Annie talk as much as she wanted, only interjecting a word or two here and there. Fletch laughed at her stories and seemed to enjoy talking to the little girl. Emily would've fallen head over heels in love with the man if she didn't know what kind of person he really was.

She also might've stormed out of his house, but the food had been a godsend. It was not only nutritious, but delicious to boot. Fletch could cook. The seasoning on the steaks was perfect, and the butter dripping off the corn only made it that much sweeter. When he pulled out the brownies he claimed to have made the day before, Emily thought her daughter was going to explode with happiness.

After they'd eaten and Fletch had read two short picture books to Annie, Emily knew it was past time to get out of there...before her heart took any more of a beating.

"Time to go, Annie."

"Aw, Mom…"

"Don't 'aw, Mom' me. It's a school night."

"Will I see you tomorrow?" Annie asked her new idol.

Fletch shrugged. "Not sure, sprite. But you know I'm always here if you need me."

Emily didn't think Fletch would hurt Annie, but she also didn't want him to give her daughter carte blanche to come over whenever she wanted. No way was that gonna happen.

"Come on, baby. Bath time, then Nancy Drew."

"Yay!" Annie ran over to Fletch and hugged him around the waist. Emily refused to be moved by the soft look that crossed the big man's face as he put one hand on Annie's small back and the other on her head.

"See you later."

"Bye, Fletch!"

"Thank you for dinner, Fletch. It was delicious." Emily might be upset at the entire situation Fletch had put her in, but the food had been wonderful. It really had been a nice break in her bleak existence.

"Do you want to take the leftover corn and salad?" he asked, leaning against the counter in the kitchen.

Emily did, but shook her head anyway. "That's all right. Thanks though."

"I said it once, but I'll say it again—it's not fair to put Annie on a diet this young. She was obviously hungry; she devoured that entire steak and the corn, and had two helpings of salad. Eat whatever the hell you want, Emily, but please don't let Annie grow up thinking she has to be skinny to be a worthy person.

Emily felt the tears well up in her eyes, but refused to let Fletch see them. Damn him. She was doing the best she could with trying to buy enough food for Annie and pay the damn two hundred a week. It was shitty of him to rub it in her face.

Her words came out bitter and harsh. "My daughter comes first in *all* things in my life, Fletch. I'd starve myself before I'd let her go hungry." The words weren't a vow, they were reality.

Emily walked to the front door and left the house, not looking back. If she had, she might've seen the frustrated and dejected look on Fletch's face.

Chapter Nine

FLETCH SMILED AT Ghost and Rayne. Truck had been visiting Ghost, and since Fletch was on a beer run, he'd offered to pick the three of them up for his barbecue. He was thrilled beyond belief that Ghost had found the woman who'd had him in such a bad mood for so many months. He and Rayne were perfect for each other, and he couldn't be happier for his friend.

"I still think you should've let me bring something," Rayne griped.

Fletch shrugged. "Got everything I need. Nothing left for you to bring over."

"But something…brownies? Chips? Something?"

Fletch laughed. "Nope. Got it all."

They pulled into the driveway of Fletch's place and Rayne looked toward the apartment over the garage. "Is your tenant going to join us?"

"No."

The word was bitten out.

"Why not? I thought you said she was nice?"

"She *is* nice. But she's busy," Fletch said flatly.

"Oh. Did you ask nicely?" Rayne pushed. "Sometimes you can be a bit abrupt. You said she had a little girl. Maybe they both could've come over."

"I *did* ask nicely. And she has a boyfriend, so get that matchmaking gleam out of your eye right now, Rayne," Fletch warned, putting his car in park.

"That's a bummer," she sighed.

It *was* a bummer. Fletch had no idea what he'd done to make Emily dislike him so much. Yes, he'd told her it wasn't cool to put Annie on the same diet she was on, but he hadn't thought it was harsh enough for her to never speak to him again. Ever since he'd had her and Annie over for dinner, she'd gone out of her way to make sure she wasn't alone with him. He'd hoped she would relent and let Annie spend more time with him, and then maybe she'd come around, but that hadn't happened. If anything, he saw less of the little girl now than he had before he'd invited them over for dinner. It sucked.

It had been about three weeks since they'd had dinner, and he'd been gone for some of that time on a mission. But the colonel had finagled them all some time off, and Fletch decided it was way past time to have the team over to his place for a cookout. He'd knocked on Emily's door earlier, biting the bullet, wanting to invite them over, but she hadn't answered.

Fletch knew she was home, because her car hadn't

left the garage since Thursday when she'd gotten home from work. It was unusual for her to take time off, or to keep Annie home from school, but she'd made it perfectly clear through her actions toward him that it wasn't really his problem.

He couldn't help but worry about them though. He wished Emily would've answered, just to put his mind at ease.

As they all entered his house, joining the others who were already there, Fletch looked longingly back at the apartment over the garage, hoping to catch a glimpse of the woman he couldn't keep out of his thoughts, and the little girl he was beginning to care for much more than a landlord should.

A FEW HOURS later, Fletch looked around at his six teammates, and Rayne, in contentment. There was nothing better than being around friends, at least in his opinion. Ghost, Coach, Hollywood, Beatle, Blade, Truck, and himself had been to hell and back...and were still alive to tell their stories. Fletch had never trusted another group of men as much as he did this one, and he knew they all felt exactly the same way.

Rayne was a fun addition to their circle. Sometimes she brought her friend Mary to get-togethers, and it was hilarious to watch her and Truck go at it. Mary was a tough woman, had been through a scary bout with cancer, and she didn't take shit from anyone. But for some reason, she and Truck were like oil and water. She'd snipe at the big man, and he'd just smile and take it, which only infuriated Mary more.

The dynamics of having women in their inner circle was interesting. In the past, when they'd all gotten together, they'd spent their time talking about hook-ups and sports, but with Rayne there, and Mary when she joined them, they had to curb that kind of conversation. The result was more personal exchanges about their lives, families, and what was going on at work.

Though tonight, no one brought up the ongoing feud with the group of soldiers, which still hadn't abated. Any time the soldiers saw any of them on base, they'd say shit under their breath; every now and then, one of their cars would be egged or keyed. It was annoying, but they had no proof who was doing it. All they could do was report the incidents to the military police and hope to catch them in the act one day. But that was talk for another time.

"Uh, Fletch, I think there's a little fairy spying on us," Rayne said softly. She was sitting on Ghost's lap, holding a glass of wine, relaxing against his chest.

Fletch looked at Rayne in confusion, and she gestured with her head to the side.

Turning, Fletch saw a little girl peeking around the side of the house.

He immediately put down his beer and held out his hand to her. "Come here, Annie. Does your mom know you're out here?"

Everyone watched as Annie cautiously made her way toward Fletch.

"Um, Fletch, I don't—"

Rayne's words were cut off as Fletch stood abruptly in concern at getting a good look at Annie.

She was wearing a pair of sweatpants, and her hair had obviously not been brushed that day, or maybe even in a couple of days. Her pajama top had a large stain, as if she'd spilled something on it. In short, she looked disheveled, not a look Fletch had ever seen on her before. Annie resembled a little homeless child, instead of the cherished daughter Fletch knew her to be.

Ignoring his friends, who had all sat up in their chairs, ready to do something, even though they didn't know what, Fletch kneeled in front of Annie. "Are you okay, squirt?"

"I'm hungry."

"You're hungry. Okay. We have some leftovers, if that's okay."

Annie nodded, but her eyes strayed to the men behind him nervously. "Do you want to meet my friends?" Fletch asked, keeping his voice soothing.

Annie nodded, but it was obvious she was uneasy. He took her into his arms and stood up, settling her on his hip. Her thin arms wrapped around his neck and she held on tightly. Fletch turned and walked the eight feet or so to the others.

"Everyone, this is my friend, and tenant, Annie Grant. She's six, and the smartest girl in the first grade." Annie smiled at him, but didn't speak. She put her head against his shoulder and gazed at him with bright eyes.

"Annie, these are my friends. I work with them every day. I trust them as if they were my brothers. There's Truck, Blade, Beatle, Hollywood, Coach, and Ghost. And sitting with Ghost is his girlfriend, Rayne."

Annie picked her head up and regarded each of the adults around her for a moment, before leaning into Fletch and declaring in a voice that was anything but private, "Your friends have weird names."

Everyone chuckled. Fletch ran his hand over Annie's unkempt hair. "That they do, squirt. You said you were hungry? Where's your mom?" He kept the words light, but deep down he knew something was wrong. Emily had been keeping Annie away from him, and there was no way she'd let her wander over here in the dark.

"She's sleeping."

"Sleeping? You're sure? You didn't sneak out?"

Annie shook her head. "She's been sleeping all day."

"All day? What do you mean?" Fletch could feel his

friends perk up at her words.

"She said she didn't feel good when we got home Thursday, and this morning when I got up, she was sleeping. She didn't want to go to work and said she was too sick to take me to school yesterday. I tried to wake her up today, but she just moaned at me. I ate the leftover noodles last night and when I tried to pour myself a cup of juice this morning, I spilleded it all over." Annie sniffed. "I ate our last apple and there wasn't more food to eat. You said I could come over if I needed anything."

"I did, and I'm glad you came over. Can you sit here with Rayne and Ghost and let them get you some dinner?"

"Where are you going?" Annie asked, even as Fletch was putting her down on her feet next to the chair Rayne and Ghost were in.

"I'm just going to run next door and check on your mom."

"She's sleeping," Annie repeated, as if he hadn't heard her before.

"I know, sprite, but I'm going to go and check anyway."

"You aren't allowed inside. No boys. It's our rule."

Fletch regarded Annie. She was smart and he needed to tread a careful line. He didn't want to scare the little girl, but she had to know her mom sleeping all day wasn't something she usually did. He kneeled down once again, so he could look her in the eye.

"I think you know this isn't a normal case, right?" At her small nod, he continued, "Mommies usually don't sleep all day. I just want to make sure she's not *too* sick. Okay?"

"Okay," Annie whispered, then leaned over and hugged him, bringing her lips to his ear. "I'm scared. She was talking funny when I woke her up before I came over here."

Fletch hugged Annie back. "Stay here, sweetie. I'm going to take Truck with me and we'll go and make sure she's okay."

Annie eyed the big man standing next to Fletch. Fletch opened his mouth to reassure Annie that Truck looked scary, but he really wasn't, at least not to little girls like her, when she climbed up on the chair next to her and tilted her head at the big soldier.

As if she'd spoken, Truck took a tentative step toward her, but didn't say a word.

Annie put her hand out and ran her small fingers over the gnarly scar on Truck's face. She traced it from the middle of his cheek to his lip and poked at it. She pulled the side of his mouth up, watching how the scar naturally pulled it back down into the perpetual scowl he wore.

"Did it hurt?" she finally whispered.

"Yeah," Truck told her honestly.

Her eyes met his. "Did Fletch help you when you were hurt?"

"Yeah. He did."

Annie laid her hand flat on Truck's cheek. It didn't begin to cover that side of his face, but Truck turned his head into her gentle touch anyway. "You'll take care of my mommy?"

"Yes."

"Okay."

And that was that. If Fletch hadn't been standing there, he wouldn't have believed it. More than once kids had run crying back to their parents after seeing Truck's wounds. Not only did Annie not run, she had touched and caressed his face. She was an extraordinary little girl.

Fletch decided then and there that Emily's time of avoiding him was over. He'd let it go on too long, but hopefully she wasn't too sick and they could talk out whatever was bothering her once and for all. Anyone who raised a child such as Annie was someone worth fighting for.

"We'll be back as soon as we can. Go on, go with Rayne and my friend Ghost. Okay?" Fletch asked, helping Annie down from the chair she'd climbed onto.

It was a measure of just how scared the little girl was for her mom, and how hungry, because she merely nodded at Fletch and allowed Rayne to take hold of her hand and lead her inside to see what they could find for her to eat.

Fletch immediately set out across his lawn, Truck close at his heels. Fletch had chosen Truck because he was the most proficient medic of them all. Oh, they all knew first aid, but if Emily was hurt, Fletch wanted to have the best care at her disposal.

He took the stairs up to her apartment two at a time and twisted the knob to the door. It opened easily, as Annie hadn't locked it behind her when she'd left. Fletch glanced at the kitchen as he entered, seeing the wet paper towels on the ground from where Annie had tried to clean up her mess. Ignoring them for the moment, he went to the bedroom.

It was empty. Where the hell was Emily?

"Fletch, here," Truck grunted in a gruff voice.

Fletch spun and looked to the couch. Truck was kneeling next to a small lump, covered in a tattered blanket. He immediately went to Truck's side, satisfied when the other man moved to give him room next to her face.

"Emily? Can you open your eyes?" he urged, putting his hand on her forehead. When she didn't move, he turned to Truck. "She's burning up."

"Get this blanket off her."

Fletch didn't argue, just helped Truck unwrap Emily so some air could get to her. She roused when the chilly air of the apartment hit her.

"Emily!" Fletch demanded, "Look at me."

Her eyes cracked open a slit but it took her a moment to recognize him. "I gave your friend his money this week. Tell him he'll have to wait until I get paid again for the next one."

"What? Emily, wake up, you're not making sense."

She closed her eyes, shivering.

"She needs a hospital, Fletch," Truck told him seriously.

"I know, but only as a last resort. I'm guessing she doesn't have any insurance. Let me get her to my place and see if we can't cool her off first. I trust you more than a random doctor at this point, Truck."

Truck sighed, not completely happy with Fletch's plan, but not disagreeing with him either.

Fletch leaned down and scooped Emily into his arms, alarmed at how thin she was. He knew she'd been losing weight, but he could feel her ribs under his hands as he held her to him. Her head rolled back and he hitched her up into his arms. "Emily, put your arms around my neck and hold on."

Surprisingly, she seemed to understand and did as he asked. She weakly grasped him around the shoulders, buried her nose against his neck, and held on as he strode out of the little apartment and down the stairs. Truck held open the front door and they quickly headed down the hall to the master bedroom.

"Go get Rayne, but don't tell Annie her mom is here yet. I want to see how it goes before we say anything."

Truck nodded and disappeared, headed for the backyard. Fletch gently placed Emily down on his comforter and smoothed a lock of her hair off her forehead. "Don't worry, you'll be good as new in a jiffy. My friends'll get you fixed right up."

Surprisingly, her eyes popped open at his words and a panicked expression came across her face. "Not your friend, please, Fletch! Not him! I paid this week. I did! I'll find a way to get the money for next week. Keep him away from Annie!"

"Easy, Em, you're safe. No one will hurt your daughter."

"But he's your friend!"

Fletch's eyes narrowed in confusion. Who in the hell did she think was his friend? None of the men sitting on his back deck would ever lay a hand in anger on a child. And what money was she talking about?

He got a sick feeling in his gut as he looked at the terror in Emily's face. There was obviously something very wrong in Emily's world and for some reason, she thought *he* was involved.

Fletch tried to reassure her. "I'll repeat. You're safe. Annie's safe. You're sick. Rayne is going to come in and help us take care of you. Trust me, Em."

"Can't," she mumbled, obviously delirious. "You used us."

"What the fuck is she talking about?" Hollywood hissed, obviously hearing Emily's last statement.

Fletch, not surprisingly, hadn't heard the other man enter the room. Hollywood was extremely light on his feet. "I have no idea, but whatever it is, it's bullshit."

"Come on you two, move so I can get in there," Rayne bossed, pushing her way between Ghost and Hollywood. "Lord, she doesn't look good."

Rayne's words were unnecessary. All three men knew exactly how bad Emily looked. She was red, as if she was blushing, and her breaths were coming in short, fast pants.

"Rayne, help me get her T-shirt and pants off. Ghost, will you start a bath? Cool water."

"Truck's already on it," Ghost assured his friend.

"Okay, good."

They quickly stripped Emily down to her undies and bra, leaving those on for modesty's sake, and Fletch was alarmed anew at just how much weight she'd lost. He hadn't seen her without clothes on before now, but he'd seen enough to know she'd filled out her T-shirts nicely. Now he could clearly see her ribs and hipbones. He'd never been the kind of man who cared one way or another how much weight a woman carried, as long as she was happy with herself, but *this* was unhealthy.

Something was up, and Fletch was pissed and frustrated at the same time that he didn't know what it was. He was going to get to the bottom of it, but first he had to make sure Emily's fever broke. Then he'd go from there.

Fletch wasn't concerned at the moment about Ghost, Hollywood or Truck seeing Emily in her underwear. They'd dealt with nudity for many different medical reasons over the years. This was a life-or-death situation, and they all knew it. He'd be an asshole to get all possessive of her right now when she needed their help.

They had to get her cooled down so her brain didn't boil. They'd all seen enough people die from heat exhaustion on their missions to know time was of the essence.

Ghost turned Rayne around while Fletch stripped down to his boxers. Fletch then leaned over, picked Emily up, and carried her into the bathroom. He awkwardly climbed into the tub with her in his arms.

Fletch sucked in a breath at how cold the water felt, but knew it was absolutely necessary. The others helped steady him as he carefully sat down with Emily in his arms. As soon as she hit the water, she arched up, trying to get away from it.

Her body convulsed in shivers and Fletch crossed his arms around her chest, his legs around hers, and held her tightly against him. Partly so she wouldn't hurt herself and partly to cover as much of her body as possible. "Easy, Em. I've got you."

"C-c-cold."

"I know, but you need this. Your body needs this. Hang in there."

"W-w-why do you hate me so m-m-much?" she sobbed between chattering teeth.

"I don't hate you, Em, why would you say that?"

"Your friend d-does."

"What friend?"

"Y-y-you know!"

"Emily, I don't. Look around you. *These* are my friends. Ghost, Hollywood and Truck. And Ghost's girlfriend, Rayne. Is it one of them who hates you?"

He could see Emily glancing at the men and woman standing and kneeling around the tub. She shook her head. "He says you don't like to be seen with him. That you're secret friends."

"What the fuck, Fletch?" Truck bit out between clenched teeth.

"I don't know!" He cocked his head until he could see her face. "What does he look like?"

"You g-g-guys."

"What does that mean?"

"M-m-military. Mean."

"Does he have any tattoos?" It was Ghost who

asked, obviously thinking like the Delta Force soldier he was.

Emily nodded.

"Where? What of?" Ghost questioned.

Emily closed her eyes and rested her head on Fletch's shoulder. "He's *your* friend…you should know."

"What. Of?" Fletch repeated Ghost's demand in a low, serious voice.

"S-s-skull. On his forearm."

Fletch looked up at Ghost, who replied, "On it," and walked out of the bathroom.

"What's going on?" Rayne asked nervously.

"I'm not one hundred percent sure, but someone is fucking with Emily, and we have a pretty good idea who it might be," Truck snarled.

"F-Fletch?"

"Yeah, Em?"

"Annie…?"

"She's here. She's safe."

"I couldn't get up to m-m-make her anything to eat." She laughed a bitter little laugh. "Not that I h-h-have anything in the house *for* her to eat."

"Why? Why don't you have money, Em?" Fletch hated taking advantage of her current mental state, but knew it was the best way to get the answers he needed.

"You know!"

"I don't."

"You d-do, Fletch! Damn, you flat-out told me out-side the PX t-t-to do what your friend wanted."

"Pretend I don't know. Lay it out." Fletch tightened his hold on Emily when she squirmed as if she wanted to pull away from him. "Please, Em, don't hold back. Tell me what you think of me. Tell me everything. Get it off your chest. You know you want to tell me to fuck off. So do it."

"What are you doing?" Rayne asked in a soft voice.

Truck took Rayne by the elbow and pulled her up-right. "Come on, Rayne, this is between Fletch and Emily."

Fletch nodded in thanks at the large man leading Rayne out of the room. He gestured for Hollywood to stay then turned back to Emily and continued to goad her. "You said I hated you. Why? What did my friend tell you? Why don't you have money?"

Emily growled deep in her throat. It was a frustrat-ed, angry sound that Fletch hadn't heard come out of her before. "Y-y-you bastard! You made m-me think you were a good guy. I actually wanted you to like me. Hell, I even m-masturbated to the thought of you w-watching me get off. I thought you were g-giving me a break on the rent 'cause you were nice."

"Go on," Fletch urged when she paused. He ignored her statement about being attracted to him and getting

133

herself off in front of him for the time being. As much as he liked it, he had more important things to find out at the moment. He pushed one more time. "Tell me why I gave you a break on the rent. Do it."

"Because you n-needed me to pay your gambling debt. I never would've m-m-moved in if I knew five hundred would turn into thirteen hundred a month. I can't afford it, b-b-but you don't care. Your f-f-friend told me you knew all about it and planned it. Damn you, F-Fletch. Because of you, I c-c-can't afford to feed my baby!"

Emily's words seemed to echo off the walls of the bathroom. She continued to struggle in Fletch's arms. "P-p-please, let me go. I need to get up so I can w-w-work tomorrow. I have to work so I can pay your f-friend so he won't hurt Annie or have her taken away from me. I don't know why I thought y-y-you'd care…it's not l-l-like you give a shit about m-me."

"How's her temp?" Fletch asked Hollywood with no emotion in his voice. He saw the concerned look his friend gave him, but ignored it. The few conversations he'd had with Emily were shooting through his brain with marksmanship accuracy.

"My job isn't the safest…and sometimes there are others that get…irritated with me. I'd hate for something to happen to you or Annie."

"You aren't going anywhere."

"We've spent a lot of time discussing this. You're better

off where you are."

Every single time they'd had a conversation, she'd obviously thought his "friend" was whoever was threatening her, instead of Ghost, who he'd been talking about. Damn it all to hell.

Hollywood pulled the ear thermometer away from Emily's head and looked down at it. "One-oh-one."

"Good enough for now. Grab hold of her. Give me a chance to hop out," Fletch ordered.

Hollywood put the thermometer on the floor and hovered over the tub, pulling Emily upright and holding her against him as Fletch scooted out from under her. He grabbed a towel and quickly dried himself off, not caring how thorough he was. He reached for Emily and wrapped a fresh, dry towel around her before sweeping her up in his arms. He strode back into his bedroom and laid her back down on his bed. He went over to a drawer and changed out of his wet boxers into a pair of dry ones, then immediately went back to Emily.

He kept the towel around her for now, not caring if the sheets got damp, and got her under the covers. He then joined her, wrapping himself around her from behind.

"Let me go," Emily said drowsily. "I need to get up."

"No, you don't. You're fine. Annie's fine. Sleep, Em."

SUSAN STOKER

"But—"

"No buts," Fletch told her resolutely. "We've had one hell of a communication breakdown over the last few months, but it stops now. When you're better, we're going to hash this out once and for all."

"Maybe if you weren't addicted to gambling I wouldn't be in this position," she grumbled, a hint of the old Emily returning.

Even though he hated her words, Fletch was glad to see she seemed more lucid.

"I have never bet on anything in my entire life, baby. Ever. You can take *that* to the bank."

Emily struggled in Fletch's hold and managed to turn onto her back. She looked up at him with such confusion swirling in her eyes. "But your friend—"

"He's not my friend."

"He *is*. He said—"

"He lied, Emily. He's been using you because he's pissed at me."

"He lied?"

"Yeah, he lied," Fletch repeated. "I've got you now. Your days of not eating so Annie can are over. No more giving your money to some asshole who claims to know me. No one will take that little girl away from you. I swear. I'm pissed at the entire situation, but not at you, Emily. At the asshole who used you to get back at me and my team. Now, close your eyes, relax. You still have

136

a fever."

"Annie?" she repeated, obviously still not quite trusting him.

"She's safe here with my friends...my *real* friends. Nothing is going to happen to her."

"She ate?"

Fletch drew his fingertip down her nose. "She probably stuffed herself like a little pig."

Emily didn't even smile. "Good."

The thought that her daughter was safe, and fed, was obviously enough to make Emily fully relax for the first time. She fell asleep quickly, probably from a combination of the weakness in her body, relief at Annie being safe, and the fever.

Making sure she was completely asleep and comfortable, Fletch reluctantly scooted out of bed, pulling the covers snugly up around her shoulders.

"Team meeting?" Hollywood asked from the doorway. He'd never left, but had given them some privacy.

"Tomorrow," Fletch told him, pulling on a pair of jeans and T-shirt. "I need to get Annie settled first and see what she can tell me. But I'd appreciate it if Ghost contacted Tex and started to sort this shit out."

"Done. You want us to stay?"

"Maybe not everyone, but yeah, I'd love some back-up."

"Anything you need, it's yours."

"Thanks, I appreciate it."

"No thanks needed, you know that. And I'll tell you right now, anyone who fucks with one of our women has to be certifiably insane. I don't care that they don't know we're Delta. They should know just by looking at us that we won't stand for it and we take care of what's ours."

"Insane—or jealous." Fletch's words were flat and toneless, which made them all the more lethal.

"Are you shitting me?" Hollywood breathed as they made their way back down the hall to the rest of the team.

"I'm not sure yet, but I have a bad feeling the little shit those infantry guys have been doing is only the tip of the iceberg."

"Mother*fuckers*." The word was bitten out, and all the more jarring because it was Hollywood who said it. He'd been named such because he looked like a pretty boy. He was six feet tall, not quite as muscular as the rest of the team, and depending on the day, could be mistaken for either Tom Cruise or Colin Egglesfield.

"They won't get away with this," he said through clenched teeth before they went back out to the patio.

"No, they fucking will not," Fletch agreed. No one messed with his woman and got away with it.

Chapter Ten

"WHERE'S MOMMY?" ANNIE asked when Fletch went back outside. She was sitting on two thick books on a chair at his patio table. Her little legs were swinging back and forth and she had what looked like chocolate smeared all around her lips and cheeks.

"She's upstairs, sprite. She's going to be fine."

"She was sick." It was a statement, not a question.

"Yup."

"I won't get in trouble for coming over here, will I?"

Annie looked scared when she asked, and Fletch hated that. He pulled up a chair next to her and stole a piece of brownie from her plate, smiling when she giggled at him. "No, Annie. You will absolutely *not* get into trouble. In fact, you coming over here was the best thing that could have happened. You absolutely did the right thing. I told you if you ever needed anything you could come to me. You got your mom the help she needed tonight. Thank you for trusting me."

The little girl tilted her head to the side and regarded Fletch critically. Her eyes held a lot of worry, too much for a six-year-old. She broke eye contact and looked around at his teammates. Ghost was sitting back in the chair he'd originally been in, and Rayne was on his lap once again. The others were standing or sitting around the small patio, looking anything but relaxed. Annie looked at each one before meeting Fletch's eyes again.

"Your friends aren't like Mommy's friend."

Knowing who she was talking about now, Fletch tried not to leap up and find something to punch. He merely asked, "How so?"

"Everyone here has nice eyes."

"And he didn't?"

Annie shook her head.

"When did your mommy first meet him?"

Demonstrating her intelligence, Annie didn't immediately shrug her shoulders or say she couldn't remember. She looked up and to the right, trying to remember. Biting her lip for a moment, she rested her tiny elbows on the table, barely missing her plate. "You were on a trip. I think the first one you took after we moved in. Remember? I wanted to know if you brought me a present?"

Fletch nodded immediately. He'd thought that was it. How he'd misinterpreted that video, thinking Emily was meeting a boyfriend, was beyond him. He was an idiot and he'd let his heart overrule his training. "I do remember. He was here when you guys got home from school and work, right?"

"Uh-huh. Mommy made me go upstairs. After she came up to our apartment, she told me anytime I saw him I was supposed to go upstairs. I had to treat him like I did our old landlord."

Fletch knew a little about *that* asshole from what Emily had told him, and it made him want to have five minutes alone with him. If Emily had told her daughter to hide whenever she saw their old landlord, he was totally bad news. He forced his thoughts back to the issue at hand. "When did you see him last?"

This time, Annie did shrug. "It's been a while."

Fletch changed his line of questioning. If he was going to help Emily, he had to know as much as possible about her situation. He hated to use her daughter to find out the information, but he knew to the marrow of his bones, Emily wouldn't be forthcoming about anything. Shit, she'd kept silent about someone blackmailing her for the last four months or so. She'd probably try to blow this off like it wasn't a big deal and would continue to try to take care of it by herself.

"What did you have for dinner last night?"

Annie looked surprised at the question, but answered anyway. "Ramen."

"And the night before that?"

"Ramen. I always have noodles. Sometimes Mommy

puts a hotdog in."

"And breakfast?"

"Sometimes toast, but lately I've been eating at school." Annie's voice dropped to a whisper. "The other kids make fun of me."

Fletch reached out and scooped Annie up and plopped her on his lap. Her sad tone was killing him and he wanted to comfort her. "Why?"

She shrugged. "They say I'm poor and only poor people have to eat breakfast at school. I know what poor is, but I don't understand why it's bad."

Fletch kissed the top of Annie's head. "It's not bad, sprite. Some people just have less money than others. It doesn't mean they're bad or good…it just means they have less money."

Annie looked up at him with big eyes, so he continued, "Starting next week you won't be eating breakfast at school anymore, I'll make sure you get a good breakfast here before you go. Is that okay with you?"

"Yeah. I like Puffy-O's." She yawned huge and snuggled against his chest.

"You can have as many Puffy-O's as you want. Tired, sprite?"

The little girl nodded sleepily.

Fletch met Beatle's eyes and motioned to the garage apartment with his head, even as he leaned down to tell Annie of the plans for the night. "Want to have a sleepover?"

Her head whipped up so quickly, Fletch barely got out of the way before he was beaned in the chin. "Yes!"

"You need stuff from your room?"

"Yes." This time the word came out as if she was saying "duh."

Fletch chuckled. "Okay, how about if you go back over to your apartment with my friends, Beatle and Coach. They'll help you carry back what you need."

"Can I bring my Army men?"

"Of course. Bring whatever you want."

Annie jumped off his lap as if she did it every day. "Yay!" She reached out for Beatle's hand and tugged at him. "Come on, bug man, let's go!"

Everyone chuckled at Annie's name for Beatle as the trio left to head over to the apartment above the garage. When they were out of earshot, Blade said grimly, "What the ever-loving fuck is going on?"

Fletch stood up and paced the small patio. "From what I can gather, Emily has been blackmailed into paying someone money every week. He told her I owed him money because of gambling debts and threatened to get Annie taken away from her or to hurt her. Emily and I have obviously had our wires crossed in our conversations…when I talked about my friends—you guys—she thought I meant *that* asshole. So she got the impression that I knew about it, and condoned it."

"The boyfriend?" Ghost asked quietly, obviously remembering some of their previous conversations.

Fletch nodded grimly. "Yeah, that's my guess. I thought she was *dating* that asshole, instead he was destroying her sense of safety and making her worry for her daughter. I have no idea what he threatened her with, but I bet it was something horrible happening to Annie. She mentioned something about Annie being shot."

"You still have the surveillance tapes?" Truck asked, knowing how Fletch kept a close eye on his property and tenants.

"Of course."

"Good. Send 'em to me. We'll take a look and see if we can't nail down this bastard. This'll get escalated to command. No fucker gets away with this on our watch."

"I'm pretty sure it's Jacks."

"Richard Jacks? That pansy motherfucker from the botched training exercise?" Truck exclaimed.

"Yeah. I hadn't put two and two together before. We know him and his friends have been doing the petty shit to our cars, but even with the hat he had on when he first confronted Emily outside her place, I bet it'll be clear it's him."

The guys nodded as if it made perfect sense. "I can totally see him doing this," Blade ground out. "Those guys don't give a shit about anything other than making themselves look good."

"Agreed," Fletch sneered.

"Send me the tapes anyway," Truck demanded. "We'll need them for evidence when we go to the colonel. No one, I mean no one, threatens to take a little girl away from her mother. Especially not when that little girl is as sweet as Annie.

Fletch breathed easier for the first time since finding out Emily was sick. His team would help take care of this for him. While one part of him wanted to be at the front of the line to crucify Jacks and whoever else was behind blackmailing Emily, the other part wanted to stay right by her side as she came to terms with him being around.

Staying by her side won out.

"Definitely send all this to Tex. If the Army won't do anything, Tex will get us the intel we need to take care of it ourselves," Fletch ordered in a deadly voice. "We all know how slow the government works. If they won't move on it fast enough, we will."

"Done," Ghost agreed. "Now, who do you want to stay tonight?"

Fletch wasn't surprised they were on the same wave-length. "Truck, Beatle, and Hollywood, I think."

"No problem," Hollywood said immediately.

"On it," Truck replied.

"As much as I hate doing it, I need one of you to

search her place, see what you can find," Fletch told Truck.

The large man nodded. "If there's anything in there that points to this asshole, it's yours."

"Thank you."

"No need, brother."

AN HOUR LATER, Fletch settled into his king-size bed next to Emily. Annie had snuggled up next to her mom, then demanded he stay too. Not able to refuse her anything, Fletch had agreed, intending to get up once the little girl was asleep and then spend the rest of the night in the guest room.

He thought about what Truck had reported when he'd come back from Emily's apartment. Annie hadn't been lying, there wasn't much food in the house at all. Some condiments and a loaf of bread. That was about it. Not only that, but there weren't a lot of belongings in the house either. The things that Fletch had supplied her were there, but not much else. It looked as if Emily had sold as much as she could to try to keep her daughter fed.

As much as that pissed him off and saddened him at the same time, the fact that Annie still had the Army men he'd given her all those months ago, still in the packaging, devastated him. He'd known how pleased the little girl had been when he'd given them to her, but for them to still be packaged up proved how much they meant to her.

Fletch knew Emily could've sold those toys and made a few bucks, but instinctively he realized she'd never hurt her daughter like that. The entire situation made his heart hurt for both Emily and Annie.

Emily had done the best she could in a shitty situation to protect her daughter. She'd gone without eating to make sure Annie could. She'd sold anything she could get her hands on, but most importantly, she'd suffered in silence. That would end here and now.

It was astonishing that, even though Emily seemed to hate him, she'd been protecting him at the same time. It proved that, deep down, she didn't dislike him. If she had, she would've sold the toys he'd gotten Annie, told Jacks to fuck off and immediately moved out. But she hadn't.

It could've been because she was scared for her daughter and what Jacks had threatened to do to her, but he hoped a small part of it was also because she had feelings for him.

Fletch thought about her words when she was in the tub tonight. She'd thought about him. Had gotten herself *off* while thinking about him. Just as he had. They hadn't had the best start, but the attraction was obviously there. He could work with that.

The sacrifices Emily had made for her daughter, and him, humbled and awed Fletch.

Looking over at the two females sleeping soundly in his bed, Fletch made a promise to himself…and them. He'd stand between them and anything, and anyone, who wanted to hurt them in the future. Never again would Emily or Annie go without. Ever. Emily's actions had solidified his resolve. She would be his. He'd fallen for her courage all those months ago, but seeing it up close and personal put his feelings in a new light.

Emily and Annie Grant were *his*. His to feed, protect, and love. They just didn't know it yet.

Chapter Eleven

EMILY GROANED AND rolled onto her back, smiling when she felt Annie's warm body next to her. She felt grubby, and would kill for a shower. She was still a bit dizzy and generally felt like crap, but it was a hundred times better than the previous couple of days.

"Good morning, Emily."

The words were soft and definitely masculine.

Her eyes whipped open and she turned her head, only to see Fletch stretched out next to her. He had his head propped on his hand and was grinning at her. The T-shirt he was wearing stretched across his wide chest, and the stubble on his face looked sexy rather than unkempt. His hair was mussed, sticking up all over his head…and he looked absolutely delicious.

Looking to her other side, Emily saw that Annie was lying on her back, one arm over her head, snoring. She was wearing her favorite Wonder Woman pajamas and Emily could see some sort of dried food stuck to her cheeks.

She tried to remember what had happened the night

before, but it was like watching a television that was going in and out in a storm. She'd get flashes, but they didn't make sense.

"What are you doing here?" she asked Fletch in a soft voice, so as not to wake up her daughter.

"You don't remember?"

"Only parts," Emily admitted.

"The short story is that Annie came over last night because she was hungry and worried about you. I checked in on you, you were well on your way to brain damage because of an extremely high fever. I carried you back here and got you fixed up. You were so comfortable, I didn't want to disturb you, so we had a sleepover."

"And Annie?"

"I thought you'd feel better if she was in here with you."

"Thank you. I do. And *you*?"

Fletch smiled and reached over Emily to Annie's face and ran his free hand over her forehead and along the side of her head. "I was going to sleep in the other room, but Annie insisted I stay here with you guys."

Emily winced. Yeah, Annie probably *did* do that. She worshiped the ground Fletch walked on. "Well, uh, thanks. We'll just get out of your hair…"

He pulled his hand back. "We need to talk."

Emily bit her lip. Damn, she'd figured she probably couldn't get out of it, but she'd been hoping to postpone any kind of conversation about anything…maybe indefinitely. But finally, she nodded. She couldn't go on the way she was. Getting sick had made that point abundantly clear. If it was a matter of trusting Fletch, or the man who'd been blackmailing her, she'd choose Fletch.

Fletch eased back and stood up next to the large king-size bed. He was wearing boxers and a T-shirt with "Army" across it. If Emily thought he was good looking in a pair of jeans, it was nothing compared to how beautiful he was first thing in the morning. He held out a hand to her and waited.

Emily leaned over and kissed Annie, who didn't even stir, and rotated, throwing her legs over the side of the bed. It wasn't until she sat up that she realized she was only wearing her panties and bra.

She gasped and gathered the quilt, clenching it in both fists to her chest.

"Oh, shit, sorry, forgot about that," Fletch said in a completely serious voice, with not even a hint at lecherousness. He strode over to a brown dresser and pulled out some clothes. He came back to the bed with them, placed them on the mattress at her hip, and then kneeled down in front of her.

"They'll be big, but they'll do for now. We'll get you some of your things later this morning. I'll give you a few minutes to get dressed, but wait for me to come back and help you. You haven't eaten much for a few days and you'll be weak after the fever."

"I'll be fine," Emily protested.

"Of course you will," Fletch agreed immediately. "I'll be back in a few minutes." He put his hand on her knee and squeezed, then stood up and left her alone in his room.

Emily looked at the closed door for a moment, then the clothes he'd placed on the mattress. It was another Army T-shirt and a pair of workout shorts with a drawstring waist. They'd go down past her knees, but she'd be covered.

She twisted and looked at Annie and sighed. Emily might not remember everything that had happened in the last twenty-four hours, or in the last couple of days, but the feeling of safety she'd felt last night when Fletch had taken her in his arms was something she recalled way too easily. And Annie…it was hard to think of Fletch as uncaring when she was looking at proof that he cared enough to make sure both she and her daughter were safe and comfortable.

Knowing she didn't have a lot of time, Emily stood, took one step—and almost immediately fell flat on her face. Only the hand she threw out to catch herself on the mattress kept her from crumpling to the ground. Lord, she *was* weak. Apparently Fletch knew what he was talking about.

Emily quickly tugged the T-shirt over her head and sat on the mattress to pull the shorts on. She'd just stood to tug them the rest of the way up when Fletch opened the door again. He came to her and brushed her hands away and tied the drawstring with capable fingers. Without asking permission, he wound an arm around her waist and helped her from the room.

They went down the hallway and into Fletch's kitchen. She was surprised to see three other large, obviously military men already seated around the table. Fletch settled her on a chair at one end of the table. No one said a word, so neither did she.

One of the men was heartstoppingly good looking. Enough that he could've been a model. Another man was large and muscular, as Fletch was. The third man was huge, even next to the others. He had a nasty scar on his face that looked extremely painful. He was scowling, or maybe it was the scar that made it look that way. Whatever it was, he intimidated the hell out of Emily.

She jumped in surprise when Fletch placed a plate on the table containing a toasted bagel with heaps of cream cheese on it and a large glass of orange juice. Emily looked up in surprise as Fletch sat down next to her.

"Eat, then we'll talk."

The smell of the food made her stomach growl,

loudly. One of the men smiled at her, but didn't mention it. Wanting only to put off the upcoming conversation, Emily ate, seeing the satisfaction in Fletch's eyes as she did.

"Emily, I'd like you to meet three of my teammates. The big man across from you is Truck. He might look mean, but he's probably the gentlest of us all. Annie had him eating out of her little hands the moment she met him. Hollywood is the pretty man to my right, and to your left is Beatle. *These* are my friends."

Emily didn't miss the emphasis on the word, but didn't comment. Fletch didn't give her a chance anyway as he continued.

"I'd trust these men with my life, and have on many occasions. But more importantly, I'd trust them with *your* life. Or Annie's."

Emily expected him to continue again, but he didn't. It was awkward sitting there eating while four pairs of eyes watched her, so she tried to break the tension. "It's nice to meet you all."

"You too."

"Same."

"Likewise."

When they didn't say anything else, Emily looked back down at her bagel and tried to eat as fast as she could. The sooner Fletch got out what he felt he needed to say, the better. Although, the longer she spent in his company, the less sure she was of her convictions about him, and what had been going on.

She finally finished the last bite of her breakfast and wiped her hands on the napkin Fletch had included.

"Good?"

Emily nodded at Fletch and pushed the plate away. "Okay, I'm done. Can we please get this over with?"

Fletch didn't beat around the bush. "I have never gambled a day in my life, Em. I have a pretty good idea who's fucking with you, but I have *nothing* to do with it. And I want to know exactly how much you've given this asswipe and you'll get every cent back—with interest."

Emily bit her lip in consternation. From the first day she'd met Fletch, she'd gotten "good guy" vibes from him. Then, after her conversations with him, it was harder to deny that he was involved with whoever was blackmailing her up to her eyeballs. Now she wasn't so sure. She ignored his statement about the money for now.

"He said you made my rent so low because you knew my payments to him would make up the difference."

"He lied."

"He said he worked with you, you guys were close, and that you talked about me all the time."

"He lied."

"He said if I paid every week that you'd be notified

and Annie would be safe. But if I talked about all this with you or didn't make a payment he'd call CPS and get Annie taken away from me."

"Dammit, Emily, he *lied*. I don't gamble, I'd never do *anything* to hurt you or Annie, or any other woman either. What's this guy's name?"

Emily looked at Fletch without answering. She wanted to believe him. So badly. But she was confused. Hell, yesterday she'd thought Fletch was one of the bad guys; she couldn't just switch her feelings so easily...could she?

"Mommy?"

Emily whipped around at the sound of Annie's voice. She immediately scooted back from the table and held her arms open. Annie ran into them and snuggled in sleepily.

"Are you better, Mommy?"

"I'm better."

"I knew Fletch would take care of you."

Emily closed her eyes at her innocent daughter's statement. It was obvious she trusted Fletch down to her bones. Annie had seen evil, and was pretty good at recognizing it, but she had nothing but trust in her eyes when she looked at Fletch.

As if reading her mom's thoughts, Annie leaned toward Fletch with her arms out.

Emily allowed him to take Annie from her and swallowed hard at the affection in Fletch's eyes as he looked down at her.

"Hey, sprite. Sleep okay?"

"Uh-huh, but you snore."

One of the guys around the table chortled, but Emily didn't take her eyes off the man holding her child.

"I do, huh? Well, I hate to be the one to break this to you, but you're a bed hog."

Annie giggled uncontrollably for a moment. "You're silly!"

"Hungry?" Fletch asked when she'd quieted down.

"Uh-huh."

"You like waffles?"

"Waffles?" Annie's eyes got huge in her face and she immediately looked at her mom for a moment, then back up at Fletch. "We only get waffles on special occasions."

"I think today *is* a special occasion…it's the first time you had a sleepover at my house. That seems pretty special to me," Fletch told her seriously.

"Yeah," Annie breathed.

"How about you and Beatle head into the kitchen and whip some up? And you should know, these guys eat a ton, so you'll have a lot of batter to stir."

"I'm a good stirrer."

Fletch lifted Annie and put her on her feet next to his chair. "I'm sure you are."

Annie ran over to Emily and threw her little arms around her. "I love you, Mommy. I'm glad you're not sick anymore."

"Love you too, Annie."

"Come on, Beatle. We have waffles to make!"

Emily watched as Fletch's eyes followed her daughter into the kitchen. Finally, they came back to her and he continued their conversation as if they hadn't been interrupted. "His name?"

"I don't know. He never said."

"But you'd recognize him if you saw him again?"

"Of course. He's expecting the weekly payment Friday."

"How does he usually collect it?" It was Truck who asked this time.

Emily shrugged. "If Fletch is out of town, he comes here. If not, he shows up at the PX."

"Fucker," Hollywood swore under his breath.

Emily jerked when she felt Fletch take one of her hands in his.

"Sorry, didn't mean to scare you. You don't have to worry about this anymore, Em. We'll take care of it. Here's the thing. We know who this guy is. He's a soldier on the base who's pissed that we made him and his squad look like a bunch of amateurs during a training mission."

"What? Really? Was it a competition?"

"No. Just a regular training thing the Army does. But he's taken it personally for some reason. He's got to be either mentally ill, or just an extreme asshole who doesn't like to lose."

"I bet he was a bully when he was growing up," Emily grumbled softly, but bitterly. "People like that don't just wake up one day and decide to be an asshole. He probably stole lunches from kids at school when he was little, and in high school he probably beat up nerds behind the bleachers."

Fletch didn't want to laugh, but Emily was so cute in her disgruntledness. She was also most likely correct. He didn't comment, so she continued.

"He said he was a sniper. That Annie wasn't safe, that he could find her, even at school."

Fletch's hands jerked in reaction at hearing the threat against Annie, but he didn't let go of her. "You've had a hard time of it, haven't you?"

His sympathy was almost her undoing. Emily felt tears in her eyes, but ruthlessly beat them back and didn't say anything.

"Here's what's going to happen," Fletch told her gently but resolutely. "Hollywood is going to go up to your place and get a few days' worth of clothes for you and Annie. I have a guest room you can move into, but I want you and your daughter here, in my house, where I know you'll be safe, and maybe more importantly, where *you* can feel safe. My team is going to take care of this for you."

"We can't stay with you!"

"Why not?"

"*Because.* It's not right."

"Em, this isn't the fourteenth century. No one is going to care."

She bit her lip in indecision.

"I'll keep you safe."

"He said he'd get Annie taken away. I don't want to do anything that might make me look bad in their eyes if he *does* call CPS because I told you about what was happening. I can't lose my daughter!"

"Look at me, Em." Fletch waited until she raised her eyes to his, then told her, "No one will take Annie away from you. You aren't doing anything wrong by moving into my house. There's been a threat against you and you're moving in so you can be protected. If he does follow through on that insane threat, the investigator will see that. I'll take care of you *and* Annie. And if he thinks he can get to you while you're under my protection, he really *is* insane."

When she didn't say anything, Fletch went on, trying to convince her. "You know I have an alarm. If anyone tries to break in, all my men will know about it and come roaring in here like they're storming the beaches of Normandy. No one will touch you or Annie.

Not while I'm around to prevent it."

"I want to believe you."

Fletch turned to Truck and Hollywood, who had been quiet during his conversation with Emily, and gestured with his head to give them some space. They nodded and got up without a word.

Fletch scooted closer to Emily, his knees touching hers, and put one hand on the back of her neck, forcing her to meet his eyes. "I'm going to tell you something I've never told another woman before in my life. In fact, the only people who know this are the men you met today, and a couple others—the rest of my team, who you'll meet later. That asshole who was lying to you definitely doesn't know this, and if he did, he wouldn't be bothering you right now." Fletch paused, letting the seriousness of the moment sink in.

Finally, he told her, "Me and my friends are Delta Force."

Emily's eyebrows came down in a frown.

"You ever heard of Delta?"

"In the movies."

Fletch snorted. "Fucking actors. What it means to you is that we're the best of the best. Nothing gets past us. *Nothing*. There is no one who can protect you and Annie better than me and my team."

"Why?"

"Why what?"

"Why would you?"

"Because you need it. Because the asshole who has been threatening you is doing it because he's jealous of us. Also, because Annie is the sweetest, cutest, most wonderful child I've ever met, and she should live a life full of new toys and as much food as her belly can hold. But mostly because when I look at you, I see a woman who has put her daughter first, no matter if that hurt her. A woman who would try and protect a man she thought had done her wrong. And if you aren't freaked out enough already, you should know that I'm also doing this because I want to get to know you better. You have no idea how destroyed I was when I thought that asshole was your boyfriend. I thought I'd lost my chance."

"Your chance?" Emily was confused. She liked what he'd said about Annie, but she didn't understand the look in his eyes. It was...interest. She wasn't so clueless as to not be able to recognize when a man found her attractive, but she was currently wearing a T-shirt three sizes too big and a pair of baggy shorts. She needed a shower, like yesterday, and she hadn't even been very nice to this man since she'd met him.

"My chance to win you."

"Is it a contest?

"I don't know. I hope not. I have no idea where Annie's father is, but it's obvious he's not a part of her life, or yours. But wherever he is...he's an idiot for letting you both go. I like you, Emily. I like that you'd bend over backwards to give your daughter everything she needs in her life, even if it means you go without. I like that you've taught her to be careful. And I love watching you two interact. It's obvious she loves you very much and she's flourished in her short six years...and I know that's all because of you.

"You probably don't remember this, and I'm not bringing it up now to embarrass you, but last night you told me that you'd fantasized about me. Well, the feeling's mutual. You've been driving me crazy since the day you moved in. I have made love to you in my mind more than I'm comfortable admitting. But it's not just about sex. I want to take you out. I want to tuck Annie into her bed at night and read her a bedtime story. I want to sit across from you at the table and watch you smile at something I've said. In case I'm not making myself clear, I want to date you, Miracle Emily Grant. You and your daughter."

"Oh." Emily blushed a fiery red, but didn't comment further.

Fletch pulled back and gave her a little bit of room. "Oh? That's all you have to say?"

"Yeah, I think so."

"One more thing."

"Oh God."

"Nothing bad, promise. But please, when I say me and my team will take care of this for you, believe me."

"I want to."

"Good. So you believe that I had nothing to do with this asshole?"

Emily nodded. She didn't really have a choice *but* to believe him. He'd made his case very clear. When she'd thought he'd been talking about the man who was blackmailing her, he'd been talking about his Delta Force teammates all along.

The relief she felt must've shown in her eyes because Fletch nodded and remarked, "Yeah, you see it now. He won't come near you again. I can't wait to get to know both of you better."

"It's ready!" Annie's little voice rang out from the kitchen, breaking the intense connection they had going on.

The little girl ran into the room, sliding on the laminate floor. "Come on! Truck says everyone has to serve themselves...like a boo-fey."

"A buffet?" Fletch asked, catching Annie up in his arms.

"Yeah, that's what I said. Come on, Mommy! We even put cimamin on yours!"

"Cinnamon? Oooh, that sounds yummy, but I already ate, baby."

At the crestfallen look on her daughter's face, Emily

quickly added, "But I'm sure I can eat at least one."

"Yay! Come on!"

Fletch stood with Annie and held out his hand to Emily. "Ready for your second breakfast?"

"I guess I am." Emily put her hand in Fletch's and marveled at how much lighter she felt, knowing she wouldn't have to come up with two hundred dollars this week.

Annie was safe…and being fed. The rest she'd figure out later. For now, she had a cinnamon waffle to eat.

Chapter Twelve

FLETCH AND HIS teammates sat around the table with the colonel and waited for his reaction. Fletch had laid out what had been going on for the last few months with Emily. The officer knew about the harassment from the infantry squad after the training exercise, but he was extra pissed with the new information.

"You mean to tell me Sergeant Jacks has been blackmailing this woman? Making her pay him money every week to keep her daughter safe?"

"Yes, Sir," Fletch responded grimly.

"Give me everything you've got. I'll take this to the division commander this afternoon. But I want to have my ducks in a row. I need proof. Will this woman be willing to testify against him, if it comes to that?"

"I think so, but she's very concerned about her daughter. She doesn't want to do anything that could blow back on her," Fletch told his commanding officer solemnly.

"Rightly so. I think I can safely say his career as an Army soldier is over, but you all need to watch your backs. He's obviously gone beyond what anyone thought he'd do, so there's no telling what will happen once he's chaptered out. We can't monitor or punish him once he's discharged."

"Understood," Ghost said, nodding. "Truck will pay him a visit and make sure he knows not to go near Ms. Grant or her daughter again, or he'll have us to deal with."

The colonel didn't answer for a moment, just studied the seven deadly men. Finally, he breathed out and cautioned, "You all understand that I respect you and know that you'll protect those around you—but watch yourselves. As of now, this is all on him, not you. Don't do anything stupid that will ruin *your* careers as well. Got me?"

"Yes, Sir," Fletch agreed immediately reading between the lines loud and clear. His teammates echoed their agreement as well.

"Good. I'll be in touch later. Don't go rogue on me here," he warned again.

The team stood up and shook hands with their commanding officer. Satisfied for now that something was being done, through official channels, about Jacks and his crazy-ass behavior, Fletch left the room and walked down the hall.

"You headed home?" Ghost asked, walking beside his friend.

"Yeah. I want to spend the day with Em. I convinced her to take the day off."

"And she agreed?" Ghost asked incredulously.

"I know, right?" Fletch laughed. "She's been really ill, and has enough sick leave to cover another day. Now that she doesn't have to worry about paying that asshole, she can take the time to get one hundred percent better before pushing it too hard."

"Annie in school?"

"Yeah, I dropped her off before I came here. Had a talk with the principal about her safety and what was going on. Security has already been increased since the shooting incident at the school, so she's on it. She promised to talk with Annie's teacher and make sure to keep an eye on her and to take extra precautions."

Ghost nodded and they stopped after they went through the door into the parking lot. "I'm happy for you, man."

Fletch looked over at Ghost questioningly.

"Emily. I know you've had your eye on her for a while and how much it bugged you when you thought she had a boyfriend. For what it's worth, she likes you."

Fletch snorted. "What are you, a mind-reader now?"

Ghost didn't get upset at his friend's tone. "No, but it's obvious to us all, even with the short amount of time that we've been around her, that she follows you with her eyes when you walk into a room. Even when she was out of it with fever, you were the one she looked to. Her eyes got all soft and gooey when she heard you took care of her daughter. If I had to guess, she's been fighting her feelings for you for a while, thinking you were the bad guy. But now that she knows you're not? That you had nothing to do with Jacks? Things are going to go well for you, my friend. Now go home and woo your girl. We'll take care of Jacks."

Fletch couldn't help but smile. "Thanks, I appreciate it. Keep me updated."

"Of course. Tell Emily that Rayne would love to come over and get to know her sometime soon. I think having a girlfriend who's with another Delta would be good for her. Mary is awesome, but we both know it's different being able to talk with someone who knows firsthand what it means to be dating a Delta."

"I'm not sure we're actually dating, Ghost."

"I give it a week."

Fletch smiled and shook his head at his friend. He would've argued, but if luck was on his side, he'd be officially dating Emily in *less* than seven days. "I'll talk to Em about getting together with Rayne. Thanks again for everything."

"Anytime."

Fletch smiled all the way home. It was crazy how much he was looking forward to spending time with Emily and getting to know her better.

"Peanut butter or chocolate?"

"Peanut butter. Cold or hot weather?"

"Cold." Emily smiled at the look of disgust Fletch gave her at her response. Somehow Fletch had convinced her to call in sick, again, from work. She'd agreed and had taken a nap on his couch while he took Annie to school and went to work for a few hours.

He'd arrived back home around eleven and they'd made a light lunch together. They were now sitting on opposite ends of his couch playing a game he'd called, "Get to know you." They took turns giving each other a choice of two things and the other person had to say which they liked better with no explanations.

It had seemed silly at first, but it was amazing how much insight she'd gotten into Fletch as a result. She knew he was probably getting just as much information about her in return, and surprisingly enough, it didn't bother her.

"Coke or Pepsi?" she asked him.

"Neither." He paused for a moment, then asked, "Will you tell me about Annie's father?"

Emily sighed and rested her head on the couch behind her. He was breaking the rules of the game, but she was ready to move on to more detailed answers anyway. It was only fair that he ask what he wanted if she was going to get to ask what she was curious about.

"I met him when I was twenty-three. He was in the Army and I thought he was so grown up. He was twenty-seven and seemed into me. He said all the right things and swept me off my feet. We dated for about six months before I slept with him. He seemed as interested in me as I was him. Even though he wore condoms, I somehow still got pregnant and was over-the-moon excited. I dreamed of becoming an Army spouse and PCSing with him all over the country. I couldn't wait to support him as he moved up the ranks."

Emily stopped and took a drink of her water, remembering how devastated she'd been when she'd found out about his true nature, and how he told her he didn't want her following him after he'd made his permanent change of station.

"I take it he didn't have the same thing in mind."

"Not hardly," Emily snorted. She hurried to finish up the story. "I told him I was pregnant and he said he wasn't ready. I thought he'd come around, but the next thing I knew, he'd requested to move posts, and I haven't seen him since."

"He never met Annie?" Fletch asked incredulously.

"Nope. I tried to track him down on my own, albeit not very hard, with no luck."

"You know the Army would force him to pay child support," Fletch said, looking relaxed on the outside, but Emily could see his hand clenched in a fist on his lap. He was obviously more upset about the entire situation than she was.

"I know, but I didn't want that. If I forced him to pay child support, then he'd have rights. If he could so easily turn his back on his own flesh and blood before she was even born, I didn't want him anywhere near her." Emily shrugged, trying to dismiss it. "The last few months notwithstanding, I think I've done a pretty good job on my own."

Fletch leaned over and smoothed a lock of her hair behind her ear. "You've done a wonderful job, Em."

She cleared her throat, embarrassed for some reason, and hurried to ask a question of her own. "Why did you rent that apartment to me?"

"You needed it."

"Did I look that desperate?"

"No. But it was obvious that you were looking for a safe place for you and Annie. I could give that to you. Besides, thinking about someone being a dick because Annie asked questions was more than I could stand."

Emily looked down at her hands, not meeting Fletch's eyes. "I'm ashamed of myself for thinking the worst of you."

"Don't be," Fletch reassured her immediately.

"But I am. I can't just turn it off."

Fletch put his glass of water down and got up to sit

on the coffee table in front of her. He took her own glass away from her and put it safely aside, then took her hands in his.

"Don't be," he repeated. "You did what you had to do. You didn't know me. You saw what that asshole wanted you to see. Don't feel bad for protecting your daughter."

"But I let him win."

"He didn't win."

"But—"

"Emily, he didn't win. He might've had the upper hand for a while, but you know what he really did?"

"What?"

"He made me that much more determined to earn your trust. To make you see me as the man you want in your life rather than the asshole landlord who gambled too much." Fletch winked, taking the sting out of his words. "And to win *you*."

"There's that winning thing again," Emily teased with a smile.

"I'm serious. It's been torture for me knowing you were right across the way and you seemed to hate me. I'm a pretty likable guy." He grinned. "And there was nothing I wanted more than for you to like me."

"I *do* like you, Fletch."

"Good. Go out with me this weekend."

"What?"

"This weekend. Go out with me."

"Like on a date?"

Fletch smiled at her and squeezed the hands he hadn't let go of. "Yeah, a date."

"But Annie—"

"Rayne and Mary will come over and babysit her."

"I don't know…" Emily was torn. She was attracted to Fletch. That was a part of why she'd been so disappointed in him. He was sexy and buff, and she knew he'd be able to take on the world for her, so when she'd thought he was a "bad guy" it had nearly broken her. "I'm a package deal, Fletch."

"I absolutely know that, and I'm thrilled about it. I adore Annie. She's a mini you. I can see you sometimes looking out through her eyes. She's smart and funny and caring. I love that you've taught her to be that way. There will be lots of times we'll all go out together. But I would love for our first real date to be just you and me. I promise I won't keep you out late. We'll have dinner, make out a bit, then I'll bring you home." He smiled to let her know he was teasing…mostly.

"Maybe I should move back into the apartment. It's weird that we're over here."

"No. Stay. I love having you both in my house, under my protection."

"Annie's loud. She's been on her best behavior since you're new to her, but you have no idea what it's like to live with a six-year-old."

"Stop trying to talk me out of liking you, Em." Fletch said it with a smile, but she still blushed.

"I just…I've only known you to be a good guy for about a day and a half. It's too fast."

"I get why you'd think that, but I've wanted to be with you since the day you knocked on my door that first time. I thought I'd waited too long and lost my chance. We'll take it slow. No more sleeping in my bed…until you want to, that is."

"Annie will become attached."

"She already is," Fletch chided gently. "And the feeling is entirely mutual. Emily, I know you're cautious, and I applaud that, but I'm not her father. I'm not some young prick who is looking to get into your pants and will bail the second something goes wrong. I'm thirty-three years old. While I can't promise being with me will be all sunshine and roses, I can be a hard-headed son of a bitch sometimes, but I *can* promise that while I'm home, I'll put you and Annie first in my life. Before my friends, before the Army, before my job."

Emily saw the sincerity in Fletch's eyes. If she was honest with herself, it was a huge turn-on. Most of the men she'd dated in the past, pre-Annie, had been all about themselves and had bragged about their jobs or how important they were. Fletch didn't do any of that. He was honest and sincere, and stated his flaws up front.

"Okay."

"Okay?"

"I'll go on a date with you this weekend."

Fletch smiled, and Emily's insides did a little flip at the pleased look on his face.

"A kiss to seal the deal?"

Emily nodded shyly. She'd been wondering how his lips would feel against hers for months. She'd felt the same attraction when she first met him that apparently he did for her.

Fletch didn't let go of her hands, but leaned into her slowly, drawing out the moment. Emily smiled at him right before his lips met hers. They weren't touching anywhere other than their lips and hands, but she felt the electricity arc throughout her body nevertheless.

The kiss started out chaste, a simple touching of lips. He drew back momentarily, smiled, and then swooped back in. This time his tongue ran across the seam of her lips and Emily opened to him. Not wasting time, Fletch moved in. He caressed her, made love to her mouth with his tongue. He tilted his head to get a better angle, and that only increased Emily's pleasure.

She moaned and tried to get closer to him. Fletch hadn't let go of her hands, and the fact that she couldn't touch him as he devoured her, made it all the more erotic. Finally, he pulled back, licking his lips as if trying to memorize her taste.

"Wow," Emily murmured to break the silence.

"Wow," Fletch agreed, letting go of one of her hands for the first time, bringing his up to her face to run the backs of his fingers over her cheek. "Hungry?"

Emily blushed. She knew he wasn't asking what she thought he was asking, but it sounded dirty all the same. "Actually, yeah. I could eat something again."

Fletch laughed, obviously having mind-reading capabilities as well as superhero make-out ones. "Come on, perv, let me feed you."

Emily took his hand with a smile, deciding keeping silent was the better option so as not to embarrass herself any further. As they walked toward the kitchen, Emily thought to herself that it was nice to be looked after for once, rather than always being the one who looked after others. Really nice.

Chapter Thirteen

THE REST OF the week went by quickly, and Emily and Annie got into a comfortable routine. If she was honest with herself, it seemed as though they'd lived in Fletch's house for weeks rather than only days. Emily moved into the guest room with Fletch's help. He'd carried her stuff over from the garage apartment, and only gave her a few disapproving looks at how little she had.

Emily appreciated him not making her feel worse than she already did about it. Annie's belongings took a few more trips than her own, but she was finally settled into the room next to Emily's. She still hadn't opened her precious Army men, but kept them propped up next to her bed so they were the last things she saw when she went to sleep and the first things she saw in the morning when she woke up.

Luckily Fletch was a morning person, because Annie, as Emily had warned, was not a quiet child. Much to Emily's dismay, she seemed to need less sleep than other children. Her bedtime was eight, which meant she had to be in her room in her bed, but she didn't usually go to sleep until at least an hour or two later. Then she was up around five or six. Annie had learned over the years to let Emily sleep.

But Fletch was up around the same time as Annie, so most mornings when Emily came into the kitchen, Annie and Fletch were already there chatting away while eating breakfast as if they'd been doing it their entire lives.

Seeing the big strong alpha man treating Annie with such care—and yes, love—made Emily like him that much more.

The only issue they'd had in the week they'd been living with him was the morning Emily came downstairs and saw that Annie had drawn all over her arms with markers.

"Look, Mommy! I'm just like Fletch!"

Emily had frowned and crossed her arms, glaring at both her child and Fletch. He'd held up his hands as if to say, "Don't blame me."

Emily and Annie had spent an uncomfortable twenty minutes scrubbing the marks off her arms. She'd tried to explain to the little girl that while it might be appropriate for Fletch to have tattoos, she'd have to wait until she was at least eighteen.

Fletch had come home that night with some temporary Army tattoos for Annie, and all Emily could do was roll her eyes. Annie had been so excited that Emily didn't have the heart to forbid them, her only rule was that they had to be placed somewhere others wouldn't see them. Annie was now the delighted owner of an "Army Proud" temporary tattoo on her upper thigh.

Emily hadn't had a talk with Annie about everything that had been going on yet, but it was on her agenda. She'd meant to do it before her date, but now it was Saturday and Rayne and her friend Mary had arrived early to get to know Annie and Emily better. Emily decided to talk to her daughter on Sunday, after seeing how things went on her date with Fletch.

He'd left to do some errands, but Emily knew it was more to give her time to chat with the other women.

"So...you and Fletch, huh?"

Rayne hadn't wasted any time in teasing her about her relationship, whatever it was, with Fletch. Emily blushed. "I guess so."

"For the record, you've picked a good one."

"I'm not sure I really picked him. It just kinda happened."

"Well, however it happened, it's a good thing."

"Whatever you might think, we're not really *together*-together. We haven't even been on a date yet."

Mary put her drink aside and leaned her elbows on the table. "When you click with someone, you click. It's something that you just know, deep down, is right."

"Have you felt that way about someone?"

"Yeah."

"And what happened?" Emily asked.

"It's complicated," Mary said with a sad smile.

"You've heard the story about me and Ghost, right?" Rayne interrupted, obviously knowing more about Mary's situation than Emily did, and trying to steer the conversation away from her friend.

Emily shook her head and checked on Annie. Her daughter was sitting in front of the television, mesmerized by the GI Joe cartoon she'd run across ten minutes earlier. "Not really, just that you were caught up in that thing in Egypt, and Ghost and the others went in and got you out."

"I'd met Ghost six months before then. We had a one-night stand during a layover in London."

Emily couldn't have been more shocked if Rayne had told her she was actually a mermaid or something. "Wow, really?"

"I know, I don't seem like the one-night stand kind of person, do I?"

Emily could only shake her head. She really didn't. Rayne was younger than she was, and seemed way less...jaded or something. Maybe it was the fact that Emily had been a mom for four years by the time she was Rayne's age, but she couldn't put her finger on it.

"I'm so not. That was my first one, and it hurt when

he left the morning after, even though I knew going in that it was only going to be for one night. But as it turns out, Ghost was upset too. He'd never wanted more with a woman before."

"So how did he know you were in that Egypt thing?"

"He didn't. It was a complete coincidence."

"Wow," Emily breathed. "A lucky one, I'd say."

"Best and worst thing that ever happened to me," Rayne agreed. "Look, here's the thing, we spent one day and night together and then didn't see each other for six months. But when we did? I think we both knew we were it for each other. We still went through some shit, but in the end, we had a connection that couldn't be broken. I see that same sort of connection between you and Fletch."

Emily wanted to protest, but she couldn't. She felt it too.

Rayne went on in a lower voice just in case Annie was listening. "When Annie came over the other night, you should've seen Fletch. He immediately took charge, soothing her and getting to you as soon as he could. Now, he's an alpha Delta Force guy, so that's something any of the guys would do, but it *wasn't* any of them. It was Fletch. He wouldn't leave your side until he knew you were out of danger. He got Annie settled into his home as if he wanted her there forever. My advice to you? Go with it. You'll never find a better man, one more devoted to you and your daughter's happiness."

When Emily opened her mouth to speak, Rayne hurried on. "I'm not saying he won't be a jerk sometimes. He will. He'll think he knows what's best for you and Annie, and you'll have to speak your mind, otherwise he'll run roughshod over you. But they're used to taking charge and fixing things. They think like guys. Ghost has mellowed some, but he'll always be the kind of man who will take charge of any situation. Let go of what you can, but put your foot down on the things that really matter."

Emily nodded. She'd already seen that side of Fletch...and liked it. She was a capable woman, had been on her own for a long time, had done a darn good job of raising Annie, if she did say so herself, but it was very nice to not always have to be responsible for everything all the time. She could easily give some things to Fletch.

"I can do that."

Rayne beamed. "Good. And I have to say, I'm so thrilled to get to know you. Mary and I have talked about it a lot. We're best friends, but we'd love to have more girlfriends. We've kinda been in a bubble."

"Bubble," Mary laughed. "Yeah, that's a good way to describe it. I love Raynie like she's my sister, but it'd be great to have a group of friends we can hang out with."

"And now that you know what Fletch and the others do for a living, I figure it might be nice to have someone else to talk to about it," Rayne told Emily.

"I'd like that," she confessed. "I have so many questions about what Fletch does, and I know he can't tell me most of them."

Rayne nodded. "Yeah, that's true. Most of the soldiers on the base have no idea that Ghost and the others are Delta Force, it's something you can't talk about to anyone who isn't married to a Delta. Mary knows, simply because I flat-out told Ghost there was no way I could keep it from her...and she almost castrated him after he'd landed in the hospital but didn't tell me he was hurt on a mission. I'm sure Fletch will give you 'the talk' about this, as Ghost did me, but the bottom line is that we're kinda an island. We can talk to our men, and the others on the team, but not anyone else. To outsiders, we're typical Army girlfriends."

"He's already brought it up. They can't tell us where they're going, can they?" Emily asked, remembering the missions Fletch had been on.

"Nope. It's top secret. Are you understanding now why I'm thrilled to meet you?"

Emily smiled shyly at Rayne and Mary and nodded. "Yeah, definitely."

"Great. Now that that's out of the way, come on, let's go see if we can pry Annie away from her show and make a mess in the kitchen. I'm sure between the three of us, we can figure out something fun to teach her to bake."

"Sounds good to me!" Emily agreed.

The rest of the day went by quickly, between Annie's nonstop chatter and getting to know Rayne and her friend. As Emily was getting ready for her date later that afternoon, she thought about what Rayne and Mary had told her. She did feel a crazy connection to Fletch…and she could see with her own eyes how he felt about Annie. Those feelings had been there from the start.

Emily wasn't an idiot. She wouldn't have gone along with what Jacks had forced her to do, and wouldn't have felt such a sense of disappointment in Fletch, if she didn't care about him in some way. It wasn't just that he'd given her a place to live when she'd desperately needed one, it was *him*. His goodness rang out loud and clear to her. He'd probably deny it, claiming he was a bad-ass soldier, but Emily saw it anyway.

Tonight could be the start of a wonderful relationship—or it could prove that all they had was affection, and no deeper connection. Emily took a deep breath and readied herself to go into the other room.

She was hoping for the connection. She liked Fletch. A lot. She could only hope he felt the same by the end of the night.

Chapter Fourteen

EMILY TOOK A sip of her coffee and smiled over the rim at Fletch. Even though they'd left from the same house, he'd made an effort to treat it like it was a conventional date. Much to the delight of Annie, he'd walked out of the house, shutting the door behind him, and had actually rung the bell, as if he'd just arrived to pick her up.

He was wearing a pair of khaki pants with a polo shirt. The tattoos on his arms and the five o'clock shadow he always seemed to have kept him from looking preppy. He'd taken her hand in his and led her to his truck, which he'd pulled up to the house earlier. It was a little thing, but somehow made it less awkward than just waltzing out of his room and telling her he was ready.

He'd taken her to a hole-in-the-wall steak place and Emily had eaten the best meal she'd had in a long time, partly because she didn't have to worry about the cost. A tender filet, mashed potatoes full of cheese, bacon and onions, steamed broccoli, and they'd topped it off by sharing a plate of fruit for dessert. They'd been sitting talking about nothing, just getting-to-know-each-other stuff for the last forty minutes, and Emily felt more comfortable than she had in a long time.

"If you could change one thing about your life, what would it be?" Emily asked Fletch. They'd been asking more and more serious questions of each other as the night went on, and this one was a doozy.

Fletch didn't even seem to have to think about his answer. "I would've asked you about Jacks the second I got back from that first mission."

"What?"

"I'd have confronted you about the guy you'd met up with in the driveway. Annie told me that was the first time you met him. I saw it on my security camera footage, but completely misinterpreted it. If I had asked you about him when I got back, you wouldn't have given him so much money, wouldn't have been stressed out, and you wouldn't have had to starve yourself."

Emily was speechless for a moment. "Out of your entire life, *that's* what you would change?"

"Yup."

"But...Fletch, there has to be something else. Something you'd do differently while on a mission, something you've said to someone."

"Nope. You said one thing. That's the biggest regret I've got. We wasted months because I was a pansy. I should've just come out and asked you about him. What about you? What would you change?"

Emily hadn't recovered from Fletch's answer. Trying to think of what she might change was tough. Lots of things ran through her mind...not saying "I love you" to her parents more often before they'd died, not being smarter about Annie's father. But right that minute? She'd have to agree with Fletch and say she wished she'd confronted him about Jacks, and stood up for herself and asked what the hell was going on.

She opened her mouth to tell him when a shadow fell over the table.

The very man they'd been talking about stood by their table, smirking, as if he knew something they didn't.

Fletch didn't even give him a chance to open his mouth, he was standing and holding onto Jacks by the collar of his shirt before he'd said a word.

Emily stood up herself, but didn't leave her spot by the table, just stared as Fletch pushed the man backwards through the restaurant, ignoring the gasps of the other people eating dinner. Not sure what she should do, Emily stayed put and watched from a distance.

"Is everything all right?" their waitress asked nervously, coming up beside the table.

"Uh, yeah, I'm sure it's fine," Emily told her, not sure herself.

"Okay," the young waitress fretted, clearly not reassured.

Emily kept her eyes on Fletch and Jacks as they had a discussion outside the window of the small restaurant. She supposed it was inevitable that the two men had words, but it was unfortunate that it had to happen during their first date.

Finally, after what seemed like forever but was probably only a few minutes, Fletch re-entered the restaurant and came back to the table. Instead of sitting across from her this time, he motioned for her to scoot over and joined her on her side of the booth. Emily could see his jaw flexing and noted his clenched fist behind her on the booth. Other than that, he looked completely in control of himself.

Taking a risk, she put her hand on top of his on the tabletop and squeezed. "Are you okay?"

"No." The word was flat and pissed off.

"What'd he say?"

"Nothing I'll repeat to you," Fletch told her matter-of-factly.

"But Fletch, I—"

"You ready to go?"

Emily cocked her head at him. He looked ready to explode. It was definitely time to get out of there.

"Yes."

"Good." Fletch pulled out his wallet and put

enough bills on the table to cover the cost of their dinner and a sizeable tip, and then stood. He held out his hand and Emily took it. She knew she was looking at Fletch the soldier, and not Fletch her date at the moment, but it didn't make a difference as to how she felt about him.

Actually, that was a lie. It did. It *totally* made a difference.

She felt safe. Even though Fletch was pissed off, he was being gentle with her, and even polite to the waitress, who they passed on the way out the door. He hadn't thrown anything, hadn't even raised his voice to her. He'd simply dealt with the situation and he obviously wanted to get her out of there as soon as he could.

Emily couldn't fault him for that.

He was one hundred percent in control of himself— and for some reason that turned her on. Annie's father hadn't had nearly the control that Fletch did. Emily had seen him punch a wall once. Why did guys do that, anyway? It wasn't as if it would do anything other than hurt their own hand, and he'd even trashed his apartment when he was drunk.

Fletch led them outside to his truck, but not before checking to make sure Jacks was gone. He opened the door and assisted Emily in, then stalked around the vehicle and got in on his side. Without a word to her, he pulled out his phone.

"Hey, Coach. It's Fletch. Jacks just waltzed into the restaurant where Em and I were having a nice dinner…I have no idea how he knew where we were. Yeah, we had words… Thanks, appreciate it." He clicked off the phone and threw it on the dash. He put both hands on the steering wheel and took a deep breath.

"Is it wrong that I found that extremely sexy?" Emily asked in a quiet voice, smiling broadly when Fletch's head whipped around to stare at her incredulously.

She held up a hand to forestall anything he might say. "I know, I know, I'm sick, but you totally took charge, and even the vein pumping in your forehead is turning me on right now."

A small smile crept across Fletch's face. "How can I want to laugh when I'm so pissed off?"

Emily reached out a hand and put it on Fletch's arm. "Thank you."

"For what?"

"For dealing with that so I didn't have to. For protecting me, even when I don't really need it because I've been taking care of myself for a long time now. For being pissed on my behalf…and yours. For just…all of it. Thanks."

Fletch's face relaxed and Emily could almost see his muscles unclenching.

She went on before he could say anything. "And I was being serious. Everyone's eyes in the restaurant were on you. You commanded everyone's attention but you didn't even seem to notice. That's sexy as hell."

"Come here, Em," Fletch growled, reaching out with a hand and putting it on the back of her neck as he pulled her to him.

Emily didn't hesitate, but leaned over the middle seat of the truck toward him at the same time he bent into her. The kiss didn't start out sweet like the only other time they'd kissed. This one was carnal and hot.

Fletch held her to him and devoured her mouth. He plunged inside as if he was claiming his prize, caveman style. Maybe it was the adrenaline, maybe it was what guys did after the heat of battle. But it didn't matter. Emily didn't protest, she simply opened more and let Fletch take what he wanted. She felt herself grow slick and her nipples hardened under his passionate deluge.

Shifting in her seat to try to assuage the ache between her legs, Emily groaned in frustration and ecstasy as he fucked her mouth with his tongue. He wasn't making love to it, he was claiming it, marking her to the world as his own...and Emily loved it.

Finally, he pulled back, looking down at her, taking all of her in...from her peaked nipples to her heavy breathing. "Jesus, Em. You have me so worked up I have to keep reminding myself that we're parked in a public lot outside a fairly busy restaurant. But...even that's not really helping. I want you. I want you under me, writhing like you were just now, begging for my tongue, my cock. I've never wanted anything more than I want you right now."

Emily closed her eyes at his words for a moment, feeling them zing down to her core. She flexed her fingers against the seat under her, then opened her eyes and met his gaze straight on. "Yes."

She was fascinated at the way his pupils dilated at the one word. Oh yeah, he liked that.

"Damn." The word was guttural and came from the depths of his belly.

Confused when he pulled back, Emily could only stare at Fletch.

"Don't look at me like that, Em. I'm holding on to my control by a thread here. I want you. I want nothing more than to push you back, strip off your shirt and suck on those nipples I can see pushing out toward me. I want to feast on your pussy more than I want to breathe. I've imagined what you'll look like naked and panting for me over and over. But…not here. When I get between those succulent thighs of yours, it'll be when I can take my time.

"Not only are we in a public place, but Annie, Rayne, and Mary are waiting for us to get home. I need to talk to Ghost and the rest of the team and figure out what we're going to do about that fucker Jacks. Coach will contact them and get the ball rolling, but I need to give them a heads up on what went on here tonight. Oh, and my colonel needs to know about this latest play on Jacks's part as well.

"Lastly, I'm not going to rush this. I want you, but I also don't want this to only be about sex. I'm in this for the long haul. We have time to get to know each other before we jump into bed together."

At the look of obvious frustration on Emily's face, he went on, "But, mark this, it's not going to be six months like it was with Annie's father. I'm thinking a week or two, max. I'm all about anticipation, but I'm not *that* patient. I've wondered what you'll feel and taste like for too many months to drag it out much longer."

Emily could only nod and swallow painfully. She had no spit in her mouth at all. She could picture Fletch lying between her legs, smirking up at her right before he lowered his head. She'd gotten herself off more than once just thinking about that very thing. At least...before she thought he was an asshole. Having the real thing just might kill her, but what a way to go.

Emily clenched her teeth and shifted back to sit properly in her seat. "Okay."

"Okay," Fletch confirmed, reaching out a hand and brushing her hair away from her face tenderly. "Thank you for a wonderful time tonight. You're easy to talk to, not demanding at all, and beautiful to boot. I'm a lucky man."

Emily bit her lip, but didn't say anything.

"Come on, let's get home. I'm sure Rayne and Mary are dying to hear how our date went."

"I like them," Emily said, both relieved and sad that the sexual tension eased from the cab of the truck. "I mean, I don't know them all that well yet, but they seem nice."

"They *are* nice. I know Rayne better than her friend, but I think you'll like her. She's a lot like you…down-to-earth and can be snarky as hell sometimes."

"I'm not snarky," Emily exclaimed huffily.

Fletch laughed as he pulled out of the parking lot. "Don't get me wrong, I like snarky…at least on you. It means you're tough."

"I let Jacks walk all over me," Emily pointed out a bit sadly.

"No, you were protecting your daughter. That's completely different."

"I should've confronted you."

"Yeah, maybe so, but I should've asked you about him, so we're even in the blame game. We've been over this. It's done."

"You like when I'm snarky?" Emily asked, trying to get back to the mood they'd had.

"Yup."

"Even when it's with you?"

"Yup."

"You're weird."

Fletch chuckled. "Guess so."

Emily laid her head back on the headrest and sighed. "Thanks for the date, Fletch."

"You're welcome."

"I have a question."

"Shoot."

"Are you going to kiss me at the doorstep then pretend to drive away to complete the illusion that this was a conventional date?"

"You'll have to wait and see. Can't let you know *all* my secrets."

Emily turned her head without lifting it. "I can't wait."

It turned out that Fletch did almost exactly that. He pulled up to the front of his house and shut off the engine to his truck. He asked her to stay put and walked around to open her door. They held hands as they approached the front door, and he kissed the hell out of her. It wasn't a "thanks, I had a good first date" kiss. It was an "I want to fuck you right here against the door" kiss.

Emily stood breathless for a moment, happy to see that Fletch was just as out of breath as she was.

"Go inside, Em. I'll be in there in a bit."

She looked down at his obvious erection and nodded. It would be awkward to walk into the house with the other women and Annie there to see him like that. He tipped an imaginary hat to her and backed away toward his truck. Emily let herself inside and quickly tapped in the code. She was getting more comfortable with the alarm system…not all the way, but enough so that she could input the numbers without having to think too hard about them.

Rayne and Mary smiled at her from the couch and both stood up as Emily entered. "Have a good time?" Rayne asked.

"Yeah."

"Fletch parking?"

"Yup."

"If I had to guess, I'd say you look…satisfied," Mary observed with a smirk.

"Then you'd be wrong," Emily retorted before she could think. Smacking a hand over her mouth, she smiled as both women laughed.

"Give it a day or so, I'm betting that's how long he'll be able to stay away from you," Rayne quipped.

"*He* said a week or so."

Rayne barked out a laugh. "He's dreaming."

Emily could only smile at the other woman. She turned when the door opened behind her and Fletch strode in. She stared at him in wonder. How he got better looking every time she saw him was beyond her.

"Everything all right tonight?" he asked Rayne and

Mary.

"Yup. No problems," Rayne told him easily.

"Ghost coming over to get you two?"

"Yeah, I just need to call him."

"No need, I texted him and Truck before I moved my vehicle."

Rayne rolled her eyes at Fletch, but didn't protest.

Mary, on the other hand, *did* protest. "Why the fuck did you text Trucker? I'm going with Rayne."

"Actually, no you're not," Fletch told the riled woman with a smile. "Truck told me to let him know when I got back so *he* could drive you home."

"Well, he's not my dad or my boyfriend, so he can just go to hell," Mary stated emphatically with her arms crossed.

"Deal," Fletch ordered unsympathetically. "Ghost had duty tonight. He's tired, and even though you don't live that far away, it would take an extra thirty or so minutes. Truck volunteered to pick you up so Ghost could get home with Rayne and get some much needed sleep." Fletch was putting more emphasis on Ghost's need for sleep than was actually necessary, but he'd do anything for his buddy Truck. And if Truck wanted to spend some time with the prickly Mary, he'd make it happen.

"Humph." It wasn't actually a word, more a sound, but Mary didn't protest further.

"What time did you get Annie to bed?" Emily asked, wisely changing the subject.

"Did you know your daughter can read at a fifth-grade level?" Rayne asked.

The question was unexpected, but Emily simply smiled. "Yeah, it's crazy isn't it?"

"She's delightful, but I don't envy you. She's gonna be a handful."

"I know, but I look forward to every second," Emily stated proudly.

"As you should. I read to her for about thirty minutes, then told her she could stay up as late as she wanted...as long as she was in bed reading."

"Hey," Emily gushed, "that's a great idea. You're a genius!"

Rayne laughed. "I don't know about that, but I figure you can use it for a while before she cottons on to the fact that her friends and classmates can stay up late and don't *have* to read."

Emily shrugged. "Yeah, but if it gives me extra time now, I'm happy."

The two women smiled at each other and Emily knew that they'd just solidified a start to a good friendship.

The four of them chit-chatted about nothing in particular for twenty or so more minutes until Ghost and Truck arrived.

"Stay here a minute, yeah?" Fletch asked the women. "I'll be right back; I need to talk to my teammates for a second."

"Of course," Rayne agreed immediately. When he was out of sight, both she and Mary turned to Emily with raised eyebrows.

Emily sighed. "Yeah, so that Jacks guy showed up at the restaurant tonight."

"He didn't!" Rayne exclaimed.

"What a fucker," Mary swore at the same time.

"He did. But Fletch took care of it. I'm sure that's what he wants to talk to the guys about."

"What an ass," Rayne said, disgusted. Then clarified, "Jacks, not our guys."

"I knew who you meant, and I agree," Emily reassured her with a smile.

Fletch came back into the house not too much later, followed by Ghost and Truck. Emily watched as Ghost immediately went to Rayne and pulled her into his embrace as if they'd been apart for days instead of a few hours.

"Ready to go?" he asked.

Rayne nodded.

Mary stood and crossed her arms, glaring at Truck. "Don't make this a habit, Trucker."

The large man merely smiled with that half smile of his and gestured toward the door. "After you."

Mary rolled her eyes, hugged Rayne, but went out the door without any other comments.

"We'll talk more tomorrow," Ghost promised Fletch before he left the house, his arm around Rayne's waist.

"What's up with Mary and Truck?" Emily asked Fletch once everyone had left.

He shrugged. "They like each other, but neither will admit it."

"They're acting like grade-school kids."

"Yup." Fletch was smiling. "But it's amusing as hell. I can't wait until they both let go of whatever it is that's holding them back and go for it. It's gonna be explosive."

Emily nodded and looked up at Fletch nervously. She hadn't felt like this when she'd been alone with him over the past week, but somehow the kisses she and Fletch had shared tonight made everything different. He walked over to her and kissed the top of her head gently.

"Get some sleep, Em. I'm sure Annie will be up at the crack of dawn wanting to know how our dinner went. I'll keep her quiet for as long as I can so you can sleep in."

"I can get up with her," she protested.

"No need. I'm up anyway."

It was one of three hundred and two ways Fletch had made her feel cherished in the last week.

"Okay, thanks."

Fletch stood back and turned to head into the kitchen and the words came blurting out before Emily could stop them. "You aren't going to kiss me good night?"

Fletch turned slowly, but didn't come closer. "No. And don't get that pouty look on your face," he teased, then got serious. "The next time my lips touch yours, I won't be stopping. I'll take you to my bed and make love to you all night. So no, no more kisses tonight. But you've been warned, Em."

His words once again made Emily's woman parts sit up and take notice. She smiled at him. "So noted. Good night, Fletch."

"Night."

Emily fell asleep in the double bed in Fletch's guest bedroom with a smile on her face, knowing she'd dream about Fletch hovering over her as he thrust in and out of her satisfied body. She couldn't wait.

JACKS PACED HIS apartment, his phone to his ear. "It's almost time...Don't be a pussy, it has to be this way...No one is gonna get hurt, but we have to do it if we want to get them out to the battlefield...I *told* you already, it's not gonna hurt them, it's just going to make them more compliant...Fine, we'll talk about it later...*No.* You're in this up to your eyeballs, just like I am. We'll get this done and show them they aren't the only soldiers on this base who're badass. Get the others and we'll meet at the battlefield to rehearse in an hour...Good. Later."

He hung up the phone and threw it onto his couch, putting his hands over his ears to try to drown out the voice that had gotten louder and more insistent over the last couple of months.

Eliminate the threat.

They're in the way.

If you don't, you'll look weak to the enemy!

Nodding, Jacks stalked into his bedroom to change into the black clothes he wore to blend into the darkness. He might've told the naïve and gullible privates in his squad that they were only playing a trick on the other soldiers, that the woman and kid wouldn't be hurt, but he knew the truth. It was up to *him* to show those super-soldier fuckers that he was better than *all* of them. And if there were casualties...so be it.

Chapter Fifteen

"**T**HIS NEEDS TO end," Fletch demanded in a deadly tone to the colonel. "He needs to be in the brig until he's chaptered out. He threatened Emily and her daughter to my face! He doesn't give a shit about authority and he's escalating."

Fletch and the rest of the team were sitting around the table with the colonel, discussing the incident from the other night.

"He flat-out told me he was planning some grand scheme, and if he touches one hair on Emily or Annie's head, I can't guarantee his safety."

The colonel held up his hand. "Look, I get that you're pissed, but don't overreact."

It was Hollywood who spoke up this time, his words all the more effective because he was usually the quiet one who backed up his teammates, but never really started anything. "That's bullshit and you know it, Sir. What would you do if this was *your* wife he was harassing? Would you like for someone to tell *you* not to overreact?"

"Of course not, but it's being handled."

Beatle shook his head. "Not very well. With all due respect, Sir, this needs to be moved up the chain of command."

The older man sighed and ran his hand through his hair. "I know, and I'm doing everything I can. All I'm asking is for you to not go crazy. So far it seems like, other than the money thing, he's been all talk."

"Talk leads to other shit," Truck observed dryly.

"I know," the colonel conceded. "I have a meeting with the general today. He'll fast track this."

"And lock him up until it's done?" Fletch persisted.

"Yes. I will highly suggest he take that into consideration."

Fletch wasn't happy with the conversation, but honestly hadn't thought it would go any other way. After being cut off from Emily, Jacks hadn't really done anything that broke the law. There was nothing against showing up at the same restaurant where they were having dinner, but Fletch knew it was an intimidation tactic on the other man's part. At least he wanted it to be. Unfortunately, or fortunately, he picked the wrong group of men to try to intimidate. It was one thing to be able to blackmail a mother with a young child, it was another altogether to try to do the same to a team of Delta Force soldiers...even if he didn't *know* they were Delta.

"Appreciate anything you can do with this," Ghost said, always the peacemaker. It was why he was their leader, he could schmooze with the best of them—but then turn around and stab them in the back if necessary.

After the colonel left, the team stuck around to try to figure out what their next step would be.

"Can we just beat the shit out of him and be done with it?" Truck asked, obviously pissed off.

The fact that his friends were upset on his and Emily's behalf went a long way toward calming Fletch down. "We need to play this cool. We'll put Tex on him and see what he can come up with. Otherwise it needs to be status quo on our parts," Fletch stressed. "I'll make sure Em knows to be on the lookout for anything odd. Annie too."

"You'll tell Annie what's been going on?" Truck asked incredulously.

"Not the details, but she's not stupid. She already knows that her mom had a 'not nice' friend and that he's bad news."

At the grim look on Truck's face, Fletch continued, "Seriously, the kid lives for Nancy Drew and GI Joe. I'll make it a game to her, she'll be fine."

"If you're sure."

"I'm sure, Truck. I wouldn't do anything to hurt or scare that little girl. She means the world to me. I wouldn't do *anything* to mess with her head."

His teammates nodded, knowing what Fletch said came from his heart.

"I do need a favor though."

"Anything."

"You got it."

"Whatever you need."

The reassurances from his friends made him thankful for the millionth time that he was privileged enough to work with these men. "I need someone, or a couple of you, to entertain Annie for a day, preferably as soon as possible."

Seeing the smirks and sly grins, Fletch knew his friends knew exactly why he was asking.

"Movin' in on that, huh?" Hollywood asked.

"Hell yeah. But I know Em will be uneasy if Annie's around. I need her to understand how much she means to me…and I can't do that if there's the possibility of her daughter interrupting us."

At the nods around the table, Fletch relaxed. He'd been ready to defend his escalation of his relationship with Emily if need be, but he shouldn't have worried. After the team saw what Ghost and Rayne went through, and how Fletch was with Emily the night she was sick, everyone realized that she was it for their friend.

"How about this weekend? There's that carnival thing on base. We could take her there," Blade suggested.

"Yeah, and she likes military stuff, right? We could show her the museum," Beatle added.

"And what about the PT grounds? She'd probably get a kick out of the obstacle course, right?" Truck chimed in.

"Thanks you guys, she'll love it."

"Think Emily will agree?" Ghost asked seriously. "It *has* been fast, and she doesn't really know all of us that well yet."

It was a legitimate question. "Yeah, I think so. I'll talk to her. She knows that I'd trust you all with my life, so I think she'll be okay with it. I'll make her understand that the only people Annie would be safer with, other than me and her, is you guys."

"It's a plan then," Beatle stated resolutely. "Anything else?"

"Not for now. Thanks."

"Come on, the colonel wants us to go over the latest intel from the state department and give our thoughts. We have a long day of reviewing crappy surveillance and satellite video to get through," Ghost told the group, standing.

Everyone groaned good-naturedly, but didn't protest. In actuality, they all lived for this kind of thing, and they couldn't wait to delve into the world of espionage and prevent terrorists from carrying out their pathetic attempts to hurt others.

LATER THAT NIGHT, after dinner and a lively conversation with Annie describing in minute detail how a bee makes honey, including lots of hand gestures and buzzing noises, when asked what she'd learned at school that day, Emily sat with Annie on her bed and tried to think of the best way to discuss with her all that was going on.

"How're you doin', baby?"

"Good, Mommy."

"You like living in Fletch's house?"

Annie nodded vigorously.

"And you like Fletch?"

"Yeah. He's really smart, and I get to make breakfast with him every morning."

Emily smiled at her daughter and ran her hand over her blonde hair lovingly. "I like Fletch too."

"But you didn't always."

Emily shouldn't have been surprised at Annie's words, but she was. "Here's the thing, baby. That other man—you know which one I'm talking about, right? The one I told you to run from if you ever saw him?"

Annie nodded solemnly.

"Well, he was telling me bad things about Fletch.

Things that weren't true. I'm ashamed to admit that I made a mistake and didn't ask Fletch about them. I just believed the other man."

"Like rumors?"

Emily nodded, remembering how she'd had to have a talk with Annie earlier that year because she'd come home telling stories about one of the other kids' moms that she'd overheard some of the teachers talking about at recess. She'd explained that rumors can sometimes not be true and very hurtful to the person being talked about. "Exactly. I listened to rumors when I shouldn't have."

"But you like him again, so it's okay now, right?"

"Right."

"Are you gonna marry him?"

Emily laughed. "How about I start by going on a few dates with him first?"

Annie tilted her head in thought, then proclaimed, "Ten."

"Ten what?"

"Ten dates. Then you can marry him. But I'm not wearing a dress. I want to wear an Army costume."

"How about this," Emily bargained, knowing better than to agree. If she agreed, she knew Annie would be demanding a wedding after exactly ten dates. "I'll date Fletch, and after ten dates, I'll update you as to how it's going. Yeah?"

"And the dress?"

Emily leaned down to kiss Annie. "And I promise *if* Fletch and I get married, you don't have to wear a dress. You can wear whatever you want."

"I love you, Mommy. You look happy."

"I *am* happy, baby. I'll go get Fletch so he can read to you. Love you."

FLETCH SMILED DOWN at Annie. Emily had called him upstairs and left him and her daughter alone for their new routine. She loved it when he read to her from the latest version of the *Army Survival Manual*. He'd finished chapter fourteen on tropical survival techniques—including things such as finding water and food and what plants to avoid—and left the book for Annie to read on her own during her "stay up as late as I want as long as I'm reading" time. He kissed her on the forehead and said, "Good night, squirt. See you in the morning."

The little girl didn't answer, she was too engrossed in finding out how to tell the difference between an edible plant and an inedible one.

Fletch entered the living room and sat on the couch, settling in to watch a rerun of *Seinfeld* with Emily. This had become their custom over the last few days, after finding out they both loved the show. They'd commiserated over the fact it'd ended, but decided it was for the best. The worst thing to happen to good shows, or a book series, was when they went on too long.

"Saturday the guys are taking Annie to the carnival on base," Fletch informed Emily. "They'll spend the day with her and will make sure she's safe the entire time." He knew his words weren't questioning, they were matter of fact.

"They are? Why?"

"Because it's time. Because I want you all to myself, and that seemed the best way to get what I want."

Emily was quiet for a moment and Fletch could see her mulling over his words. She glanced at him out of the corner of her eye then looked back at the television. "All day?"

Fletch smirked. "Yeah, Em. All day. I think their plan is to pick her up around eleven, then take her to dinner after the carnival. They'll return her sometime early evening."

This time Emily bit her lip and he saw her shift in her seat as if she was uncomfortable. She seemed to want to say something, but was hesitating.

"Say what you're thinking. If you're having second thoughts about us, don't be afraid to tell me."

"It's not that," Emily blurted out. She gave up her pretense of watching the sitcom and turned so she was facing him, tucking one leg under her as she shifted. "I just…it's perfect. I've been racking my brain to figure out how it was going to work. I mean, I wasn't comfortable with the idea of sneaking down the hallway after Annie fell asleep, like I was in high school, or doing it out here on the couch while she was upstairs. I know you said you wanted to do it in your bed, but I figured we'd have to resort to your truck after all."

Relieved more than he could put into words, Fletch relaxed. "There's no way I want us to feel any anxiety over this, Em. The thought of Annie walking in on us is something I don't think I'll ever get over, even after we've been together for years, but our first time should be fun and exciting. I don't want you to think about anything other than how I'm making you feel." Fletch purposely threw in the line about being together years in the future, and was pleased as hell when it didn't seem to bother Emily at all.

"Should I pencil this into my calendar?"

Fletch read the snark loud and clear and chuckled. "Doesn't matter if you do or don't…it's happening regardless."

Emily smiled at him, happily. "Thank you. I swear I feel like I spend half my life thanking you for something or other, but seriously. I'd love to spend the day with you. Even if all we did was sit around like this. There's just something…calming about being around you. As if

I don't have to worry about anything, that you'll take care of everything. Of me."

"I will on both counts. And Annie. You're my responsibility now. One I take very seriously."

"I don't want to be a responsibility, Fletch," Emily protested, frowning at him.

"That came out wrong. I don't mean it in a bad way at all. It feels good, here," Fletch told her, putting a fist to his chest. "I like knowing you'll be here in my house when I get home from work. When Annie yells my name and runs to the door when I come in? You'll never know how much that means to me. The thought of anything happening to either of you makes me crazy. But the fear that I'll do or say something that will hurt you also tears at me. *That* kind of responsibility. The kind that makes me want to be a better man. A better male figure in Annie's life. A better lover."

"Oh." The word came out on a breath of air and Emily stared at him from across the couch.

"I'm looking forward to Saturday." His words were the understatement of the century, but it seemed Emily was on the same wavelength.

"Me too. But now I'm nervous."

"Don't be."

"Fletch, you can't just tell a girl that you're going to spend the day rocking her world and not expect her to be a bit freaked out about it."

He chuckled at that. "I'm not nervous in the least."

Emily snorted. "Well yeah, because you're built like a real-live Ken doll. Perfect abs, perfect legs, not an ounce of—"

Fletch cut off Emily's words by leaning over and grabbing her under the arms and laying back, hauling her over him in the process.

"Fletch! What are you doing?" Emily chided, laughing.

"You have nothing to worry about, woman," he growled, holding Emily against him, letting her feel how hard he was and how much he wanted her. "We haven't discussed this…I didn't want to bring it up because I knew you'd be embarrassed, but I've seen you mostly naked, Em." He ignored her gasp and continued on. "That night you were sick we had to get your temperature down. The fastest way was to put you in the tub. I held you in my arms as you shivered against me."

"But…that…" Emily sputtered, looking everywhere but at him.

"Even though you'd been starving yourself, I liked what I saw. But it definitely wasn't the time or place. You're perfect for me, Em."

"I'm too skinny," she protested.

"Maybe, but I'm doing my best to fix that."

Emily looked at him for the first time and wrinkled her nose. "Yeah, I noticed. You're constantly making me food. Delicious food that I can't turn down."

Fletch brought the conversation back around to what he wanted her to understand. "I like your body, Em. Every inch. I love how you're so much smaller than I am, it makes me feel good to be so much bigger and stronger than you. That might make me a Neanderthal, but I can't help it."

"What if I gain a hundred pounds?" Emily asked with a hint of sass.

"I'll still be bigger than you, won't matter." When she opened her mouth to say something asinine again, Fletch pulled her hips against his. She gasped and he made his point. "Feel that? That's me loving what I see each night as we eat dinner. As we sit here and watch TV. As I see you tucking Annie into bed. I can't control it, my dick has a mind of its own, and it wants to be right here. In you. And starting this weekend, I'll make it my mission for you to love your body as much as I do."

He felt it as Emily relaxed in his hold, squirming until his hard cock nestled into the sweet spot between her legs. He knew it was his imagination, but Fletch swore he could feel her heat through both of their jeans.

"Are you going to kiss me?"

Fletch smiled up at her. "Nope."

"But don't you think this has gone well past the kissing stage?"

"Maybe so, but I told you the other night that I wouldn't kiss you again until I could take you immediately to my bed, and I'm holding to that."

"Bummer," Emily pouted.

"Thank you for giving me Saturday," Fletch told her seriously.

"Thank you for giving *Annie* Saturday," Emily returned. "She's going to be in heaven. Not only will she get to spend some time on base where there will be 'real live soldiers,' but she'll get to be with your friends."

"They're taking her to the obstacle course," Fletch informed Emily with a smile.

She dropped her head onto his chest and groaned. "Great. She talked about the course her gym teacher set up for weeks, that's how much she loved it. If they take her to a real one, she'll never shut up about it. They're gonna make her GI Jane."

Fletch heard the smile in her voice. Even though she was complaining, she wasn't really. "She'll love it."

"I know." Emily picked up her head and licked her lips, unknowingly taunting him to break his promise about kissing her. "Am I going to have to worry about you jumping me the second the door closes behind her?"

"Probably," Fletch asserted in a completely serious tone.

"Good."

Fletch sat up suddenly, holding onto Emily so she

didn't pitch off him and onto the floor. "And on that note, it's time for you to go to your room."

"Reached your limit?"

"You have no idea, Em. Please, have pity on a poor soldier man, would ya?"

Emily laughed and got up off the couch and took a step away from him, blowing him a kiss and turning to the hallway. "See you in the morning."

"Yes you will, Emily. Yes you will."

Fletch groaned and reached down to adjust himself as soon as Emily was out of sight, flopping back onto the couch. He wasn't sure he would make it another few days, but what sweet agony it was. He smiled as he settled back to watch the end of the show. Somehow he knew the rest of his life would start on Saturday, and he couldn't wait.

Chapter Sixteen

"I'M GONNA RIDE the ferry-go-round and the merry wheel and eat cotton candy and see myself in the mirrors and then I get to be an Army man and crawl in the dirt and run through tires!"

Emily smiled at Annie as she sat not-so-patiently at the kitchen counter waiting for Beatle, Blade, and Truck to arrive and take her to the carnival. The little girl was oblivious to the looks Fletch had been giving Emily all morning. They were carnal and impatient at the same time.

Emily had taken her time in the bathroom that morning, primping and getting ready for her "date" with Fletch. She'd shaved her legs carefully and even trimmed up her pubic area. She'd put on a hint of makeup and some of the perfumed lotion she rarely used as well.

Dressing carefully for seduction, Emily had put on a pair of jeans and a shirt that buttoned down the front. The thought of Fletch slowly undoing each button had made her bite her lip in anticipation.

She'd picked a pair of bright red bikini panties and a matching lace bra. It was a push-up jobby that did what it was supposed to. She looked at least a size bigger. Emily worried for a moment about false advertising, but then decided that Fletch had seen her with very little on before, so he knew what he was getting. She was just prettying up the package for him. She might still need to put on some weight, but that was the last thing she wanted Fletch thinking about when she was standing in front of him.

The bottom line was that when she entered the kitchen about an hour after the time she usually did, she felt good. Pretty. And the look in Fletch's eyes only reaffirmed those feelings. He'd been leaning against the counter, listening to Annie talk about something, but after seeing Emily, he'd immediately gone to her, leaning in. He'd brushed his lips against her cheek and moved to her ear.

"Fuck, is it eleven yet?" he whispered.

"You look nice, Mommy. Do you have a date?" Annie asked innocently.

Emily glanced at Fletch, who'd put his hands in his pockets, trying to hide his erection, and smiled at her daughter. "Yes, baby. Fletch and I are hanging out today."

"Good. That's two."

"Two?" Fletch asked Emily in a soft voice, confused.

"Don't ask," Emily told him as an aside. "Good?" Emily queried to her daughter, settling on the stool next to hers.

"Yup. I like Fletch. I want him to be my daddy," Annie stated without missing a beat.

Emily froze in her seat and glanced over at Fletch. She wasn't sure what she expected to see, shock, maybe a bit of terror, but the look on his face as he gazed at her daughter was an endearing mix of longing and tenderness mixed with humor at Annie's straight talk. The thought of her daughter calling Fletch "daddy" didn't strike fear into Emily's heart as it had with other men she'd dated on and off over the years.

She cleared her throat and managed to croak out, "I like Fletch too," she told Annie, ignoring the daddy thing for now.

"When I grow up, I'm going to be a soldier, just like Fletch and his friends. They're gonna show me all I need to know today to be just like them, then I'm going to—"

For once in her life, Emily tuned out her daughter's ramblings and stared at Fletch. He was beautiful. He was wearing a simple T-shirt and jeans, but he was so rocking them. All Emily could think of was ripping the shirt over his head and putting her hands on his chest for the first time. She'd wanted to check out his tattoos for a while, but hadn't really had the opportunity. She hoped that today she'd get that chance.

His feet were bare, and the raised eyebrow he cocked her way when he saw her looking at his feet seemed to say, "Why put on shoes when we're going to be in bed the second Annie leaves?"

"What do you want for breakfast, Em?" Fletch asked, sounding completely normal, which was annoying since she was all jittery and excited.

"I had cereal," Annie piped in. "Fletch said that I probably shouldn't eat too much so I could save room for all the crap I'm gonna eat at the carnival today."

"Smart. But remember, baby, if you're going to go and run an obstacle course, if you eat too much junk beforehand you'll probably barf it up," Emily told the little girl honestly.

Annie seemed to think about that for a moment, then told her mom seriously, "Yeah, but if I puke it up, that'll mean I worked really hard. I've seen some cartoons where soldiers do that."

Emily only laughed and shook her head. Annie could out-talk her mom more and more, but she didn't mind. "True, but it's still gross."

"Yeah…"

Emily looked up at Fletch and saw the grin on his face as he looked affectionately at Annie. The thought that he cared as much for her daughter as she did, did funny things to her insides. He seemed to be the total package, even with his flaws…which honestly didn't seem too bad when compared with all the good things. Yes, he was a neat freak, he was bossy, and he wanted to always get his way. He didn't ask her what she thought about a lot of things, just did whatever *he* thought was the right thing. But he also never seemed to tire of listening to Annie talk, and he'd spent hours reading to her. Gorgeous, loyal and, hopefully, a master in bed. She'd find out soon enough. Yeah, she'd take him as he was.

"I think cereal for me too, please," Emily told Fletch.

His eyes came back to hers. "Are you sure? You might need something to keep your energy up today."

Lord love a duck, he was lethal.

Emily ate her cereal and watched Annie as she pulled out her precious Army men, still in their packages, and acted out a whole awkward war scene with them. Fletch stood next to Emily with his hand on her lower back. He caressed and rubbed her the entire time Annie babbled at them. If Fletch's touch over her shirt made goosebumps pop out all over her legs, Emily knew she was in for one hell of a day when her daughter left.

Finally, Annie heard a truck pull up outside the house. Fletch looked up at the security camera monitor and acknowledged that it was indeed Annie's dates for the day. He nodded at her, giving her permission to

SUSAN STOKER

open the front door, and the little girl raced away.
Fletch took the opportunity of being alone with Emily
to lean down and suck on her earlobe for a moment.

Emily groaned and tilted her head to the side, giving
him more room.

"Hold that thought, Em. Five more minutes and
you're mine."

Emily didn't know how her legs held her, but she
managed to get off the stool and make her way outside.
She greeted Fletch's teammates as if she wasn't thinking
about tearing her clothes off and attacking their friend.
She hugged Annie tightly.

"Be good today, baby."

"I will."

"I love you. I'll see you tonight."

"Have fun on date number two with Fletch," Annie
sang out innocently before hugging Fletch quickly, then
climbing up into the backseat of the truck.

"Yeah, have fun on your *date*," Truck teased.

Emily blushed, but didn't say anything, simply
waved at Annie again as Beatle got into the driver's side
and Blade climbed into the front seat. Truck settled
himself into the back with Annie, and Emily waved at
the truck until it turned out of Fletch's driveway and
disappeared.

Emily felt Fletch's arms go around her from behind
and his lips brushed her ear. "Two, huh?"

224

"It's a long story."

"Hmmmm, I want to hear it, but at the moment I've got other things on my mind. I'm trying really hard to be good. I'm so hard, I hurt. I want to do a million things to you at once, but don't know where to start."

She turned in his arms. "How about a kiss? I've been dying to feel your lips on mine since the last time on your front porch."

She didn't need to ask twice. Fletch's mouth came down on hers and they kissed as if it was their first time...and their last. By the time Fletch pulled back, they were both breathing hard.

"Wow."

Fletch didn't say a word, simply leaned down and picked Emily up. She threw her arms around his neck and held on as he started for the house.

"This feels familiar," Emily told him seriously.

"I carried you this way from your apartment when you were sick."

"Huh, I didn't remember it until just now."

"I'm not surprised; you were out of it."

"I just..." Emily paused, then continued. "It feels nice. I'm sorry I forgot it. No one's ever carried me like this before."

Fletch put her down on her feet just inside the door, keeping his hand on her back as he leaned over and punched in the alarm code. When he was done, he turned to her. "I like carrying you. Shirt. Off."

"What?" The change in topic was abrupt and Emily wasn't ready for it.

"Take your shirt off."

"But—"

Fletch was obviously done asking because he reached for the first button and undid it. Then the second. And the third. Emily smiled. Okay then. She helped and started from the bottom, working her way up until their hands met.

Fletch didn't take his eyes away from her chest as he parted the shirt and pushed it off her shoulders. Emily shrugged, letting it drop to the floor, and waited for Fletch to say something.

He didn't. He reached for the button to her jeans, and undid that as well. Emily wriggled her hips and helped him get them off. She kicked them to the side and waited for whatever Fletch was going to do next.

She'd obviously chosen the right underthings, because his breathing visibly sped up and she watched as his pupils dilated so much she could barely see the blue of his eyes. His hands came up and he lightly skimmed her breasts with his palms. Emily could feel the warmth of his hands against her sensitive peaks. Her nipples swelled in their cups as if reaching for him.

"You are so fucking beautiful, I'm almost afraid to touch you," Fletch whispered.

"I'm small."

"You're perfect." Fletch didn't waste any more time with words, he leaned down and kissed the peak of each breast with a chaste kiss. Emily thought her legs would give out when he plumped both breasts with his hands and buried his face into her cleavage and inhaled.

Lifting his head, he declared, "You smell delicious."

"It's my lotion."

"It is," Fletch agreed, "but it's also you."

Emily reached behind her for the hook to her bra, ready to get the show on the road, but Fletch stopped her.

"No, that's my job. And if we don't get to my bed now, we might not make it there."

"I'm okay with that."

"Nope, I've wanted to see you in my bed again ever since that first night. Come on," Fletch leaned down and picked her up again and Emily shrieked in laughter. She wound her arms around him as he walked them to his room, leaning in and sucking on his earlobe as they went.

Emily had never thought of herself as sexy, but being held in Fletch's arms as he carried her to his bed, and feeling him shudder as she caressed and teased his earlobe, was heady stuff. She was slick and more than ready for him.

The mattress bounced as Fletch dropped her onto it.

SUSAN STOKER

Emily laughed as Fletch stripped off his clothes. He didn't break eye contact with her as he undid and dropped his jeans and boxers. His shirt came off just as quickly and the next thing she knew, he was crouched over her before she could get a good look at him.

"Here's the thing—I can't go slow." Emily felt his hand caress her side, then move to her belly as he spoke. "I feel like I've waited forever for you. For this moment."

Her back arched as his fingers dipped under the waistband of her undies and brushed against the hair there.

"Are you wet for me?"

"Yes," Emily moaned, wrapping her arms around Fletch's neck as his fingers continued to flex and tease, but never touch her where she needed him most.

"Are you sure? Because I'd sooner face a hundred Taliban soldiers with no weapon than hurt you."

"I'm sure. Touch me and I'll prove it."

The words were barely out of her mouth before his fingers were there. They slid between her wet folds as confidently as if he'd been doing it every day of his life.

"Lord, Em. You're soaked."

"Told you."

"All for me." It wasn't a question.

Emily answered him anyway. "Yes." She bucked her hips up when one of his fingertips entered her hot

228

cavern. The action pushed his finger deeper and they both groaned at the sensation.

"It's been months for me," Fletch told her, easing another finger inside. "I've been busy with work and interested in a hot neighbor. After I met her, I had no desire to be with anyone else."

Emily groaned in ecstasy. He felt great. Awesome—but she needed more. Her panties were restricting his movements, and she wanted him as out of control as she currently felt. She sat up, pushing him back, and dislodging his fingers in the process.

Talking as she pushed her panties down her hips and off, she told him, "I'm on the pill. I have heavy periods and horrible cramps if I'm not on it. But that being said, I also haven't slept with anyone in at least two years. I've been too busy myself, and honestly, as much as I love my daughter, she's not conducive to having any kind of sex life. After today, we'll have to get creative. I'm not an exhibitionist, but I swear if we have to sneak out back while she's watching GI Joe, I'll do it."

Emily reached to undo her bra, and once again Fletch stopped her.

"Leave it. Lie back."

Emily did as he asked and looked up into his eyes. He was once again crouched over her, and his hand went back between her legs and was caressing her harder now that he had more room to work, spreading her wetness up to her clit, making her squirm under him.

"I'm clean, Em. I wouldn't hurt you in that way."

"Me too."

"I have a condom. I'll use it if you want."

"You swear you're clean? I can imagine you've been with lots of women."

"I swear on the life of my teammates, I don't have anything. And I can't remember any of the women I've been with before now. Ever since a certain woman and her little girl crashed into my life, my only thoughts have been for them." He smiled down at her, all the while lazily caressing her, stretching out her enjoyment.

"Fuck me, Cormac. I need you."

It was as if her words loosened the restraint he'd been holding on to. He shifted, pushing her legs farther apart and easing the tip of himself into her. He stopped, holding himself still as Emily writhed under him. She dug her nails into his sides, trying to pull him into her.

"What are you waiting for?" she panted, looking at him in confusion.

"I'm memorizing this moment. The first moment you took me inside." Steadying himself on one hand, he used the other to pull the cups of her bra down under her tits, pushing them up. The cool air hitting her nipples caused them to pucker tighter. He lightly flicked the right one, then the left, smiling at her groan and how her back arched.

"Can you memorize faster?" Emily whined, "I thought you said you couldn't go slow?"

"Once I get all the way inside you, I won't."

Emily was done. She used her inner muscles to squeeze the tip of Fletch's cock as hard as she could. Her movements actually pushed him out, but he immediately pressed back in, gaining the ground he'd lost and then some.

"Jesus, you have no idea how fucking amazing this feels. How *you* feel," Fletch gritted out between clenched teeth. "I wish this moment would never end, but it's gonna end way too quickly, I'm afraid."

"Then we'll just have to do it again; we've got all day," Emily told him, using her fingertips to caress his nipples, which were quickly turning into hard points with the attention she was giving them.

"Oh yeah, fuck, I like that."

Emily pinched them, grunting in satisfaction as he buried his cock deep into her body. It stung a bit, as it had been a while, but the slight discomfort disappeared quickly as she adjusted to his size. She shifted under him, widening her legs and hitching her knees up his body, allowing him to push in even farther. Emily felt his balls, hot and heavy against her ass, and she arched her back, baring her neck to him.

Without opening her eyes, she urged, "Fuck me,

Fletch. Make me yours."

"You *are* mine, Em," Fletch groaned.

He pulled back and his first thrust made Emily moan as he bottomed out. After that, there was no stopping the train they were on. They were going full steam ahead and nothing was going to stop them until they were finished.

Fletch was a considerate lover, caressing and squeezing her tits as he rode her hard. He watched her face and adjusted his thrusts to make sure he hit her clit as much as possible.

"I'm not going to last much longer, you feel too fucking perfect," Fletch bit out, holding himself still for a moment.

Emily swore she could feel him pulsing inside her. She felt raw and almost bruised, but also tingly at the same time.

He moved his thumb down to where they were joined and stroked her clit once. Emily jerked in his grasp and he started thrusting into her again. "Yeah, that's it, Em. Fuck, you're gorgeous."

Emily shifted, frustrated that Fletch wasn't putting quite enough pressure on her clit for her to orgasm. She brushed his hand aside and took over. She could feel the orgasm just out of reach and she'd be damned if she wasn't getting there with him this first time.

"Oh yeah, that's so sexy. Show me how you like it.

Hard and fast, huh? God, you have no idea what you're doing to me. That's it…take yourself there. Let me feel it. Don't wait for me, Em."

Emily could barely understand what Fletch was saying. She was lost in sensation. She masturbated on a regular basis…had touched herself just like this while imagining him doing just what he was doing now…but this was so much better. And it was *way* better to have a real live cock inside her rather than a plastic one. Fletch was warm and hard, and his hands holding her still as he thrust into her were only increasing her pleasure.

"Harder, Fletch. Harder!"

Amazingly, he did as she demanded. She felt his hipbones slamming into her thighs as he pumped. She closed her eyes but opened them at his harsh words.

"Look at me, Em. I want you to look at me the first time you come with me."

Emily looked down at where they were joined. Her middle and index fingers were frantically rubbing against her bundle of nerves and she could see his cock sliding in and out, shining with her juices.

Her eyes bounced up to his at the exact moment she felt herself going over the edge. She groaned and barely managed to keep them open as it hit her. She twitched in his grasp and clenched around him as her muscles spasmed with her orgasm. Emily's free hand grabbed onto one of his biceps and she hunched up toward him as *la petite mort* continued to move through her body.

It was one of the most intimate things she'd ever done with anyone in her life. It. Was. Amazing.

And it wasn't even over.

"So fucking beautiful, Em. I actually felt you melt all over my cock." Fletch's thrusts continued to be hard against her, but she could tell a difference. He glided in and out of her easier now, her orgasm easing his way even more than before.

"I'm coming, I'm going to coat you with my come. You're mine now, Em. Mine. I'm marking you, inside and out."

Fletch groaned and held himself deep inside her as he came.

Smiling, thinking he was done, Emily relaxed.

She jerked in surprise when Fletch pulled out of her body abruptly and held himself over her belly. He squeezed out one more stream of come and she sighed at the carnality of the move. Fletch kept hold of his cock and fit himself to her folds and managed to push back inside her, even with his softening body working against him. He lay down on her, not caring about the mess he'd made on her belly.

Emily sighed in contentment and wrapped both arms around Fletch. They lay like that for several moments, breathing in synch, enjoying the aftermath of monster orgasms.

Finally Fletch pushed up on his elbows and grinned affectionately at her. "On a scale of one to ten, that was definitely a twelve."

Emily smiled up at him. "I was going to say a fifteen."

"I can go with that. Thank you, Em."

"For what?"

"For trusting me. For being here with me. For giving your body to me. All of it."

"You're welcome. But honestly, I think I should be thanking *you*...again." Emily looked down at her belly, now smeared with his orgasm. "What was that about?" At his look of chagrin, she hurried to reassure him. "I'm not complaining mind you, just wondering."

Fletch pushed up farther, and they both groaned as his actions dislodged him from inside her. He used his hand to caress her belly, massaging his come into her skin. "I'm not sure. I just wanted to see myself on you."

"Guys really are visual, huh?"

"Yeah, but it's more than that. I shot off inside you, but I wanted to mark you on the outside too."

Emily smiled up at Fletch. He was a badass soldier, but such a horny teenager too. The juxtaposition was alluring as hell. "Okay."

"Okay?"

"Yeah. Okay. You know what this means, right?"

"What?"

"That we need to shower now."

"Oh yeah, we definitely need to shower."

Emily felt his interest against her inner thigh and looked at him in surprise. "Really? Already?"

"I have a feeling it's going to have a mind of its own when it comes to you."

"What time is it?"

Fletch leaned over and looked at the clock on his bedside table. "Eleven-thirty."

Emily chuckled. "You were right, that didn't take long."

"Hey, I warned you."

"You did."

"But now that we've taken the edge off, we have plenty of time for other things."

"As I said, it's been a while for me."

Fletch caressed the side of her cheek for a moment. "I know, and you'll never understand how appreciative and thankful I am of that. I'm a lucky son of a bitch and I know it. There are plenty of other things we can do when you get too sore. I can't wait to taste you and feel you explode on my tongue. But I do have to say, I'm not nearly done with you yet. We have hours before Annie gets back. I plan to take advantage of every second."

Emily looked up at the man who'd changed her life. She'd tried to hate him. Tried to think the worst, but ultimately, deep down, she'd known he was a good man, and not the asshole Jacks had tried to make her believe he was.

"Come on." Fletch sat up. "Let's get you out of this torture device," he motioned to her bra, which was still bunched up under the curves of her tits, pushing them up and presenting her nipples to him in a way that made him want to spend hours showing her how much he loved her body, "and get in that shower. Ever had shower sex?"

Emily rolled her eyes and shook her head. "Sounds complicated."

"I don't think so. I've never done it either, so it'll be a first for both of us. I'm not that much taller than you, so I think it'll work."

Emily stood up and shed the lacy bra, enjoying the lustful look Fletch gave her body as she displayed it to him. "You expect me to believe you've never had sex in a shower?"

Emily swore she saw a slight sheen of red blossom across his cheeks before he answered. "Well, self-induced orgasms excluded, it always seemed too intimate. Before you, I wasn't much into that sort of thing. Now come on, before I take you back down to that bed and we never leave."

"No complaints from me, although you get the wet spot."

Fletch leaned in and took her head in his hands. "I have no problem with the wet spot, Em. None whatsoever. Because it means we've both been satisfied." He grinned at her. "You can't be blushing."

"Hush. Are we going to stand here all day or what?"

"Or what."

Emily smiled as Fletch led the way to his bathroom. It was going to be a long, delicious day, and she couldn't wait.

THAT NIGHT, AS Annie chattered on and on about what a wonderful day she'd had and all the rides she'd ridden, food she'd eaten, and how she'd put on "real live" Army man face paint, Emily tried to ignore the new aches and pains in her body. Every time she shifted in her seat she was reminded of how hard Fletch had loved her all day.

After the third time, she'd protested that she was too sore for any more sex. Fletch hadn't even argued, he'd simply eaten her out until she'd exploded all over his fingers and tongue. She'd reciprocated and found that going down on Fletch was an experience in itself. She'd not particularly enjoyed giving blow jobs in the past, but he made it fun, and she felt more powerful than ever seeing his knees get weak as she got him off.

All in all, the day had been amazing. Fletch was a

considerate and attentive lover. Giving more than he took. And between bouts of loving, they'd cuddled in his bed, on the couch, even on the back porch for a while. It was almost overwhelming, but he'd warned her that once he was in, he was *in*. He hadn't lied. Not in the least.

As Annie wound down, Emily looked over at Fletch. He was smiling at the two of them as if he couldn't imagine being anywhere else other than right where he was at that moment. Emily thought to herself that the feeling was entirely mutual.

Chapter Seventeen

EMILY KNEELED DOWN by her daughter and pretended to brush some wrinkles out of her T-shirt. She really just wanted to be eye to eye with Annie so she could best gauge her reaction.

"Are you excited about today?"

"Uh-huh."

Emily looked into Annie's eyes for a long time, trying to make out what the little girl was thinking. They were headed down to Austin for the day…Fletch had wanted to take them on a double date. Emily had tried to talk him out of it, saying Annie would be just as happy to go to McDonald's with them one day, but he'd knocked any further argument out of her by saying, "If I'm willing to spend the time and energy on her mom, why wouldn't I want to do the same for Annie?"

But Emily had more concerns than just her daughter getting a sugar high and spazzing out all day. Annie was already extremely attached to Fletch. It was one thing for Emily to get hurt if their relationship ended, it was another thing altogether for *Annie* to get hurt if things didn't work out.

"Remember when I went on a few dates with Rodney?" Emily asked her daughter.

"When we were at the other place," Annie said with a solemn nod.

"Right. And you liked him too. But adults sometimes date each other and don't get married. I know you like Fletch, and you want us to get married, but that doesn't always happen."

"Rodney told me once that when you and him got married, that I was gonna be sent off to a boring school," Annie told her mom seriously with absolutely no hint that she was kidding.

"What? He did? *When*?"

The little girl nodded. "He was there to pick you up for a date to the funny singing place and you weren't ready yet."

Emily felt the tears behind her lids, but controlled them. She put a hand on Annie's cheek. "The opera?"

Annie nodded.

Emily felt sick inside, knowing exactly when Rodney had said that to her child. She'd been upstairs finishing getting ready before he'd arrived to pick her up. She never would've guessed that he'd say something so horrible to her daughter. "I would never send you anywhere, baby. We stick together. Always. I'd never send you off to a boarding school. Ever."

Annie nodded solemnly. "I know. I told Rodney that. He laughed at me."

Emily brought Annie into her embrace, hating that she was just learning about this now. She pulled back and held her daughter's shoulders tightly. "Annie. Listen to me. I love you. You're everything to me. I don't like that you kept this secret from me."

"I know, Mommy."

"Did he tell you not to tell me?"

She shook her head. "No. But it's okay. I was gonna tell you, but then you stopped going on dates with him, so I didn't have to."

Emily eyed her daughter critically. There was still something she wasn't telling her. "We only went on one more date after that."

"I know."

"What'd you do?"

Annie bit her lip and looked away from her mom.

"Annie. Look at me." Emily waited until the little girl had looked her in the eyes again. "What'd you do?"

"I didn't want to be sent away. I didn't think you would, and I could tell you didn't really like him. He smelled funny, like fried food. And you always say that fried stuff wasn't good for us. Your boss called and you went into your room to take his call."

"Go on," Emily urged when Annie paused.

"I just told him how hard it was being a kid," Annie

protested, her little eyes tearing up, obviously afraid her mom was going to be mad at her. "I told him about the time I got the lice bug things in my hair, and how you had to help me all the time with my homework. And that time I got sick and barfded all over my bed and you. But then I told him how much I love to sing in public, and that I couldn't wait to be able to be old enough to have a sleepover with all ten of my best friends, and how Chuck E. Cheese's is my favoritest place to eat in the whole world."

Emily wanted to laugh, but held it back. She'd already decided that things with her and Rodney weren't going to go any further than they had, but it seems her daughter helped him break up with her, rather than the other way around.

"Ann Elizabeth. You know better than to do something like that."

Annie pouted and looked at the ground. Her words came out in a small whisper. "I didn't want you to love him more than me and send me away."

Any trace of laughter Emily might've had was washed away in an instant. There were times she honestly forgot that Annie was only six years old. She put her fingers under her daughter's chin and raised her head until they were looking into each other's eyes. "I will *never* send you away. No matter what. I love you, baby. You're the best thing that's ever happened to me.

No man will ever come between us. Ever."

Annie sniffed and ran the back of her hand over her nose. "Promise?"

"Pinky swear." Emily held out her hand and smiled when Annie hooked her smaller finger around hers. "Now, about today. I like Fletch, and I'm pretty sure he likes me back. But adults sometimes like each other, and when they've been dating for a while, decide they don't like each other as much anymore."

"Like Tommy's parents. They don't live in the same house anymore. He spends school days with his mom, and weekends with his dad."

"Sort of like that, yes," Emily agreed.

"But you've been on four dates with Fletch. I think he likes you."

Emily smiled. "I want you to have fun today, but I just want you to realize that we aren't getting married. At least not right now. The last thing in the world I want is for you to be disappointed if it never happens. Okay?"

"Okay. But Mommy?"

"Yes, baby?"

Annie leaned into her mom and whispered, "I have a good feeling about Fletch."

Emily laughed and shook her head. She'd tried. She stood up, wincing at the creak in her knees as she did. "What are you most excited about for today?"

They were going to the Millennium Youth Entertainment Complex in East Austin. It was a huge building that had a movie theater, bowling, roller skating, food, and even an arcade. Emily knew it was going to be an exhausting day, for both Annie and her, but when Fletch had suggested it—and seemed so excited to have thought of it—she didn't have the heart to turn him down. The man had no idea what he'd gotten himself into. None. He'd first suggested laser tag, but Emily had vetoed that. As much as she knew Annie would love it, she thought her daughter was still a bit too young to be running around trying to shoot people.

"Roller skating. I've never done it before," Annie said.

"You think you can stay up and not fall?"

Annie shrugged and turned to the mirror, grabbing her brush and running it through her hair. "Don't know, but Fletch will be there to help me."

Emily couldn't argue with that. "What about bowling? You like bowling."

"Yeah. Me and Fletch have a bet."

"What? What kind of bet?" Emily demanded. It looked like she was going to have to have a talk with Fletch about a few things.

"I guess it wasn't really a bet since you told him he wasn't ever allowed to bet in his entire life. But he said you and me together couldn't beat him by himself."

"Oh he did, did he?" Emily asked, leaning down to hug Annie again. She put her face next to her daughter's and they both looked at each other in the mirror. "You didn't tell him that I've been taking you to the free family bowling night since you were three, did you?"

"Nope."

They grinned at each other.

"He's so going down," Emily told her daughter.

"Yup."

Mother and daughter smiled at each other. This was gonna be fun.

EMILY WATCHED AS Fletch "instructed" Annie on how to bowl. They'd arrived at the entertainment complex and had started with some food. It wasn't a long drive to Austin, but of course Annie was hungry. Ever since Fletch had found out how little they'd been getting along with, food-wise, he'd made it his mission in life to always have healthy snacks around and to prepare nutritious meals for the two of them. He vowed that neither of them would ever go hungry again.

After making quick work of an order of nachos, Annie declared she wanted to bowl first. Emily knew it was because the little girl was gonna burst if she couldn't "trick" Fletch soon.

They had exchanged their shoes and found an empty lane. Fletch was standing behind Annie, showing her the holes in the ball and pointing down the lane at the pins. Emily tried to hide her smile behind her hand. Fletch happened to look back at her right at that moment.

"What?"

"What *what*?" Emily asked, trying to sound innocent.

"What are you smiling about?"

Emily thought fast. "I just love seeing you with Annie."

Fletch leaned down to the little girl and said something to her. Annie smiled back and nodded.

Walking back toward Emily, Fletch had an intense look on his face, one Emily couldn't read. He came right up to her and put both hands on her waist. He leaned in and said in a voice only loud enough for them to hear, "You've raised an amazing child, Em. She's funny, smart, and sensitive to the feelings of those around her."

Emily beamed. There was nothing that made her feel better than hearing someone compliment her daughter.

"She's also sneaky, underhanded, and a cheat. Just like her mom."

Trying not to laugh, knowing he was right, Emily

did her best to play it off. She pouted and tried to look hurt. "What do you mean?"

"Don't give me that hangdog look. You know what I mean." Fletch turned them so he was standing behind Emily and they were both watching Annie at the bowling lane. He had one hand on Emily's stomach and the other at her hip. He pulled her back into him, and Emily snuggled in close.

"Go on, Annie, see what you can do," he called out to the little girl, who was practically dancing in place, anxious to throw the ball down the lane for the first time.

They both watched as Annie confidently strode up to the line, she held the ball, granny style, and lined it up.

"She's done this before," Fletch said unnecessarily as they watched the bowling ball roll lazily down the lane and knock down seven pins. "I'm gonna lose, aren't I?"

They watched as Annie turned to them with a huge smile on her face. "Is seven good, Fletch?"

"Shit. I'm so gonna lose." It was a statement that time.

Emily turned in Fletch's arms and leaned up to kiss him lightly on the lips, loving that he felt comfortable with the public display of affection, and that every time she did something like kiss him or hold his hand, Fletch's eyes glittered with desire. "You're going down,

Cormac."

An hour and a half later, Fletch slumped against the seat in defeat. "You guys win. Heck, you had me beat from Annie's first spare."

Annie danced a victory dance and Fletch couldn't hold back his laugh. He leaned over and grabbed the little girl, holding her upside down on his lap and tickling her. Annie's giggles rang out through the busy bowling alley as she wiggled and screeched, trying to get away from Fletch's nimble fingers.

Finally, he pulled her upright and sat her sideways on his lap and looked over at Emily.

Seeing the tears in her eyes, his entire demeanor changed. "What? What's wrong?"

"Nothing," Emily reassured him immediately, wiping away the moisture.

"Em, what?"

"I'm just...happy, Fletch. These are happy tears."

Understanding what she wasn't saying, Fletch leaned over, Annie still in his lap, and put his free hand behind her neck and pulled her into him. He kissed her, hard. The kiss probably wasn't appropriate for their surroundings, especially considering how closely Annie was scrutinizing them, but Emily couldn't care at the moment.

He placed his forehead against Emily's and whispered, "As long as they're happy tears, I'll take 'em. It's the other kind I can't stand."

"Come on, Fletch. You said after I beat you, you'd show me how to roller skate," Annie begged, squirming off his lap to the floor.

Fletch pulled back and brushed his thumb under Emily's eye. Without looking away from her, he told, Annie, "I did, sprite. Can you return our shoes? We'll go after that."

"Yay!" Annie chirped in excitement.

Emily smiled at her daughter as the little girl plunked herself on the ground and ripped the rented bowling shoes off her feet. She waited impatiently as she and Fletch removed theirs as well.

"We'll be right here. Don't go anywhere else but the return counter," Fletch warned. "I want you in our sight the entire time."

"I won't!" Annie reassured him.

Fletch and Emily watched as the little girl skipped up to the counter and got into the short line.

"Thank you, Fletch," Emily said quietly. "She's having the time of her life."

"I feel like I should be thanking *you*," Fletch said seriously. "I haven't really thought about kids. Not with what I do. I figured it was either a pipe dream, or that it would be many, many years before I'd ever have the chance to have any. Today has been amazing. I mean, I know that Annie is awesome. But seeing her like this, seeing her without a care in the world, it's…" His voice trailed off. He cleared his throat once, then continued.

"It's everything. It makes me feel that what I do has meaning. Seeing her happy and carefree, makes me realize something that I didn't get before. Every mission has a purpose."

Emily laid her hand on Fletch's tattooed forearm. He kept his eyes on Annie as she crept forward in the line. She leaned up and kissed Fletch's jaw. Then his temple. Then leaned forward so she could whisper in his ear.

"You're *so* getting lucky tonight."

Fletch's head whipped around so fast Emily couldn't even catch a breath before his lips were on hers. His tongue plunged into her mouth and his hand once more came up to rest behind her neck. But this time it wasn't in a tender caress. It was to hold her still for his sensual assault on her mouth.

It didn't last nearly long enough, but Fletch was obviously more than aware they were sitting in a bowling alley surrounded by families. He turned his head back to where Annie was, and murmured without looking at Emily. "Damn straight. You set me up, woman. You owe me."

Emily giggled, feeling the goosebumps break out over her arms as Fletch's thumb caressed the side of her neck. He hadn't taken his hand away, and she put her head on his shoulder.

They sat like that for several moments, watching Annie as she returned their bowling shoes and came skipping back toward them, her arms full with their regular ones.

"Here they are! Hurry! I wanna skate!"

The tender moment gone, Fletch slowly sat up and reached for his boots. He put them on as leisurely as he could, just to torture the little girl. Emily followed suit, until Annie was literally dancing around them, begging for them to go faster.

Fletch stood and held out his hand to Emily. Her warm hand against his own made his heart swell, but it was Annie's smaller hand, which grabbed hold of his, that made it melt. The little girl was affectionate, but she'd never held his hand before.

He wasn't a mushy man, but at that moment, he knew he'd do everything in his power to keep both Emily and Annie for his own.

EMILY WATCHED AS Fletch and Annie made their way slowly around the roller-skating rink. Annie had only let go of Fletch's hand long enough for them both to tie up their skates, and as soon as they were securely fastened, she'd grabbed hold again. The duo made their way around the floor with about what seemed like five thousand other kids and adults.

Leaning against the wooden rail, Emily watched as Fletch steered Annie away from a pile-up of kids who'd fallen. Then, as he got between her and another kid who was recklessly racing around the far end of the rink, not caring who was in his way. And as Fletch threw his head back and laughed at something Annie said, she sighed.

The man was amazing. Granted, she'd never really been on a date with both a man and Annie before, but somehow she knew this wasn't exactly normal. Annie was exhausting. She'd be the first to admit it. Emily loved her child, but her never-ending questions, unrelenting energy and enthusiasm for life, and her stubbornness weren't conducive to a relaxing day by any stretch.

But watching Fletch with her, Emily wouldn't have guessed he'd gotten up at four-thirty to do PT, after being awake until two making love to her. The man was a robot. He was able to do it all. And Emily was falling in love with him.

No. She *was* in love with him.

The thought should've scared her, but strangely it didn't. People always said that when you found your soul mate, you just knew. And Emily knew.

"Mommy! Look at me!" Annie called out as they skated past.

"You're doing great, baby!" Emily dutifully responded, waving.

Fletch smiled lazily at her, but didn't say anything.

"They're really cute," a woman next to Emily noted.

"Oh, thanks. Yeah."

"Looks like she's got her daddy wrapped around her little finger."

Emily opened her mouth to explain that Fletch wasn't her father, but closed it, nodding instead. "Yes, she does."

"Lucky," the other woman observed. "Have fun." She ambled away.

She hadn't corrected the stranger, one, because it just seemed too complicated, and two, because it felt good to have someone think that Fletch was hers. It was juvenile and stupid, but there it was.

After what seemed like another fifty laps, Annie had finally had enough. She and Fletch skated over to where Emily was waiting. Fletch helped her step over the wooden lip of the rink and smiled at Emily as Annie talked nonstop.

"Did you see me, Mommy? That was so fun! At first I couldn't do it good but Fletch helped me keep my balance. Did you see that he could go *backwards*? I wish I could do that, but Fletch says that if I keep pracmacing that I'll be doing it in no time. And then he let go but he was still right there. Did you see that? I did it by myself! It's like when you taught me to ride my bike. I was scared, but you were there holding the bike until I could do it on my own. When can we come again?"

Emily let Annie prattle on and looked over at Fletch. The love inside her seemed to grow when he mouthed, "Thank you," and his lips turned upward in a smile bigger than she'd ever seen on his face before.

She grinned back and mouthed, "Lucky tonight," and pointed to herself, then to Fletch.

Emily didn't think it was possible, but his smile got even bigger.

THE CAB OF the truck was silent and dark as they headed back home after dinner. Fletch had drawn the line at Chuck E. Cheese's, refusing to step foot in the notorious restaurant, finally winning Annie over by telling her that all good soldiers needed to keep their protein intake up by eating a nice large steak at least once a week.

Emily should've been concerned at how good Fletch was getting at manipulating Annie into doing what was best for her, but she wasn't. It was nice to share the responsibility for raising her daughter for once. Very nice.

"Mommy said I could wear combat boots when you

get married," Annie announced when they were on I-35 headed home.

Emily almost choked. Good Lord. She opened her mouth to say something, she wasn't sure what, when Fletch beat her to it.

"I'm okay with that."

"Fletch," Emily hissed. "Don't encourage her."

He looked over at her and said in a serious voice, "Why not?"

"Want to watch your movie?" Emily asked Annie, ignoring Fletch and the entire conversation.

"*Small Soldiers*!" Annie yelled, happy to be distracted by her favorite movie. She knew every word in it and could recite it anywhere, anytime.

Emily got it cued up and handed her daughter the headphones and tablet, provided by Fletch, to watch. Within ten minutes, Annie was out.

"I think she had a good time," Emily told Fletch dryly, glancing in the backseat at her daughter, who was sleeping the sleep of the exhausted in her booster seat. The tablet still clutched in her hands, the light from the video flickering over her lightly flushed cheeks.

"I did too," Fletch said softly. "Thank you for letting me take you both out."

"We had fun. But you know," Emily said hesitantly, "you shouldn't encourage her."

"What do you mean?"

"The wedding thing. She's at that stage where she gets fixated on stuff. I don't want to set her up for disappointment."

"What if I'm not?"

"Not what?"

"Setting her up for disappointment." Fletch's tone was low and urgent. "I like you, Emily. A lot. I'm not dating you just so I can have sex. I have every intention of following through with this relationship. All the way."

"Fletch—"

"I know, it's still early. But I want you to know, I'm not messing with the two of you. Okay?"

"Okay." There was more Emily wanted to say, but she couldn't bring herself to mention any of it.

Fletch put his hand on Emily's leg as they continued the rest of the way home in a comfortable silence.

When they pulled up back at the house, Annie was still sound asleep. Fletch turned to Emily. "Will you let me help you put her to bed?"

"Of course."

"Then you'll let me put *you* to bed?"

Emily smiled and leaned toward Fletch, brushing her lips against his softly. "I did say you were getting lucky tonight, didn't I?"

"You did," he confirmed with a smile, keeping his hands on the steering wheel.

"Then you can put me to bed afterward."

The look of lust in his eyes made Emily squirm in her seat. Lord, she wanted this man. Her nipples got tight under her shirt and she wanted nothing more than to straddle him right there in his truck and have her way with him.

"Are we home?" Annie's sleepy voice asked from the backseat.

"Yeah, sprite. We're *home*," Fletch affirmed, emphasizing the word "home" without breaking eye contact with Emily.

"Good. I'm hungry."

Emily laughed at the look of surprise in Fletch's eyes. As much as she wanted to go straight to bed, now that Annie was awake, and apparently hungry, they'd both have to wait a bit longer.

"Soon," Emily told Fletch softly as she reached for her seatbelt.

"Soon," Fletch agreed as he climbed out of his side of the truck.

SEVERAL HOURS LATER, Emily lay in Fletch's arms, replete and satisfied.

"Best day ever," she stated resolutely.

"Best day ever," Fletch agreed, hugging Emily's naked body to his even tighter. "But, I plan on every day from here on out being the best ever."

"Knock yourself out, soldier," Emily teased. "I won't stop you."

Fletch kissed Emily lightly on the forehead, then settled himself back down on the mattress. "You'll never know hunger again. You and Annie are safe with me. I'll do everything in my power to make sure Jacks never gets near you."

His words were somewhat out of left field, but Emily went with it. She was getting used to how Fletch's mind worked. "What he did wasn't your fault."

"Yes and no. We've talked about this," Fletch argued. "He got to you once. He's still out there. I won't let him get to you again."

"You're not God, Fletch. You don't know what will happen."

"I know I'm not. But I promise, you and Annie are protected."

"Okay," Emily agreed. She knew in her heart that there was no way he could guarantee their safety. Heck, the shooting at Annie's school showed her that. People were responsible for their own actions, and unless Fletch was around them twenty-four/seven, he couldn't guarantee anything.

"Okay," Fletch repeated. "Go to sleep, Em."

"Good night, Fletch. Thanks for an awesome day.

For me and Annie."

"You're welcome. We'll do it again soon."

"Yay."

Fletch smiled against Emily's hair as she fell asleep in his arms. He tightened his hold.

His. She and Annie were his.

He fell asleep, content in the knowledge that the two most important females in his life were safe under his roof.

Chapter Eighteen

EMILY SMILED AS Annie babbled in the backseat on their way home from school. It had been an amazing month. Not only were she and Fletch getting along—well, more than getting along, if she was honest with herself—Annie was blossoming under the attention of not only Fletch, but his teammates as well.

They did have to get creative in order to spend time with each other. Emily still wasn't completely comfortable having sex with Annie in the house, but since her daughter slept like a log, she was feeling more at ease with each day that passed.

Emily had fallen hard and fast for Fletch. He seemed just as happy lying in bed with her, cuddling, as he was making love. He didn't push if she was feeling uneasy, but the times they *had* made love were unforgettable.

Emily had woken up one night, she wasn't sure why, but she hadn't been able to resist waking Fletch by sucking him off. Within minutes, he'd been pounding into her from behind while she muffled her moans in her pillow. He was creative and giving, and Emily couldn't be happier with how their relationship was progressing, both physically and in general.

It wasn't often she and Annie were alone in the house. If Fletch couldn't be there for some reason, he'd send one of his teammates over to be with them. The other men had spent quite a bit of time listening to Annie talk about what she was learning in school, or reading to her. For some reason, she loved it when one of the guys would read out loud to her. Emily would've been jealous, but, if she was honest with herself, she loved hearing their deep voices as they "acted" out the scenes in the books they were reading.

After they'd read a chapter in Nancy Drew, Annie would want to discuss it. The guys had been very patient in letting her talk out what Nancy had done, and what maybe she should've done to keep herself out of trouble. Everything spy and self-defense seemed to fascinate the little girl. Emily might have been worried, except the guys had all kept what they'd taught her age-appropriate.

It was all very touching for Emily, since Annie had never had any kind of long-term positive interaction with men in her life. There had been too many people like Jacks and her former landlord.

Peeking in on Annie one night and seeing her sitting on her little bed with Truck had almost made her lose it. Truck was way too big for the little girl's bed, but he didn't seem to care. Annie was lying next to him, watching the book as he read, but her arm was across his broad chest and her hand was resting on his cheek. She was unconsciously rubbing his scar with her small thumb, as if trying to soothe him. Emily had backed away from the room, leaving the two alone, before she could burst into tears and embarrass Truck, and herself.

Rayne was also a very nice surprise. Whenever Ghost came over to the house, Rayne came too. She was down-to-earth and funny, and Emily could see them becoming very good friends in the future…at least she hoped they would. She hadn't seen Mary since the time she and Rayne had looked after Annie, but Rayne promised to bring her over again soon.

All in all, Emily was very happy. She hadn't planned on living with Fletch indefinitely, but she felt safe and content in his house, and especially in his bed.

They were almost home, and Emily couldn't wait to see what Fletch thought of the picture Annie drew for him. The little girl had shown it to her the moment she'd gotten into the car. It was of a crudely drawn man hiding in some bushes. Under it, Annie had written, "Daddy Fletch." Emily knew Fletch would love it. He said he was hoping to get off work early today and should be home by the time she and Annie got there.

"…and then Mrs. O said it was time for math, and Crissy cried. She actually cried because she didn't like math! I said I'd help her, but—"

Annie's words were cut off abruptly when a car, seemingly out of nowhere, slammed into them from behind.

Emily felt herself being flung forward, and the sound of her head thunking against the steering wheel as the other car made contact with her bumper was sickening. The seatbelt did its thing, but not soon enough for her to not whack her head against the wheel.

After taking a few moments to gather her wits, Emily's first thought was for Annie. The little girl had screamed when they were hit, but hadn't made a sound since.

The sound of a window breaking made her spin around in her seat to look back at Annie to make sure she was all right—and she couldn't believe what she was seeing.

A man she'd never seen before, dressed all in camouflage, literally from head to toe, had reached through the broken window he'd just smashed toward Annie, and was holding a white cloth over her nose and mouth. With his other hand, he was unbuckling her seatbelt, clearly intending to lift her out of her seat.

Annie's eyes were huge, and her fingers were trying to pry the man's hand away from her face, with no luck.

Emily thought about slamming on the gas, but quickly dismissed the idea, not wanting to risk the man dropping Annie onto the ground as she sped away. She fumbled with her seatbelt and opened her mouth to scream bloody murder, when a hand came in from her left and covered her own face with a cloth.

She struggled against the tight hold and her gaze lifted to see Jacks, also dressed in camo, standing by her door.

"Don't fight it, bitch."

His words seemed to come from far away, but Emily didn't listen. Like hell she wouldn't fight. She struggled against his hold but slowly, whatever was on the material did its job, and she lost the battle against consciousness. Her last thought was for her daughter.

FLETCH PUT A couple of slices of apple on a plate for Annie, as he did every afternoon that he beat Emily and Annie home, which unfortunately wasn't often. They usually arrived a little after three, and most of the time he wasn't done on base until at least five-thirty. But today, after he and Ghost spoke with the colonel about the situation with Jacks and the infantry squad, the colonel told them to take the rest of the day off.

It seemed that even though Jacks was being processed out of the Army for his asinine blackmailing scheme, he wasn't letting the matter drop. He continued his junior high school games of taunting Fletch and the team with vague threats, and even following the members of the team home every now and then. He wasn't doing anything illegal, per se, but Ghost made sure everyone reported every single incident.

They couldn't prove that Jacks was working with some of the other soldiers in his squad, but it was likely. He'd probably convinced them it was some sort of game and they'd all just gone along with it because they thought it wasn't real.

The colonel was getting sick of dealing with the bullshit as well, and had escalated the feud to the general in charge of the post. The best case scenario was that all of the soldiers involved in the petty jealousy shit, whether they were doing it out of maliciousness or as practical jokes, would get moved to another post, the worst was that all they'd get was a note on their officer or noncommisoned officer evaluation that they didn't play well with others, which could derail their promotions for quite a while.

Neither was acceptable to Fletch. Jacks had scared Emily. He'd caused her to not *eat*, for Christ's sake, because she didn't have enough money to buy food. He'd threatened to take a six-year-old little girl away from her mother. Jacks and his friends had made Fletch lose out on months of being with Emily—and that sucked most of all. When he thought about how he could've had her in his bed, and Annie in her room down the hall all along, he got pissed.

Fletch still hated that he'd thought Jacks was her boyfriend, when in reality the man was terrorizing Emily right under his nose. That was on him. He'd never assume anything when it came to her again. He'd ask her right out.

Looking at his watch, Fletch realized for the first time that Emily was late. He could almost set his clock by her. He vaguely wondered if something had held her up at work or at Annie's school. His phone rang just as he'd closed the refrigerator after putting the apples back inside.

"Fletch here."

"Is Emily all right?" Coach asked in an urgent tone.

"What do you mean?" Fletch asked.

"I'm by your driveway and Emily's car is sitting here, pushed off the road into the dirt on the other side of the shoulder, her door open, the back smashed in."

Fletch was on the move before Coach had finished speaking. He didn't know why his teammate was on his street in the first place, but ultimately it didn't matter. "Em's not there? What about Annie?"

"No, man. There's no one. I looked around the trees a bit and didn't see them."

"I'll be there in three." Fletch clicked off his phone and raced out his front door, for once without bothering to reset his alarm. He ran full speed past the garage apartment and toward the street. He paused at the end of the driveway to see which way he needed to go, and turned right after seeing Emily's old Honda next to Coach's pickup.

Fletch tried to take in the scene as he ran up to the car. The driver's side door was open. Without touching anything, he looked inside. Em's purse was on the floor of the passenger side, as if it had been flung there by the impact of whoever had hit her. He looked down and saw a set of footprints in the dirt. The car had been pushed all the way off the road so it mostly came to rest in the dirt. The prints came up to the door, then led away again. One set. Fletch clenched his teeth at the implications.

He walked around the front of the car and to the other side. The back passenger side door was still closed, but the window was broken. Annie's seatbelt was unbuckled and glass lay on the seat as well as the dirt by the door. Again, there was only one set of prints in the dirt leading up to the car and then back the way they'd came.

But there was a piece of paper folded up and lying on Annie's booster seat.

"Gloves."

Fletch barely spared Coach a look as he held out his hand to his friend, taking the black leather gloves Coach held out to him. He pulled them on as fast as he could and reached for the paper.

Rematch.
Our city.
Old Home Rd.
9pm.
Mission: rescue the hostages.

Fletch wanted to kill those motherfuckers.

The likely scenario was that Jacks had drugged Em and Annie and was using them as bait for his sick game. That would be the only reason they were nowhere to be seen, and only one set of footprints led up to each side and away from their car. They certainly didn't disappear into thin air.

It was utterly outrageous that Jacks and his friends were taking this as far as they were. But they'd made a mistake. Fletch didn't know what "their city" was, but it didn't matter. The team had six hours to get their game plan set.

He just hoped like hell those assholes didn't hurt Emily and Annie in the meantime.

Unfortunately, Fletch knew he needed to bring the colonel in on this one. It was bigger than him. The Army couldn't have soldiers going rogue on each other. And he needed the legitimacy that the commander would give the mission.

And he knew without a doubt, this *was* a mission.

Rescue the hostages.

If he'd hurt one hair on either Emily or Annie's heads, Jacks was a dead man.

That's why they needed the colonel. Fletch knew Jacks wanted to ruin his career, but the Army wasn't going to go lightly with kidnapping on top of blackmail. The Deltas had the might of the US Army behind them on this one, and Fletch knew it.

He looked up at Coach. Their eyes met and the other man nodded once. They both knew this would end with the careers of the men involved being ruined, but neither gave a fuck. No one messed with the Deltas…or those they loved.

"I need to change," Fletch told his friend in a surprisingly normal tone.

"I'll meet you at the house," Coach assured him. "I'm going to take a few pictures first. I'll be right there." He already had his phone out and was documenting what he'd found.

Fletch didn't bother to nod, he simply turned around and ran back the way he'd came, his mind going a million miles an hour with what needed to be done.

As he raced back to the house, flashes of Annie's face as she left that morning tore through his brain. He'd kneeled down as usual to hug her goodbye and she'd put her little hands on his face and leaned into him.

"I love you, Fletch." Her words were whispered, and she had looked scared to death. Typical Annie, however; like her mom, she didn't hold back the words even if they scared her.

"I love you too, Annie. Very much."

The smile she'd gifted him with spread across her face and had warmed him from the inside out.

"I'll see you when you get home today, squirt."

"Okay, Fletch. Have a good day!"

He'd smiled at the little girl as she'd skipped out of his house. He stood and looked at Emily. The tears shining in her eyes said more than words ever could. He'd taken the three steps to her and wrapped her in his arms. The words came from his soul.

"All my life I've been about serving my country and being there for my teammates. I never thought the true meaning of my existence would come up to my door and knock all those months ago. Thank you for trusting me with Annie. Thank you for giving me a chance. Thank you for trusting *me*."

Emily had eased out of his hold and looked up at him. "I still think we should be thanking you." It was now a running joke about who should thank who.

"No way. If I hadn't snatched you guys up, some other guy would've stepped in there, and I wouldn't know this deep satisfaction that you belong to me."

Emily had merely shook her head in exasperation,

not realizing he was one hundred percent serious. "You're the best thing that ever happened to Annie."

"And you?"

"And me. I love you, Cormac. We'll see you after work and school."

Fletch pushed the memories from that morning aside, trying to concentrate on what was ahead. He opened the door to the house and headed to his bedroom for his fighting clothes, but as much as he wanted to block out his memories, he couldn't. He thought back to the kiss he'd given Emily when she'd left that morning. It was supposed to be short and sweet, but with her words of love echoing in his brain, they had a mini make-out session in his doorway. It had taken Annie honking the horn impatiently to break them apart.

"Drive safely. I'll get home as soon as I can tonight. If I'm lucky, it'll be a slow day and I can get out of there early."

"Yay."

"Go on, you know Annie hates to be late."

"Whose fault is that?" she'd said as she backed away toward her car.

"Love you."

Her face had softened. "Love you too."

As Fletch pulled on a pair of black cargo pants and a black T-shirt, his lips pressed together in fury. Emily and Annie had to be scared to death. Jacks and his minions would pay.

No one fucked with his family. *No one.*

Chapter Nineteen

"I 'M SCARED, MOMMY." Annie's voice wobbled with the words.

"I know, baby. Me too. But you know what?"

"What?"

"Fletch will find us." As soon as Emily said the words out loud, she felt better. She had absolutely no doubt whatsoever that Fletch and his teammates *would* find them.

She had no idea how much time had gone by since they'd been taken from the car, as someone had removed her watch, but it didn't matter. As soon as Fletch knew they were missing, he'd be on the warpath to find her.

Jacks. She'd recognized him when he'd reached for her at her car. Fletch had sat her down one evening after Annie went to bed and laid the entire situation out for her.

Making her pay him every week was just the tip of the iceberg in Jacks's "harass Fletch" campaign. Even being kicked out of the Army wasn't enough to make him stop. He wanted revenge against Fletch and his teammates for embarrassing him, and he obviously would go to any lengths to get what he wanted.

Annie snuggled down into her mom's arms and Emily looked around. It was impossible to tell where they were, but it seemed they were inside some sort of metal box. They'd woken up alone, with only a lantern burning in the corner to illuminate the area. There wasn't any furniture, just the two of them and the small light.

It was a bit too much like a coffin for Emily's peace of mind. But they couldn't just sit around and cry.

"Come on, Annie. We need to explore."

"Explore?"

"Yeah. We've been reading Nancy Drew and GI Joe books for a while now. We need information."

Annie perked up on her mom's lap. "Yeah, good idea. Truck told me a story the other night."

"He did?"

"Yep."

"What was it about?"

"He told me about a time him and his team were captured by the enemy. They were stuck, but Fletch was the one who found a way out. They all had to slither out through a tiny hole. Truck almost got stuck 'cause he's so big, but he squirmed and wiggled and finally he popped out. You know what else?"

"What, baby?"

"All his friends were waiting for him. They didn't run away, when they could've. They waited for Truck to get out too. He said that's what friends do."

Emily's heart swelled. She knew the story was probably a lot more harrowing than Truck had told her daughter, but she appreciated anything that could get Annie out of her own head.

"Well, if they could do it, we can too." Emily wasn't sure that was true, but it would keep Annie busy and not thinking about how scared she was. She helped her daughter stand up, then got herself up and off the ground as well. Emily held out the lantern with one hand and held on to Annie with the other. "Come on, Miss Annie Drew. Let's find out exactly what we're dealing with here."

The giggle that escaped her daughter's mouth was sweet sounding indeed, but didn't do anything to loosen the ball of dread that sat in Emily's tummy. They were in big trouble, and she hoped Fletch and the others would find them sooner rather than later. There was no telling what Jacks had in mind for his captives. Emily was terrified to find out.

FLETCH GLANCED AT his watch. Seven twenty-two.

Time was going by too quickly, and they didn't have the information they needed yet. It was maddening and frustrating. "Fuck this. Call Tex," he ordered. "We can't use Google Maps to scope out Old Home Road. The data is too old. We need current satellite data to see what those fucktards have set up and planned. I'm not going into this blind."

Ghost nodded in agreement, but didn't move. "Contacted him before we came in. I'm expecting him to call any moment."

Fletch nodded and stood up to pace the room. He tried to keep his mind on the upcoming mission, but couldn't help thinking about how Emily and Annie were probably feeling. They'd be frightened and worried, and he hoped Jacks would be smart and not hurt them.

It suddenly didn't matter if he hadn't physically hurt either one of them. He'd probably drugged them. Scared them. It was enough. Jacks was going to die.

As if he could read Fletch's mind, the colonel growled, "I know y'all are pissed. I don't blame you, I'm just as upset about this as you are. But under *no* circumstances will this become an incident if I can help it. Nonlethal ammunition only."

"Fuck that!" Hollywood exclaimed before Fletch could open his mouth. "These guys are serious, there's no way we won't have live rounds if we go in there. You know *they* will most likely have real bullets."

"There's no way I'll allow *you* to be armed with live rounds," the colonel countered immediately. "Look, we all know you're gonna kick their asses. The end of this is a foregone conclusion. I have no idea what these asswipes think they're doing; they must've been given trophies every time they lost a little league game. They obviously think they're fucking Olympic champions or something. But the bottom line is that they're gonna lose. But in order to prevent the President of the United States from having to go on air and try to explain how one team of US soldiers killed another team of US soldiers, *this* is how it's gonna go down."

The colonel didn't seem to care that he had seven pairs of irate eyes on him. He'd been around the men long enough that he knew them to the core. They were upset and angry, but they were never out of control. Ever. It's what made them such good special forces soldiers. The best of the best. The kind of men he'd want to come and find him if *he* was ever kidnapped.

He continued as if he hadn't been interrupted. "I know you're pissed, and I don't blame you, but I talked to the captain in charge of Jacks's squad. He said the men he works with are stand-up good guys. He claims that there's no way they'd purposely put any woman or child—or even fellow soldiers—in danger. He thinks, and I agree, that Jacks has been lying out his ass to them to get them to do what he wants. You know as well as I do that rubber bullets can be just as effective as real ones. Hell, you guys can use your *hands* just as effectively as a bullet."

"I'm not willing to risk Emily or Annie's life on a hunch," Fletch insisted in a low, hard voice. "Whether the infantrymen out there know anything about civilians being involved in this clusterfuck is a moot point. They *are* involved and I won't risk one hair being harmed on either Emily or Annie's head because of Jacks and his insane sense of retribution against me or my team."

Ghost's phone vibrated, and everyone in the room looked over at him as he answered it.

"Ghost. Hang on, putting you on speaker." Ghost clicked a button and placed the phone on the table in the conference room. "Okay, you're on."

The voice that rang out through the speaker wasn't the masculine, southern-accented voice everyone was expecting. It was female, and the owner jumped right into what she wanted to say without bothering to waste time on pleasantries.

"So I checked out the address you gave Tex and it looks like there's been a lot going on there over the last month or so."

"Who are you?" Fletch interjected before she could continue.

Everyone heard the woman sigh before she huffed,

"I'm Beth. And before you bitch about me not being Tex, you should know he put me on this because his wife fell down a flight of stairs. She's fine, but he's taking her to the emergency room to make sure. Now, if you'll let me continue, I'll tell you what you need to know to get Emily and her daughter out of their situation."

"Fuck," Fletch swore violently. "Excuse my French, but I don't know you. I know *Tex*. I need his expertise. We've only got an hour and a half and don't have time to deal with this."

"Guess what, Ranger Rick?" the woman on the phone broke in, sounding just as upset as Fletch. "You got *me*. Tex knows how important this is to you, that's why he called while he was on the way to the hospital with the love of his life and begged me to shut this shit down. If you'd close your hole for one second, I'll give you the information you need to find Jacks and his fucking minions and to get that woman and kid out of the middle of a massive clusterfuck and back home where they belong."

There was silence in the room for a heartbeat, before Coach chuckled. "She's got you there," he noted, smirking.

"Go on," Fletch demanded unapologetically.

"Well, thank you, your highness," the woman griped, but then went on as if she hadn't been interrupted and insulted. "As I was saying, it looks as though these assholes have built themselves an entire city made out of freight containers, you know, the ones they pile high on ships—"

"We know what freight containers are," Fletch barked, knowing he was being an asshole, but not able to stop himself.

"You got pictures?" Beatle demanded impatiently.

"Do I have pictures?" Beth asked rhetorically. The team's phones started vibrating one by one, as if on cue. "You've all just received the photos that I took from the satellite. I don't know how in the hell they got their hands on as many of those damn containers as they did, but it's a moot point right now. They've done a good job setting up a defensive position, but there are several obvious holes. They must not've been able to recruit enough buddies to cover the entire thing. All the more lucky for you.

"The northwest and the southeast are where it looks like they're expecting you to breach their little town. They've left them relatively open for you and are most likely lying in wait for you there. Along the north side, they've put concertina wire, thinking that would force you into the town where *they* want you to enter, but they're idiots, so of course that's what they'd think."

Fletch's respect for the woman on the other end of the line increased as he examined the pictures she'd sent and she continued to break down the town Jacks and his friends had built. She was right on every single item. She really didn't need to point any of it out to the Delta Force soldiers, but no one interrupted her, as they were all making their own mental plans.

"Now, I'm not one hundred percent sure where Emily and Annie are in this fucked-up scenario. The satellite didn't catch Jacks arriving with them, but I'm thinking they stashed them right in the middle. See the three containers stacked up? I'm betting they think if you guys have to come all the way into the center of their town, they'll have a better chance at coming up behind your six and taking you out. From what I can tell, they aren't planning on playing fair."

"We didn't think they would," the colonel clipped out.

"Of course not. Anyway, I'm sure I'm not telling you anything you haven't already figured out. Just don't give them a reason to grab the girls and use them against you."

Fletch had thought the same thing, but hearing it out loud made his blood boil all over again. The thought of Emily or Annie being used as a human shield almost made him lose his cool.

"Thank you, Beth. Not sure who you are or how you know Tex—"

"I work for him. He hacked into my computer and

recruited me. I'm friends with Penelope Turner."

Ghost had obviously not been expecting an explanation, and it wasn't much of one, but it made as much sense as anything else did when it came to Tex. "Tell him we hope Melody is okay. And say hey to Tiger for us, and thanks for the intel."

"I will. Thank you for not calling her the Army Princess. She hates that stupid name. And you're welcome. Get those fuckers. It's a sad day when we can't trust our own soldiers anymore."

"You can trust *us*," Fletch told her in a serious voice. "These guys don't even deserve to be called soldiers."

"Amen to that. Go be the quiet professionals we all know you are. Over and out."

There was silence in the room for a beat, before Ghost snorted out a laugh after hearing the unofficial Delta Force slogan come out of Beth's mouth. "Figures *she* knows we're Delta when no one on this base does. Tex knows how to pick 'em." Then he got serious. "Okay, we've got the intel we need. The colonel says we can't kill the fuckwads, so let's plan this."

The seven teammates, and the colonel himself, sat down at the table, pictures in hand, paper in front of them, ready to figure out how to not only safely extricate Emily and Annie, but how to shut down Jacks and his crew once and for all.

"MOMMY, LOOK. THE metal is flaking in this corner." Annie's voice was soft and excited. She'd taken her job seriously, examining every inch of the shipping container they were being held prisoner in.

Emily stood behind her daughter and kneeled down. She reached out and ran her hand over the rusted metal. Annie was right. "Stand back a sec, baby." Annie did as she requested and gave her mom some room.

She pulled hard on one of the chinks of flaking metal, and let out an "oof" when she fell backwards on her butt. Looking down at her hand, Emily saw she'd taken a chunk of the wall with her. "Turn off the light!" Emily said urgently, breathing a sigh of relief when Annie immediately did as she'd asked.

"You did it, Annie!" Emily told her daughter. "The metal is weak over here. If we can get enough of it off, maybe we can squeeze out. But we need to keep the light off as much as possible. We don't want to announce our plans to anyone who might be able to see. It's dark outside, we've been here for a while."

As a measure of how mature Annie could be sometimes, she merely said, "Long enough for Fletch to find us?"

Emily stopped yanking at the rusty side of the box and pulled Annie into her arms. Then she took Annie's head in her hands, much as the young girl had done that morning to Fletch. "Yes. Long enough for Fletch, and Ghost, and Coach, and all the others to find us." Moving one hand to Annie's chest over her heart, Emily went on, "And I know here, with all my heart," she patted her hand to make her point, "that Fletch is doing everything he can to get to us."

Emily heard Annie sniff once. "I love him, Mommy. I'm trying to be a good soldier, but I'm scared."

"And you're allowed to be. You know what I heard once?"

"What?"

"That being scared means you're about to do something really really brave."

"I'm brave."

"I know you are, baby. I'm so proud of you." Emily held back her tears by pure force of will. She wasn't scared for herself; she'd go through whatever she had to in order to protect Annie. Rape, gang rape, being beaten, stabbed, shot...it didn't matter. Whatever it took, she'd protect her daughter at all costs.

Emily had an epiphany at that moment. She suddenly "got" how Fletch must feel about his job...about *her*. She knew without a doubt that he'd stand in front of them and protect her and Annie from anything life threw their way. Jacks, bullies, bullets. When he went on a mission, she imagined he felt much the same way.

When he set out to do his job, he did it with all his heart.

Suddenly she felt bad for him...he was probably freaking out, wondering where they were. And that hurt her heart. She actually had the better end of this situation at the moment. Yes, they'd been snatched out of her car and, yes, she'd been scared, but she didn't remember anything other than that brief moment in her car, thanks to whatever drug had been on the cloth. She and Annie had woken up alone and relatively unhurt.

Imagining what Fletch was going through made Emily feel sick inside. She vowed right then and there to do whatever it took to help him. Not only did she want to have a future with the man, she desperately wanted to ease some of the angst he had to be going through.

"Come here and help me, Annie, but be careful, don't cut yourself. Some of this metal is sharp." Keeping her daughter busy seemed to be the best way to keep her mind off of what was happening.

Finally, after several minutes of pulling at the flaking metal, Emily sat back on her haunches in defeat. They'd cleared a hole, but it didn't seem big enough for either of them to fit through. She leaned down and peeked outside.

The fresh air was heavenly, even if it was hot, typical for central Texas this time of year. There was only a half moon, so it wasn't enough to fully illuminate the area, but Emily could see the outlines of several other containers. There were no sounds, other than the crickets and cicadas that were normally active this time of night.

Sitting back, Emily turned to Annie. "I guess we'll just have to sit tight and wait."

"I can fit."

Emily ran her hand over her daughter's head affectionately. "I know you want to, but we don't have a choice."

"Mommy," Annie said seriously. "I can fit. I know I can. If Truck could wiggle through his hole back when they were in trouble, I can get out of this one."

At that moment, they heard a noise above their heads. Footsteps.

Emily grabbed Annie and gathered her to her chest and flattened herself against the back wall of the room. They both held their breath as the footsteps walked to one end of the container, then back to the other. They sounded muffled, as if there was another box on top of the one they were in.

Just the thought of what Jacks or one of his friends could do to Annie, if they decided they wanted to mess with them, made her decision easy. If anyone came into this metal prison, she and her daughter were sitting ducks. Being outside wasn't exactly safe, but it might be the better option. It would give Annie a chance to get away. "Okay, baby. We'll see if you can fit."

THE SEVEN DELTA Force men gathered a bit away from the city Jacks and his infantry friends had built. It mimicked the one the Army had erected on Fort Hood that they'd spent quite a bit of time training in, and which had started the asinine one-sided feud in the first place.

There were thirty or so of the large metal containers strategically placed around the property, and no one had any doubts that the setup included booby traps as well. Now that he could see it in person, Fletch agreed with Beth's earlier assessment. He had no idea how Jacks had found the money and resources to set it up. At the moment, it wasn't important though. All he wanted to do was find Emily and Annie and make sure Jacks would never mess with them again. He shouldn't have gotten to them this time, but he had, and tonight it ended.

Ghost's voice was toneless and low, making sure it didn't carry over the quiet night. "Everyone has their targets...remember, Jacks is probably armed, so I'm assuming he'll be up high. This op is a silent one, the goal is to take out the enemy one man at a time...up close and personal. Take 'em out, leave 'em where they are. We'll mop up after we have Em and Annie safe and away from here. Any questions?"

"How long is the colonel giving us?" Blade asked Ghost.

"Twenty minutes. That's all the time he could buy us with the general. He's had enough of this soldier jealousy bullshit and is giving us time to go in and get this done without having to involve anyone else. I can't believe he's even giving us that, but he knows we're good at what we do and he'd rather keep this as quiet as possible. As it is right now, the waiting troops think this is merely another training mission. If we can't get it done in twenty, the general will inform the platoon sergeants what's really going on and go from there."

"Soldier jealousy bullshit?" Fletch bit out, pissed off.

Ghost held up his hand. "Now's not the time. We need to end this. You have your shit together?"

"Yes." It was obvious Fletch did *not* have his shit together, but every man knew he'd do what needed to be done.

"These assholes aren't going to play fair, so move slowly but with purpose, and make sure you don't find yourself locked inside one of those goddamn boxes. Got it?" Ghost asked, looking at each member of his team. They'd discussed how that was probably the other soldiers' plans...isolate and lock them up, keep them contained.

When everyone nodded, Ghost gave the signal to move out, keeping his hand on Fletch's arm as everyone faded off into the countryside.

"Seriously, Fletch, you need to lock it down. Emily and Annie need you," Ghost lectured.

"Do you remember how you felt when you realized Rayne was inside that building in Egypt?" Fletch asked in a steady voice.

"Yes."

"Then you know a little about how I'm feeling right now. I'm pissed off that we aren't allowed to kill these fuckers. *You* were able to get closure by knowing you shot that asswipe who wanted to rape Rayne. I don't know if Em and Annie are even in here. I don't know what they've done to them. I don't even know if they're together. So if I'm a bit out of sorts, you'll have to fucking forgive me."

"I *do* know how you feel, but you know as well as I do we can't go rogue on this. Jacks is going to federal prison after this is over."

The argument seemed to do nothing to calm Fletch down. "He crashed into her car. He drugged them. He's playing a fucking game with us...he deserves to die!"

"Your entire goal is to find and retrieve Emily and Annie. That's it. Period. You know we've got your back. These assholes aren't going to get away with this. *We* might not be able to kill them...but that's the only thing we promised the colonel."

At that, Fletch turned his eyes on his friend. "As

much as I want them to hurt, don't lose your career over this, Ghost."

Ghost put his hand on Fletch's back. "No one fucks with Delta. As much as Rayne is Delta, so are Emily and Annie now. When we find them, you keep Jacks's attention on you however you have to. Mess with his head, taunt him, whatever it takes. We'll have your back and he won't hurt either of them. Trust me?"

"With their lives," Fletch said immediately.

"Good. Tonight a message will be sent…loud and clear…with no blowback," Ghost reassured his teammate.

The two men stared at each other, completely on the same page.

"The back-up plan is in play, just in case," Ghost informed Fletch.

"No blowback?"

"Absolutely none," Ghost confirmed. "If things go south and that fucker gets in a position where we can't get to him, he'll be taken care of."

Fletch felt his shoulders relax a bit. He still wasn't happy, but the reassurance from Ghost made him feel a little better about the entire fucked-up situation. He wasn't sure what his team leader had in mind, but he trusted Ghost with his life.

With Emily and Annie's lives.

It was enough.

SUSAN STOKER

"Come on, it's time to end this shit. Let's go get your daughter and her mom," Ghost grunted.

The words struck Fletch hard. His daughter.

Yes, Annie was his. As was Emily.

All of his focus turned to the mission at hand. Nothing would touch his family as long as he was alive to prevent it.

Chapter Twenty

"WHEN YOU GET outside, you need to pretend to be one of your Army men," Emily lectured Annie. "Move slowly and carefully. Look around you and don't make any sudden movements. Don't forget, the enemy soldiers could be above you."

"Got it." Annie was serious as she nodded at her mom.

"Fletch is out there somewhere, I know he is. Your goal is to find Fletch, or one of his teammates. Understand? If you see one of the bad guys—the ones who took us from our car were wearing camouflage clothes—you need to hide until they're gone."

"How will I know the difference?"

It was a smart question. One, unfortunately, Emily didn't really have an answer for. She tapped Annie's head. "You're going to have to use your noggin." As far as answers went, it sucked, but Emily continued, "Fletch and his friends like to wear all black. Head to toe. You've seen Fletch's clothes, right?"

Annie nodded.

"Okay then, if you see someone out there, wait and watch them. Don't run up to them without making sure it's a friend. Not even if you think it's Truck or any of the others. Some of the bad guys *could* be wearing black, but I'm hoping they're all in camo clothes. Count to ten inside your head and see what they do. If they look as though they're coming toward you, rather than looking outward, they're probably safe."

"I understand, Mommy."

"I said *probably*," Emily warned, not liking anything about this situation, and unconsciously drawing it out. "The bottom line is, if you aren't one hundred percent sure if the person you see is Fletch or one of the other good guys, do *not* reveal yourself. Stay hidden. It's important, baby."

Annie nodded again.

"I'm proud of you, Annie. You are an excellent soldier. You've been practicing for this for a long time, yeah?" Emily tried to bolster Annie's confidence. She was feeling anything *but* good about sending her six-year-old out into the unknown, but the alternatives were almost more frightening. Almost. She remembered the looks Jacks had given the little girl. The man was sick, and the last thing she wanted was him getting his hands on her daughter.

Emily kissed Annie on the forehead and pulled her into a tight embrace, not wanting to let her go.

Finally, Emily pulled back and looked into her daughter's eyes. "I love you, baby girl. Be safe. Be smart."

"I will. I love you too. I'll find Fletch and bring him to rescue you."

Emily smiled at her daughter through her tears, suddenly having second thoughts. They hadn't been bothered so far, maybe they both should stay put.

But Annie was already lying on her belly and had her head out the small hole they'd made.

They'd waited until the footsteps above their head were at the other end of the box, trying to time Annie's escape perfectly. Her daughter wiggled and squirmed her way through the small hole until her hips popped through. It was a tight squeeze, but Annie was right, she *had* been able to fit. The little girl pulled her legs up under her and suddenly she was gone.

Emily leaned down and peered out the hole, but couldn't see Annie at all. It was as if she'd simply vanished into thin air.

One side of Emily was pleased, but the other couldn't help but freak out.

What had she done? She'd sent her six-year-old out into the dark in the middle of what was essentially a turf war between two gangs.

Emily fell back on her butt and scooted backward until her back hit the opposite wall of the container. She hugged her knees to her chest, resting her head on them, and prayed that Fletch or one of the other good guys would find Annie soon. She shivered to think about what would happen if Jacks or one of his idiot friends got their hands on her daughter.

What was done was done, but Emily couldn't help the tears that coursed down her cheeks.

"Find her, Fletch. Please." The words were whispered into the stale air, but Emily hoped someone upstairs was listening.

FLETCH GLANCED AT his watch. Seven minutes had gone by since the team had silently stalked off into the night. Thirteen minutes remaining before the colonel and the general brought in reinforcements. Twenty minutes was enough time for the Deltas to take care of business, but they would've been happier with at least forty-five. As soon as Jacks figured out he'd lost...again, there was no telling what he'd do.

Fletch had foregone night-vision goggles, knowing all it would take was one small flashlight beam to screw up his vision for too many precious seconds. There was enough light from the partial moon to allow him to see where he was going. Fletch had only run into one of Jacks friends, and the man had been rendered unconscious without even knowing Fletch was behind him. They really were a bunch of amateurs compared to the Deltas. It should've made Fletch happy that the takedown of the man in his sector had been so easy, but he was in the mood for a fight, one that obviously wasn't going to happen because of their inexperience.

Making his way silently toward the center of the city—where Beth had suggested, and the team agreed, Emily and Annie were most likely stashed—Fletch paused at the end of one of the Conexes. He went to his belly and didn't move a muscle, trying to make out what he'd just heard.

Shuffling noises were coming from around the corner of the box he was lying next to. Someone was trying to be quiet, but they were doing a piss-poor job of it. It was as if the soldier had never had any training in evasive maneuvers before. Pathetic.

Using the tactics he'd learned from spending two weeks in sniper school, Fletch moved slowly—so slowly, if someone wasn't looking right at him, they'd still never see him. Crawling on the ground, he inched his way just far enough past the end of the container to check out what the noises were.

It took Fletch a moment for his brain to process what he was seeing.

He'd been expecting to see one of Jacks's soldiers. But it wasn't. It was *Annie*. She had flattened herself against the side of the container and was slithering alongside it as if she was trying to meld herself to the metal.

Something in Fletch's belly lurched at seeing the little girl seemingly safe and sound. He didn't immediately do anything to catch her eye though. Peering past her, and all around him, Fletch didn't see anyone else. While part of him was relieved, the other part didn't like that Emily wasn't with her daughter. Why would they have been separated? Had something happened to Emily? Was Jacks using Annie as bait for some reason?

Knowing he'd never get the answers he needed without talking to the little girl, he calculated his odds and decided that getting Annie in his arms and away from her too-vulnerable position was the best move at this point. She was trying very hard to be sneaky, but unfortunately, her blonde hair, her clothes scraping against the metal container, and her upright stance were beacons pointing right to her. She might as well have been running screaming through the makeshift village.

Not knowing how the little girl would react to seeing him pop up in the middle of the darkness, and not wanting his position to be given away, Fletch moved quickly. As soon as Annie was looking the other way, he sprang upward and took a few huge, silent running steps toward her. Gathering her up in his arms, he put one hand over her mouth to keep her surprised shriek muffled, and quickly eased back around the opposite side of the container.

Moving rapidly, wanting to reassure Annie as soon as possible that it was him, he went back the way he came, where he knew with more certainty they were clear of bad guys.

Glancing around and seeing nothing, Fletch knelt with Annie still in his arms, her back to his chest. She was struggling as hard as a six-year-old could. He put his mouth next to her ear and whispered, "It's me, sprite. Fletch."

She stilled as if he'd unplugged her. To make sure she'd understood, he reassured her again. "I've got you, Annie. You're safe."

Seeing she'd heard him, and understood, Fletch turned her and barely held himself upright as she threw herself into his arms. Obviously understanding the need to be quiet, she told him in a soft voice, "I knew I'd find you."

"That you did. You did good." Fletch pried her off him and held her by the shoulders, looking into her eyes. He wanted to spend more time reassuring her, and praising her for being as quiet as she could, but he needed to know about Emily. "Where's your mom?"

"I don't know." Annie's answer was short and to the point. "We woke up in a box. The corner was rustling, and we pried the metal up but it was only big enough for me to get out."

"Rusting?"

"Yeah, that's what I said."

"What direction?" Fletch knew his questions were too brusque, but he couldn't help it. The thought of Emily being desperate enough to send Annie out into the darkness without her was enough to know how precarious the situation was.

Annie pointed back the way she'd come. It looked as if Beth had been right. Fletch had almost made it to the center of the city when he'd come across Annie. He glanced at his watch. He only had ten more minutes to end this *his* way. He didn't want to leave the little girl, but for the moment she was safe. Emily wasn't.

"You did an excellent job in finding me, Annie, but I need to go and get your mom."

She nodded solemnly. Annie was a unique little girl. She should be freaking out, crying, *something*, but instead she simply looked him in the eye and waited for whatever direction he was going to give her.

"You know I love you, don't you?" Fletch asked the little girl.

She nodded again.

"You should know, I'm going to ask your mom to marry me as soon as the time is right."

"Really?" Annie breathed, her eyes going wide. "Has it been ten dates?"

Fletch didn't know what the number of dates he and Emily had been on had to do with anything, but answered affirmatively anyway.

"Will that make you my daddy for real?" Annie whispered, tilting her head inquisitively.

Fletch had never thought he was an emotional person, but hearing the awe and hope in Annie's voice almost did him in. "If it's okay with you, and your mom, yes. I want to adopt you and become your daddy legally."

Showing how smart she was, Annie asked, practically hopping up and down in her excitement, "So I'll be Fletch then too?"

He understood what she meant. "Yes, sprite. You'll be Annie Fletcher."

"Oh boy, oh boy, oh boy!"

"But for now, you need to keep this between us...okay? Can you keep it a secret? I want it to be a surprise for your mom."

"Yeah, I'm a good secret-keeper."

She wasn't, but at the moment, it didn't matter. Fletch took a deep breath. Okay, he had shit to do. He spoke into the mic at his throat, giving his coordinates to the colonel, who was listening in and ready to send in men to assist if needed.

"Here's the plan, little soldier," he told Annie in a serious voice as soon as he was assured a Ranger was on his way to their position. It was as if his words tripped a switch inside the young girl. She stopped smiling and nodded at him seriously. Once again, Fletch thought that she acted way older than her six years.

"I need to go and get your mom, but *you* need to get to home base." Fletch turned Annie so she was looking back the way he'd originally come. "In just a moment, an Army Ranger will be here and you guys will head back to base. I cleared out the bad guys, but you still need to be careful as you make your way through, there still could be some out there. Listen to the other soldier, be stealthy, use what Nancy Drew and I taught you. Can you do that?"

Annie nodded solemnly and turned back to him, looking worried for the first time. "You'll get Mommy? She didn't want to let me go, but I squirmed out before she could change her mind."

"I'll get your mom."

Fletch didn't even need to promise. Apparently his words were enough for the little girl he ached to call his own. As soon as the words left his mouth, the Ranger appeared out of the darkness to escort Annie to safety.

"Okay." Annie told him in a firm voice. "My soldier is here. Go. Time's a-wastin'."

Fletch smiled, having no idea where she'd picked up that saying. He kissed Annie on the forehead and hugged her quickly. "Ten-four. I'll see you in a bit."

He watched as the little girl flattened herself against the container at her back and side-stepped to where the Ranger was standing. He lost sight of them as they disapeared behind another Conex.

Thankful that half his worries were assuaged, Fletch concentrated on Emily. Nine minutes. He went back to where he'd seen Annie for the first time and calculated how many of Jacks's friends were probably between him and Emily, and faded into the darkness toward his future.

Chapter Twenty-One

EMILY GASPED WHEN the door of the container was suddenly wrenched open and a light shone into the darkness, blinding her. She threw up her hand to block the light, but was grasped in a firm grip and forced to her feet before she could scramble away. Two men had stalked into her prison and had obviously expected to see both her and Annie cowering in fear.

"Where the fuck is the kid?"

Emily knew it was Jacks who'd asked. She couldn't see him that well, but would recognize his voice anywhere. She tried to pull her elbow out of the other man's grasp, with no luck.

"Gone."

"Fuck!" Jacks spat out, then shrugged. "Doesn't matter. You'll do. Come on."

Emily tried to stay upright, but it was tough when she was dragged, none too gently, across the floor toward the door. "You might as well give up, Jacks, you know you can't win," she begged, knowing he wouldn't listen to her, but needing to say it anyway.

"Fuck you. We *already* won. We stole you and the little bitch right out from under his nose. We could've done anything we wanted to you, and your boyfriend and all his friends know it. This? It's just icing on the cake."

"You can't honestly think you're going to walk away from this scot-free," Emily hissed.

When Jacks didn't respond, she turned to the younger man holding her so tightly she knew she'd have a bruise in the morning "What are you getting out of this? Because your military career is over. Kidnapping and drugging a woman and child isn't going to go over very well. You'll be spending time in federal prison, I've heard that's worse than the regular jails."

The smack came from Jacks, and Emily wasn't expecting it. She wobbled, only the other man's grip on her upper arm keeping her from falling.

"Shut the fuck up, bitch. Or I'll knock you unconscious again."

"Uh, Jacks…I'm not sure—"

"Shut up, soldier!" Jacks snarled at the younger, now nervous-looking man. "This is all part of the training. She's not really gonna be hurt. You have to man-up. You think bitches won't pull this shit in Iraq? Hell, ISIS uses women and children as shields in combat, and they're just as well trained as the men. They're playing a part, stupid. Acting, just like she is. I'm helping you get over any sympathy you might have for *anyone* in the middle of a life-and-death situation. So man the fuck up."

Emily pressed her lips together, knowing Jacks was serious about knocking her out again. He was acting completely crazy, and she was getting even more scared than she'd been before…and that was saying something. She opened her mouth to tell the other soldier that she wasn't doing anything voluntarily and that she really had been kidnapped, but Jacks grabbed her away from the younger soldier and pushed her out the door.

They went around the side of the container she'd been held in, and Jacks pointed to a ladder propped against it. "Climb."

"What? Up there?"

"Yes, up fucking there," Jacks mocked.

Emily found herself shoved toward the wobbly ladder and looked up fearfully.

"And don't try anything, or I'll knock you off so fast your head'll spin."

The last thing she wanted was to fall from the ladder. Not seeing any other option, Emily began climbing. Jacks was right behind her, one hand on her calf, squeezing painfully the entire time. When she reached the top, she quickly scampered away from the edge, breathing hard.

There weren't two shipping containers stacked on

top of one another, as she'd thought—there were *three*. They were high off the ground, about thirty feet or so, and Emily knew if she fell or was pushed from that height, it could kill her.

Jacks and the other man came over the top and she looked on in horror as Jacks pulled the ladder up behind him. There was no way for anyone else to get up there now. She was trapped on top of crazy town with the absolutely last person she'd ever wanted to *see* again, nonetheless be stuck with.

Emily didn't stand up, she stayed on all fours and crawled farther away from the two men. Jacks didn't seem to care at the moment, feeling confident that she wouldn't get away from him. And he was right.

She flinched when Jacks's voice rang loudly out over the quiet night. "I've got your bitch, Fletch! You want her? Come get 'er!"

Silence followed his gruff words, but Emily had no doubt if Fletch and his teammates were out there, they'd heard him. Jacks stalked over to her and crouched down to her level.

"So, here's the thing. We knew they'd come after you, we even told them where you were. But they think they're smarter than us. Hell, they think they're smarter than *everyone*. I recruited some privates from the base to act as the 'bad guys' around this city. They eagerly signed up to play paintball in the middle of nowhere with no rules to follow. If anyone from the base comes here, those guys are here to take attention away from what we really wanted." He paused dramatically.

Emily didn't want to fall in line, but did anyway. "And what do you really want?"

"Retribution."

Emily didn't even know what that meant, but she kept quiet, as Jacks obviously liked to hear himself speak.

"They cheated when we played this game the first time. We weren't ready and they had us beat before we knew we were starting." Jacks paused then nodded his head as if agreeing with something someone had said. But Emily hadn't heard anyone say a word, and the younger soldier on top of the containers was looking on in disbelief, so *he* certainly hadn't said anything.

"But wouldn't terrorists do the same thing? Cheat to win?" Emily couldn't help but ask. Fletch had told her the story about the training exercise a few months ago, about how embarrassing it had been for the infantry squad to get beaten so quickly and so badly.

"Shut up," Jacks growled, standing and swinging the .22 rifle from behind his back and putting his finger on the trigger. "They fucking cheated and made me and my squad look like incompetent assholes! Fucking with you was fun, but ultimately it was just buying us time. We used the money you gave us, along with our own, to create this masterpiece. When your boyfriend gets here, the *real* show'll start."

"The real show?" Emily asked.

"Yeah. I know you're fucking Fletch. So killing you in front of him while he's helpless to do anything about it will show him *exactly* what it feels like to fail."

Emily gasped in horror at the same time the other soldier on top of the container did.

"I'm here, asshole." Fletch's deadly voice rang out in the dark night.

Emily gasped and tried to stand up, but Jacks was there before she could get fully upright. He dropped the rifle, pulled out a pistol from the small of his back, put one arm around her shoulder, diagonally across her chest, and pulled her back into him. She staggered and clutched his arm to steady herself.

"Look what I found," Jacks taunted.

Flinching as the barrel of the pistol was shoved against her temple, Emily didn't dare move otherwise. Jacks was just pissed off enough to pull the trigger. He wanted revenge against Fletch? Killing her would certainly do it.

"What the fuck do you think you're doing, Jacks?" Ghost's was loud and clear and came from the other side of the container.

Daring to look around, Emily could see several dark shapes moving around the outer perimeter of the containers they were standing on. It sucked, but it was obvious Jacks had the upper ground. The *way* upper ground. He'd positioned himself well, tactically, and everyone had no choice but to wait to see what the hell he wanted.

"What am I doing?" Jacks repeated. "Showing you that I'm not the fuck-up you thought I was."

"No one thought you were a fuck-up," Coach called out.

"Bullshit! My platoon leader did. The captain and colonel did. And now the general does too, no thanks to you! You guys all think you're undefeatable, but I know for a fact that you fail all the time. I know you went on some hush-hush mission the other month. How many people were killed in it? Huh? Wasn't it two?"

"Not sure where you're getting your information from, kid," Blade taunted, "but the only people killed were the terrorists."

"Shut up!" Jacks yelled, incensed. "I have sources that say you ran like *pussies* when the bullets started flying!"

Emily tried to shift in his grasp, but Jacks pushed the barrel of the pistol harder into her temple. "Don't try anything," he hissed. "I swear to God, I'll put a bullet in your brain so fast, no one will have time to take a step before you're dead."

Emily would've reassured him she wasn't trying to

get away, but he continued his tirade against the others.

"All my life I've looked up to E-7 soldiers, thinking they were the best the Army had to offer, that if you made that rank you were the shit. But it's all a crock of bull! You guys are nothing but thugs. When push comes to shove, all you want is the limelight. Well, today it's my turn. *My* turn to show the world what real bravery is."

"What, kidnapping women and children? That's what you think bravery is?"

Emily wasn't sure who said it, but she felt Jacks stiffen behind her. She didn't know why in the world Fletch's friends felt the need to taunt the obviously mentally unstable man, but she wished they wouldn't. She *really* wished they wouldn't.

"What I want the world to know is that I bested you! The enemy doesn't care about the lives of kids or bitches…they set them up to be suicide bombers all the time. Women are expendable. They were put on this earth to bear children. They're only good for fucking, cooking, and cleaning. I'm sick of the namby-pamby, watered-down Army. You guys think the world should play by your own set of pansy-ass rules. Fuck that! There aren't any rules in war."

"We're not at war with you, Jacks." Emily heard Fletch's voice again.

"The hell we aren't! You started this that day

months ago. I'm finishing it."

"What are you doing, Jacks?" the other man on top of the container asked nervously, in a quiet voice. "This wasn't the plan."

"Yes it was, Brown. You were just too stupid to realize it," Jacks told the other soldier, laughing manically. "*All* of you were too stupid to realize it."

"Fuck this," Brown murmured, pulling the ladder toward the side of the container, obviously planning on getting the hell out of Dodge. "I thought this was all a game. You said they were in on it, but it's obvious that's not the case. I'm not cool with kidnapping women and children and especially not *killing* anyone, and I certainly don't want to get in a turf war with other US soldiers. If you have a beef with them, it's *your* beef. Not mine."

Emily dropped to her knees as Jacks suddenly shoved her forward then stalked toward the other man. She watched in horror as he shoved him hard enough that he had to take a step backwards.

Jacks pointed the pistol at him and pushed again. The other man took another step back, then another, until he had nowhere to go because he was standing at the edge.

"Fuck you, Brown!" Jacks shouted before pushing the man one last time. It was just enough to knock him off balance.

Emily shut her eyes, knowing she'd never forget the

look of terror on the young soldier's face as he wind-milled his arms, trying to get his balance back. She heard his screech of terror, then the sickening thud as he landed on the ground below them.

"What the *fuck*, Jacks!" Emily thought it was Truck who called out that time.

A loud bang rang out in the dark night and Emily flinched, ducking without thought. She heard a thud against something, and then Jacks's pained grunt.

Jacks rushed away from the ends and back over to Emily. He pulled her against him again, even though she put up a fight, trying to keep him away from her. He replaced the pistol right back against her temple. "You guys can hit me with all the fucking beanbags and nonlethal rounds you want, it won't make a lick of difference. I'm still gonna win. I know you won't shoot me. *I* know it, and *you* know it...why bother denying it? I can do whatever the fuck I want, and you can't do anything about it. *Nothing.* I know how the government works. You probably got the lecture about using nonle-thal tactics to take me and the others down, didn't you?" He answered his own question. "Yeah, I know you did. So...here's the conundrum...what are you going to do now?

"I'm up here, out of your grasp. You can't sneak up behind me, because you can't get up here without me hearing you since I pulled up the ladder. You probably have backup coming, but what are *they* going to do? I've got a loaded weapon pointed at my hostage—and you've got nothing."

"What do you want?"

Surprisingly, Fletch didn't even sound pissed. Resigned was a better word. Emily wasn't sure what to make of that. Did he think that they were going to lose? Did all his friends realize that she was going to die?

Sweat beaded on her forehead. No. She didn't want to die. Not now. Especially not like this.

"You know you're not getting out of this," Ghost's voice rang out.

"I don't have to get out of this," Jacks taunted. "Poor little *Emily* is the one who has to get out of this. Here's the thing. I know I'm going to jail—and I don't give a shit. My two brothers are there, and shit, maybe I'll be lucky enough to be put in a cell next to them. But you know what? If Em here dies...*I win*. I win, because Fletch—you'll suffer for it. I'll lie in my bunk at night knowing I beat you. That you're crying in your Wheaties every morning wondering what you could've done differently."

There was silence as Jacks's words carried out into the night. The lack of any response seemed to bother him. It was obvious he expected an outcry from the soldiers below.

Emily squirmed in his grasp. The hell she was going

to make it easy for him to shoot her. Shit, she'd rather fall off the edge of this fucking container and have a chance at living than get shot in the head.

"What? You don't believe I'll do it? You don't think I'll blow her brains out right here?" Jacks jeered, having lost any remaining composure he had. "I'll fucking do it! Then I'll throw her down for you to see what *you* did to her. Who'll be the winner then, huh? I'll—"

Emily had been silent up until then, but let out a shriek of terror at the sound of a shot echoing in the night.

Jacks's grip on her loosened as he fell to the ground and Emily felt something wet splatter across her face.

For a moment she thought he'd done it, that he'd shot her in the head, but she wouldn't still be standing if that were the case.

"Emily?" Ghost's voice was frantic as he called up to her.

"I'm okay. At least I think I am." Her voice shook, and wasn't very loud, but she was alive and in one piece. She quickly took a step away from Jacks and looked at him fearfully. The last thing she wanted was him jumping up and grabbing her again. He lay still on the metal rooftop, a puddle of blood forming underneath his head. She took another step away from him and bent over, resting her hands on her thighs, trying to catch her breath.

"Em."

That was Fletch's voice again—and he sounded so close. She whirled around and gaped. It *was* Fletch. How had he gotten up there? She had no idea how he'd appeared behind her all of a sudden, but didn't care. Emily glanced at Jacks again, he hadn't moved from the last time she'd seen him. She had no idea if he was dead or not, but at the moment, she couldn't really care.

Instead of coming to her, Fletch moved towards Jacks, securing both his rifle and pistol before turning toward her.

"How, what—" Emily didn't get anything else out before she was engulfed in Fletch's arms. Everything else faded away. She inhaled deeply, smelling Fletch's unique scent that never failed to soothe her. Safe. She was safe. Everything else didn't matter.

She felt herself being carried away from the edge of the container, and Jacks's body. Fletch's arms were tight around her, holding her to him as if he never wanted to let go. She'd never felt anything more reassuring in her life.

Remembering her daughter, Emily pulled back a fraction and frantically asked, "Annie?"

"She's fine. I ran into her playing soldier and she's safe, far away from here," Fletch reassured her in a choked voice.

"Thank God. I didn't know if I should let her go by

herself or keep her with me."

"I'd say you made the right decision." He loosened his hold on her just enough so her feet could touch the ground, but he didn't let go.

Emily nodded and snuggled back into Fletch. They stood like that for a long moment, thankful they were both alive and breathing.

"Yo, Fletch, mind putting the ladder down?"

Emily didn't want to move, but knew she couldn't stay up there forever, so she reluctantly pulled back. She started to look at Jacks again, but Fletch put his hand under her chin. "Don't look, Em. It's over. He'll never hurt you again."

"Is he dead?"

"I don't know and I don't care."

"Will you guys get in trouble?"

"No."

"But—"

"I'll explain later."

"How'd you get up here?"

"With a boost. It wasn't hard, Em. I'd climb mountains to get to you."

Emily nodded and squeezed his hand as she followed him to the other side of the Conex, where he lowered the ladder. Within seconds, Ghost and Hollywood had joined them.

"Shit's gonna hit the fan, we gotta roll," Hollywood

urged after seeing Jacks. "The colonel specifically said nonlethal."

Ghost walked over to the man lying motionless and put his fingers on his throat, checking for a pulse. "First of all, Jacks isn't dead. Second of all, it's not gonna hit the fan," Ghost reassured the other man, as if he knew something Hollywood didn't.

"Nonlethal force was our directive," Hollywood argued, repeating himself, ignoring the first part of Ghost's statement.

"I *said*, it's not gonna hit the fan," Ghost repeated firmly. "Come on, let's get Emily off this damn roof and reunite her and Annie, yeah?"

Not stupid, Hollywood gave the team leader a long look before finally nodding and kneeling down beside the ladder to keep it steady.

"Come on, Em, I'll start down, you come down after me. I won't let you fall," Fletch told her.

"I know you won't. I trust you with my life."

"Damn straight. Let's get you cleaned up, then go find our soldier girl."

Emily waited until Fletch had gone down a rung or two and followed after him. She had a ton of questions, but vowed to keep her mouth shut until she was alone with Fletch. She was thrilled to be with him again. That was all that mattered at the moment. Emily supposed later she might have a flashback, or somehow not deal well with Jacks being shot when he wasn't even a couple inches away from her, but at the moment, knowing she, Annie, and Fletch were alive and in one piece...it was enough.

Chapter Twenty-Two

EMILY SAT ON the couch with her feet tucked under her and snuggled into Fletch's hold. She'd taken a long, hot shower, it was now two in the morning, and she was dead tired, but weirdly too wired to sleep. Ghost had followed them home, obviously wanting to talk to his friend before they had to meet with the general the next morning.

Dealing with the aftermath of the events that night had taken longer than it had for the Delta Force team to take out all of Jack's recruits. Not one minute after her feet had touched the ground, the area had been lit up by two helicopters and about forty soldiers. The cavalry had arrived, but ultimately it wasn't needed to save her.

All of the men the Deltas had run across lay where they were found, unconscious. None were injured, other than the headaches they'd have when they awoke. Apparently everyone on the Delta team was skilled in ways to make a man unconscious with little to no fuss.

The man who'd been up on the container with her and Jacks, Specialist Brown, was airlifted to the local hospital, most likely with a broken back...but Hollywood had reassured her that he'd live.

And surprisingly, Ghost had been right, Jacks wasn't dead. Whoever had shot him had either been unlucky, or extremely talented, as the bullet had only grazed the side of his head. A groove had been carved out from his right temple to behind his ear, but he was alive. Fletch wasn't happy he was still living, but Emily didn't care.

The best part of the night was when Truck had walked into the clearing after Jacks and Brown had been taken to the hospital—with Annie's hand in his. The Ranger who'd taken responsibility for her had brought her to the scene after it was safe for her to be there. Emily had never been so happy to see her daughter in all her life. The little girl was beaming from ear to ear, thrilled as she could be to be in the middle of a "military op," as she'd started calling it.

Emily had seen one of the soldiers who was late to the party, unvelcro the rank from the front of his uniform and pin it onto Annie's shirt, after the whole story came out about what she'd done. Emily didn't care if her daughter told the world that she saved her mom's life...as long as she was safe, and emotionally healthy, Emily was content.

She hadn't wanted to be separated from Annie after everything that had happened, but it was obvious the higher-ranking officials wanted answers. She agreed, after Fletch's reassurance, to allow another soldier to look after Emily by the vehicles. She waited for the adults to be done, safe and out of earshot.

Emily had been surprised to find the general was out for blood and had detained everyone involved in the "incident," as he'd called it, until he had answers as to exactly what had happened that night. She kept her mouth shut as Ghost explained, in great detail, his team's role in the entire thing. She wanted to know as much as the general, what had happened between the time she'd been kidnapped and when she'd seen the Deltas while she'd been on top of the shipping containers.

"You mean to tell me Sergeant Jacks—"

"Ex-sergeant, Sir," Ghost interrupted. "He'd already been chaptered out of the Army."

"You mean to tell me *ex*-Sergeant Jacks planned to kill Ms. Grant and her daughter?" the general asked, obviously pissed off about the entire situation.

"Yes, Sir." Ghost kept his answers short and to the point, which Emily thought was probably a good idea.

"And he knew you had no-kill orders?"

"Yes, Sir."

"Does anyone want to explain to me then, if this was a nonlethal op, how ex-Sergeant Jacks was shot with a live round?"

Nobody around them said a word, which didn't

help the situation.

"Obviously, someone didn't get the memo," the general complained. "I have a conference call scheduled with the President tomorrow, when I have to try to explain just what the fuck happened with this goat-screw tonight. You're all restricted to quarters until further notice," he snarled out.

"Sir?" Emily ventured cautiously.

"What?" The word was still barked, but lacked some of the bite he'd used toward the men.

"I don't know who you think shot Jacks, but it wasn't Ghost or his men." Emily could say that with one hundred percent confidence. She continued at his doubtful look. "Jacks had his arm across my chest and his pistol pointed at my head. He was going on and on about vengeance and how he was going to kill me to get back at the guys. I can tell you, I heard every single one of Ghost's men trying to talk him down. They were on the ground below us. I knew I was going to die, and there wasn't anything they could do about it."

The general frowned at Emily and crossed his arms over his chest. "The bullet creased the side of his head. Only someone extremely trained would be able to do that. Someone like a special forces operative."

Emily nodded. "I know," she whispered. "I felt his blood spurt on me and thought for a second he'd actually pulled the trigger and it was *my* blood I was feeling."

The highest-ranking man on the entire Fort Hood base cocked his head and didn't say anything for a moment. Finally, he asked in a low voice, "Why should I believe you, Ms. Grant? It's obvious Fletch has feelings for you, and that they're returned. Maybe *he* did it and you're covering for him."

"With all due respect, while I might love Fletch and I *would* cover for him if I thought it'd work, how in the world could Fletch shoot Jacks and then be shoved up the back side of the container two seconds later? I know without a doubt that he wouldn't have risked it with me so close to him."

The general had looked away from her then, and had met the eyes of each of the men on the Delta team. One by one, without a word, he studied them.

Finally, he speculated, "I talked to Specialist Brown before he was taken to the hospital, and he backed up your stories, but the bottom line is, *someone* shot ex-Sergeant Jacks. Despite what I asked Ms. Grant, I *am* aware the angle of the bullet wasn't an upward trajectory...meaning if you were all on the ground, or getting Fletcher's ass up to the top of the containers, it couldn't have been any of you. So—who was it?"

Silence greeted him again, and finally the general sighed. "You guys are killing me. Go home. All of you. But be in my office tomorrow at oh-eight-hundred.

We'll continue this discussion then."

A chorus of "Yes, Sirs" rang out around them. Each of the men saluted the general as he turned to leave. At the last minute, before he disappeared around one of the shipping containers, he turned around and stated, "You're a very lucky woman, Ms. Grant. I'm glad you're all right."

"Thank you, Sir. I am too."

The Deltas hadn't said a word, hadn't given each other secret looks, they'd merely acted as if the fact that they'd almost lost their jobs—and everything they'd worked for in their career—was a nuisance, rather than the disaster it really was.

"Come on, Em, let's get you and Annie home," Fletch said, wrapping one arm around her waist and pulling her into his side.

It wasn't quite as easy as that, but eventually they were allowed to leave, and now Emily was sitting next to Fletch at home, safe on the couch, and it felt divine.

"So what really happened tonight?" Emily asked Ghost and Fletch, feeling oddly mellow.

"What do you mean?"

"Don't act dumb," Emily scolded Ghost. "Who shot Jacks?"

"Is that like 'Who shot JR?'"

Emily glared at the man sprawled out in the chair next to them. He looked unconcerned with everything that had happened, as if it was just another normal night for him.

Ghost finally wiped the smile off his face and leaned forward. He spoke in a soft, serious tone. "You can't ever tell anyone this, Emily."

"I won't," she agreed immediately.

"No one. Not Rayne. Not Mary. Not Annie. *Ever*," Ghost reiterated.

"I almost died tonight," Emily said, instead of reassuring Ghost again. "I knew you guys were in no position to do anything to help me. I didn't lie to the general about that. Jacks was hyped up and was shaking with adrenaline. I knew it was just a matter of time before I'd die. He was going to pull that trigger and I would've never gotten to see Annie grow up. I'd have missed out on everything in her life. I wouldn't be sitting here right now. I don't care that he was shot. I don't care that he may or may not recover. If one of you managed it, great, fine. I just…I'd like to know."

"We had a back-up plan in place, just in case. We didn't know if we'd need to use it or not. There aren't a lot of Delta Force soldiers out in the world who have retained their skills. It's tough to get in and it's even tougher to *stay* in. It's a shit job where we have to do shit things. We learn loyalty early, and that doesn't end when someone leaves the teams. There are no ex-Delta Force solders. Once a Delta, always a Delta." Ghost paused and looked Emily in the eye.

Apparently seeing the seriousness of his words was sinking in, he continued.

"I worked with a guy before I was stationed at Fort Hood. He got out, but he's a highway patrolman who works down in San Antonio. As soon as we knew who it was that took you, I called him. He was a sniper."

Those four words said it all. He. Was. A. Sniper. Thank God.

"Thank you." Emily breathed. "And when you talk to your friend again, thank him for me too?"

"I will. We good, Fletch?" Ghost asked.

Emily had left the men alone while she'd gotten Annie settled. It had taken a while, the little girl seemed to be as hyped up as the rest of them. She wanted to go over what she'd done, and how Fletch had grabbed her, and then how she'd made her way back to home base with the Army Ranger. It was one big adventure for her, one that Emily knew would be rehashed over and over again, like the shooting at her school. But since the ending was a good one, Emily didn't mind.

Obviously during that time, Ghost and Fletch had worked out what they were going to tell the general the next day.

"Are you guys gonna get to talk to the President?" Emily asked in awe.

Both Fletch and Ghost laughed. "Hopefully not."

"But that'd be cool."

"Trust me," Fletch said, kissing Emily on the nose. "It would *not* be cool."

"Whatever."

"I'll see you in a few hours," Ghost told Fletch as he stood up to leave.

"Will you tell Rayne if she wants to come over to-morrow…I wouldn't be opposed?" Emily asked, suddenly shy. She knew Rayne, they'd spent some time together, though they weren't best buds yet. But Emily thought it might be nice to talk to another woman dating a Delta. They truly were a breed unto themselves, and she knew now she could use all the help she could get in understanding them.

"Will do." Ghost leaned down and kissed the top of Emily's head. "Glad you're all right. Annie too. See you tomorrow, Fletch."

Fletch didn't bother to get up and see his friend out, he tightened his arm around Emily and asked her, "You good?"

"I'm good."

"Are you really all right, or are you just saying that because it's what you think I want to hear?"

Emily turned in Fletch's arms and said earnestly, "I'm good. Seriously. You're okay. I'm okay. Annie's okay. I'm more than all right. Promise."

"I almost lost you tonight." Fletch's words were

muffled as he buried his face in her hair. It was just dawning on Emily that she should've been asking Fletch if *he* was all right instead of the other way around.

"You didn't."

"I would've if Ghost hadn't called TJ."

"But he did. While I can't say I'm thrilled that I was that close to a bullet, I *can* say that I'm one hundred percent fine with the outcome. Fletch, look at me."

"I can't say that *I'm* thrilled you were that close to a bullet. He could've shot Jacks on the other side of the head...away from your face." Fletch ran his hand through his hair, agitated at the thought of how close the bullet from the former Delta Force operative's rifle had come to *her* skull.

"Fletch," Emily said gently.

He finally looked up.

Emily waited until Fletch's eyes met hers. "From the second I woke up in that container, until I heard and felt you behind me, I knew you'd somehow save me and Annie. That's the *only* reason I allowed my six-year-old to wander off by herself. I knew you'd be out there. I trust you with my life, but perhaps more importantly, I trust you with *Annie's* life. If tonight had to happen again, I'd want it to go down exactly the same way. I love you, Cormac Fletcher. I am so damn thankful I got up the courage to inquire about that apartment for rent."

"Me too, darlin', me too."

"Will you get in trouble tomorrow?"

"I doubt it. The general is a stickler for the rules, he has to be, but the colonel will vouch for us, and I think what you told the general tonight went a long way."

"Won't he want to know who shot Jacks?"

"Yeah, but he won't find out. TJ is back home, and from what Ghost has told me, he's too good to leave any trace that he was here. The general is going to have to get used to the idea that he'll never know who it was who shot that fucker."

Emily yawned and closed her eyes as she settled even deeper into Fletch. She felt him turn sideways and pull her on top of him. Without opening her eyes, Emily groaned in contentment. "Man, this feels good."

"I should've drawn you a bath. You're gonna be bruised tomorrow."

Emily shrugged. "Whatever. I've been bruised before. Not a big deal."

"It's a big deal to me," Fletch returned resolutely.

"You can make it up to me later," Emily mumbled, half asleep. "I love you."

"Love you too, Em. Sleep. I've got you."

"Don't you need to lock the door? Set the alarm?"

"Nope, Ghost did it on his way out."

"'Kay. Fletch?"

"Yeah, love?"

"Between losing a couple of years off my life during the school shooting, when I didn't know if Annie was in the gym or not, to being blackmailed, and then tonight...I think I've had enough adventure to last me at *least* the rest of the year."

"Me too," Fletch agreed, chuckling. "Me too."

"I just want to go to work, come home, and live my life quietly with you and Annie."

"I can give you that."

"Good." There was silent a moment before Emily spoke again. "Fletch?"

"Yes?" If Emily was more awake, she would've heard the laughter in his voice, but she was almost asleep and it went over her head.

"I want to jump your bones but I'm too tired."

"No worries, Em. My bone is available for you to jump whenever you feel up to it."

"Good. I like your bone."

Fletch almost choked on his laughter, but he held it back...barely. "I'm glad. Now, shhhhh, go to sleep. I have to get up in a few hours."

"'Kay. Night."

"Good night, love."

Emily didn't feel Fletch's lips touch her forehead, or hear his next whispered words, as she was already out, the day finally doing her in.

"I'll never take you for granted, Emily Grant. I'll

love you and Annie until the end of our days. There'll never be another woman in my life as important as you."

Epilogue

FLETCH LOOKED DOWN at the little girl standing proudly by his side. Annie was between him and Emily, holding both of their hands. She'd listened solemnly as the judge went through the questions for him, not saying a word as he'd answered what he did for a living, if he felt he could provide for Annie, and other required inquiries from the court.

The little girl hadn't flinched when the attorney was asked if he thought it was the best thing for Annie. Even when Emily told the judge she gave her support "one thousand percent" for Fletch to become her legal father, Annie hadn't moved a muscle.

She'd insisted on wearing a dress for her official adoption, which had surprised Fletch to no end. But he needn't have worried, she'd come out of her room that morning with the pink frilly dress on...with combat boots on her feet. Truck had apparently special-ordered them for her. Ghost had warned him that Annie had a surprise in store for him, and Fletch couldn't have been more proud.

It was obvious the little girl wanted to make the day special, and retaining her own personality in the face of her nervousness and excitement *was* something special.

Finally, it was Annie's turn.

"Annie, Cormac Fletcher has requested the right to become your father. To be responsible for your actions, good and bad, for the rest of your life. This is a big step and shouldn't be taken lightly. I've asked everyone else what they think, but I haven't asked you yet. Do you want the man standing next to you to be your daddy?"

"Permission to approach the bench?" Annie asked solemnly.

Taken aback by her words, the judge could only smile and nod.

"What are you doing, Annie?" Emily asked as her daughter passed in front of her.

Fletch beamed with pride. Annie had asked him a million times about how today would go. They'd watched some videos online of other adoption finalization hearings and he'd thought she was finally confident as to what would happen. It was obvious by her question of the judge, Annie had somehow gotten ahold of other videos of courtroom dramas.

"Don't worry, Mommy, I got this," Annie reassured Emily.

Emily moved closer to Fletch and grabbed his hand. He could feel how nervous she was.

"I have no idea what she's gonna say," she whispered to him.

"It's gonna be epic," Fletch declared, looking back at Coach to make sure he was getting whatever Annie was going to say on film. The whole team was there, as was the colonel and Rayne and Mary. Fletch's chest swelled with more feelings than he could put words to. He was about to officially become a daddy, and he couldn't wait.

They all watched as Annie walked around the side of the bench and up into the witness box. She held up her hand as if she was swearing on a Bible, another clue that she'd somehow watched some sort of courtroom drama show.

"Your honor, my name is Annie Elizabeth Grant. I'm six and a half years old and in the first grade. For all my life, as long as I can member, it's been me and Mommy. She bought me food and made sure I was safe. We moveded into Fletch's apartment and it was great. Then a bad man made Mommy sad and she gave me all her food. I was worried, but didn't know what to do. I can't work…you know?" Annie turned to the judge and gave her a "what can you do" look and a shoulder shrug, before turning back to the courtroom and continuing her speech.

"Fletch gave me my first Army man toys. New. Brand new still in the box. They're amazing, but you know what? It didn't mean that I didn't like the toys Mommy gave me. They might not have been new, but my mommy did her best. She never made me eat the weird green vegetables that look like balls. I could play in the dirt and she never made me wear icky girly clothes."

"You're wearing a pretty dress today," the judge interjected, smiling.

Annie looked irritated that her speech had been interrupted, but answered anyway. "Because today is a *special* day. I only get one day to get a daddy, and I wanted to look pretty for him. I'm wearing my soldier boots though." She held up a leg and propped it on the chair next to her, showing off her shiny new combat boots to the judge, who looked like she was gonna burst out laughing. Seeing the judge nod in appreciation, Annie asked, "Now, can I continue?"

Fletch thought the judge was gonna bust a gut, but somehow she kept a serious look on her face when she gestured at Annie to continue and told her, "By all means,"

"So, as I was saying, Fletch gave me presents, but that's not why I liked him. I likeded him because he made Mommy smile. She worked so hard to take care of me, but no one was taking care of *her*. I'm only six. There's only so much I can do. So while I'm happy to have Fletch as my daddy, I'm happier because if I belong to him, that means so does Mommy. And then they can get married and Mommy can be happy too." Annie finished her speech with a broad grin and went to step down, but stopped and quickly took her place again and held up her hand once more.

"I forgot...I can't wait to be Annie Elizabeth Grant Fletcher...and be called Fletch, just like my daddy. So help me God." She nodded, as if her words were law, and stepped down out of the witness stand and back to Emily and Fletch.

"Well, I think that settles that. I grant you, Cormac Fletcher, full joint custody of Ann Elizabeth Grant, from—"

"Fletcher!" Annie called out.

The judge simply shook her head and continued, "Custody of Ann Elizabeth Grant *Fletcher*, from this day forward. Congratulations."

Fletch leaned over and kissed Emily, happier than he could ever remember being in his entire life. Then he kneeled down and took Annie in his arms. He heard the clapping from the spectators in the courtroom, but he only had eyes for his daughter. "I love you, Annie Fletcher."

"I love you too...Daddy."

"THAT WAS INTENSE," Blade remarked to Coach later that night. Annie's speech had been priceless and both men knew they'd be laughing about it with Fletch for years to come.

"He's a lucky son of a bitch," Coach agreed, lifting his beer in salute.

Blade clinked his bottle against Coach's and they both drank. They'd spent the afternoon at Fletch's house celebrating with his family. Annie had changed out of her dress two-point-three seconds after she'd entered the house and reemerged in a battle dress uniform, complete with the camouflaged hat and everything. She loudly declared, "Let's play soldier!" and the rest of the afternoon was spent with men trained to be lethal killers, playing hide-and-go-seek with the six-year-old.

"We've got two weeks off, what are your plans?" Blade asked Coach as they watched the Dallas Cowboys game on the television above the bar.

Coach shrugged. "I agreed to help a buddy out at his skydiving club."

"Really? You hate that shit."

Coach laughed. "I know, ironic, huh? But he's down an instructor, the guy went and broke his leg or something, and he needed someone to take the guy's place. He's got someone ready to step in, but not for two weeks. I told him I was getting two weeks off...and voila…I'm in."

"Sucker," Blade teased.

"Whatever. It could be worse."

"Yeah, how?"

"I could be roped into teaching a six-year-old how to rappel."

"You suck," Blade griped.

Coach laughed at his friend. "You walked right into that one, and you know it."

"It's not as though *Fletch* is going to do it. He panics when she jumps from the second stair to the floor. He's such a pansy around her."

"That he is." Coach tilted the bottle back and finished up his beer. "I'm gonna get out of here. I'll see you later?"

"Yup. Give me a yell and let me know how the parachuting thing is going. I'd hate to turn on the news and see that you'd splatted on the ground or something."

"Ass. I'll text ya." Coach slapped his friend on the back and headed out of the bar.

He wasn't thrilled about skydiving. It wasn't as though he wasn't proficient at it, he was, as were all the Deltas, but there was just something not right about jumping out of a perfectly good airplane if it wasn't necessary.

Coach mentally shrugged. Oh well, it was only two weeks. What could possibly go wrong?

Look for the next book in the *Delta Force Heroes* Series, *Rescuing Harley*.

<u>To sign up for Susan's Newsletter go to:</u>
http://bit.ly/SusanStokerNewsletter

<u>Or text:</u> STOKER to 24587 for text alerts on your mobile device

Discover other titles by Susan Stoker

Delta Force Heroes

Rescuing Rayne

Assisting Aimee – Loosely related to Delta Force

Rescuing Emily

Rescuing Harley

Marrying Emily (Feb 2017)

Rescuing Kassie (May 2017)

Rescuing Bryn (Nov 2017)

Rescuing Casey (TBA)

Rescuing Wendy (TBA)

Rescuing Mary (TBA)

Badge of Honor: Texas Heroes

Justice for Mackenzie

Justice for Mickie

Justice for Corrie

Justice for Laine

Shelter for Elizabeth

Justice for Boone

Shelter for Adeline (Jan 2017)

Shelter for Sophie (Aug 2017)

Justice for Erin (Oct 2017)

Justice for Milena (TBA)

Shelter for Blythe (TBA)

Justice for Hope (TBA)

Shelter for Quinn (TBA)

Shelter for Koren (TBA)
Shelter for Penelope (TBA)

SEAL of Protection
Protecting Caroline
Protecting Alabama
Protecting Alabama's Kids
Protecting Fiona
Marrying Caroline
Protecting Summer
Protecting Cheyenne
Protecting Jessyka
Protecting Julie
Protecting Melody
Protecting the Future

Ace Security
Claiming Grace (Mar 2017)
Claiming Alexis (July 2017)
Claiming Bailey (TBA)

Beyond Reality
Outback Hearts
Flaming Hearts
Frozen Hearts

Connect with Susan Online

Susan's Facebook Profile and Page:
www.facebook.com/authorsstoker
www.facebook.com/authorsusanstoker

Follow Susan on Twitter:
www.twitter.com/Susan_Stoker

Find Susan's Books on Goodreads:
www.goodreads.com/SusanStoker

Email: Susan@StokerAces.com

Website: www.StokerAces.com

To sign up for Susan's Newsletter go to:
http://bit.ly/SusanStokerNewsletter

Or text: STOKER to 24587 for text alerts on your
mobile device

About the Author

New York Times, USA Today, and *Wall Street Journal* Bestselling Author Susan Stoker has a heart as big as the state of Texas, where she lives, but this all-American girl has also spent the last fourteen years living in Missouri, California, Colorado, and Indiana. She's married to a retired Army man who now gets to follow *her* around the country.

She debuted her first series in 2014 and quickly followed that up with the SEAL of Protection Series, which solidified her love of writing and creating stories readers can get lost in.

If you enjoyed this book, or any book, please consider leaving a review. It's appreciated by authors more than you'll know.